THE BEGINNING OF HOME

LANGLEY PARK SERIES

KRISTA SANDOR

CANDY CASTLE BOOKS

A NOTE TO THE READER

This book is intended for mature readers. It contains descriptions of adult relationships, sexually graphic situations, and adult language. If such things offend you, this book is not for you.

To the women who have suffered and survived abusive relationships.
Your stories matter.
Your words are important.
Your lives are valuable.

1

16 YEARS AGO—SUMMER

"You are one lucky girl, Lindsey Hanlon. I'd kill to be going to Camp Clem with Nick Kincade!"

Lindsey glanced over at Monica with her jet-black ponytail and mischievous eyes. She gave the girl a distracted nod, adjusted the straps of her backpack, and stepped into the shade of one of the old burr oak trees standing tall above the Langley Park Community Recreation Center. Ten preteen girls, in a frenzy of blooming hormones and tittering excitement, buzzed around her, hitting each other, pillow fight style, with their sleeping bags.

She shifted the straps of her pack again. It was hot. It could get warm in her hometown of Camden, Maine, but this summer, she wasn't spending her days photographing the scenery along Penobscot Bay. No, this summer, she was staying with her godmother, Rosemary Giacopazzi, just a stone's throw from Kansas City in the quaint town of Langley Park, Kansas.

Her godmother had pulled some strings and gotten her a job as a camp counselor at the day camp so she could, as her godmother would say, "make new friends and experience the wonders of Langley Park."

Unfortunately, in the two and a half months she had been there, the closest she'd gotten to wondrous was a double scoop of rocky road at the local ice cream parlor.

The majority of the counselors were sixteen like she was, but most of them were from the area and went to the same high school. She and Nick Kincade were the only camp counselors from out of town. At the beginning of the summer, she had thought this commonality would have made Nick an ally, maybe even a friend. On top of that, she was put in charge of the preteen girls, and he had the preteen boys. They were two fish out of water, thrown together in a town they didn't know, doing essentially the same job. They should have been instant friends.

She couldn't have been more wrong.

Monica nudged her playfully. The community center allowed fourteen-year-olds to volunteer as junior counselors. Since Lindsey's first day on the job, the junior counselor, Monica Brandt, always made an effort to talk with her while the older counselors stuck to their cliques.

Lindsey nudged Monica back. "I'd trade places with you if I could. Nick's barely spoken to me all summer—and when he has—he's usually a total jerk. I can't imagine what's going to change about that at Camp Clem." She glanced Nick's way. He towered above a group of preteen boys who were picking red berries off the shrubs and throwing them at the girls.

Monica's gaze flicked to Nick. "He doesn't talk much, but when he does, that Kentucky drawl is about the hottest thing I've ever heard. And it's not like he's spoken much to me either this summer. But who needs the guy to talk when he looks like that? He's like a southern version of Brad Pitt and Justin Timberlake's six-foot-four-inch lovechild. He's like all the hotness of Bay Watch crammed into one guy."

Lindsey bit back a laugh. "I'm not sure it's possible for Brad Pitt and Justin Timberlake to have a lovechild—southern or otherwise."

Monica leaned in and lowered her voice. "Camp Clem is four hours away, hidden deep in the Missouri Ozarks. It's sleepaway camp. You'll be with Nick 24/7 for the next five days! And what'll I be doing? I'll be stuck here in Langley Park playing junior counselor and taking the six-year-old day campers to the Langley Botanic Gardens for another scavenger hunt. It's better than being trapped in my grandmother's bakery, I'll give you that. But I still wouldn't mind five uninterrupted days staring at Mr. Pitt-Timberlake."

"I hate to burst this Nick Kincade fantasy you've created for me, but I don't think there's going to be a whole lot of alone time. There's me, my ten twelve-year-old girl campers and his ten twelve-year-old boys. Real intimate, all twenty-two of us," Lindsey said, stealing another glance at Nick. He was staring down at his iPod. His campers had joined the girls in the sleeping bag fight, and Nick was utterly oblivious to the preteen mayhem unfolding around him.

The shrill shriek of a whistle halted the commotion, and Nick looked up to find Lindsey and Monica staring at him. Lindsey turned away. The last thing she wanted was for Nick Kincade to think she liked him. But that didn't stop a hot blush from creeping up her neck.

Another whistle shriek pierced the air.

"Time to start the day and go collect my pack of nose pickers," Monica said with a wide smile. "I want to hear all about how you cracked the hard shell of Nicholas Kincade's brooding outer layer the minute you get back!"

Lindsey shook her head and watched Monica jog over to where the younger children were waving goodbye to their parents and lining up in front of the counselors. This had been Lindsey's usual routine for the last ten weeks. But not today. A yellow school bus pulled up and stopped in front of her. The words *Camp Clemens* were painted on the side of the bus in bold lettering.

Beads of sweat pooled in the space between her breasts. How was she going to get through five days with Nick constantly by her side? It had been relatively easy not to interact with anyone her age this summer. She was always with her campers during the day, and there was never a lack of something to do; a squabble to be sorted, or an activity that needed to be completed. The kids took up all of her time at Kids' Camp, and, when she wasn't working, she'd explore Langley

Park on her own, snapping photographs on her dad's old Nikon camera along the way.

She tried to remember the last interaction she'd had with Nick. A few days ago, she had asked him to keep an eye on her campers while she used the restroom. He didn't even properly answer, only gave her a quick, detached nod—the cocky jerk.

The bus doors opened with a mechanical whoosh, and the tinny sound of Journey's "Don't Stop Believing" drifted out the door. The driver said something, but Lindsey couldn't make out his words over the music. She put her hand to her ear, and the driver turned down the volume on a radio duct taped to the dash.

The driver squinted at her through a pair of thick, filmy bifocals. "Are you Mrs. Quigley?"

"No, I'm just a camp counselor," Lindsey answered. She hoped this guy was qualified to drive a bus. Behind the grimy glasses, the driver's right eye oscillated back and forth like a bowling pin teetering in slow motion.

"Hello, you must be Mr. Robbins. I'm Mrs. Quigley," came a voice calling out from behind. It was Karen Quigley, the Langley Park Kids' Camp Director.

The gray-haired bus driver extricated his considerable girth from behind the steering wheel and shifted to face them. He cleaned off his glasses with the hem of his shirt. "Hello there, Mrs. Quigley. Are your children ready for Camp Clemens?"

Karen juggled several pieces of paper and two large binders. "They certainly are! I just need a moment to speak with my counselors, and then we'll start loading the kids onto the bus."

"Take your time," Mr. Robbins said, shifting back into driving position.

Karen waved Nick over and handed each of them a thick binder. "This is everything you'll need. Emergency contact numbers. Allergy and diet information. The camp schedule and planned activities. And remember, there are going to be other day camps attending Camp Clemens this week. You'll always want to be counting heads and taking attendance. You leave with twenty children. We'd like you to return with the same number," she added with a shrill laugh.

Lindsey nodded. Mrs. Quigley was very big on calling roll. Monica shared that, eons ago when Mrs. Quigley was a camp counselor, she'd accidentally left a child on a canoe for four hours before realizing she was one kid short.

Mrs. Quigley clapped. "Lindsey, you go first."

Lindsey hated doing this. Every morning of Kids' Camp, she had stood next to Nick and endured his smirks and muffled laughter as she took attendance.

She opened the camp binder and glanced at the camper roll call sheet. "All right. Rachel?"

"Here, Miss Lindsey!" called a smiling girl with sandy blond hair.

"Taylor?"

"Here."

"Heather?"

"Here."

She kept going, calling name after name, but paused and bit her lip when she got to the last four.

"Keep going, Lindsey," Mrs. Quigley said, gesturing with her hand. "We need to get these kiddos on the bus."

Lindsey nodded. "Megan?"

Nick released an amused huff.

She ignored him.

"Here, Miss Lindsey."

"Meghan with an H?" Lindsey continued.

Nick looked down. He had a smug smirk plastered across his face.

"Here," the second Meghan replied.

"Hanna?" Lindsey said.

"Here."

"Hannah with an H?" Lindsey called out. Thank god this was her last camper.

"I'm here, Miss Lindsey."

Mrs. Quigley made a few notes on a clipboard. "Your turn, Nick."

"I called roll right before you got here, Mrs. Quigley. All my campers are present and accounted for."

What a kiss ass! Nick did the absolute bare minimum. His campers were always the ones causing trouble or pulling pranks. But in front of Mrs. Quigley, he played the part of the conscientious, prepared counselor.

"Good thinking, Nick," Mrs. Quigley said, barely glancing up.

Lindsey threw him a sharp glance. "I don't know what's so funny about my roll call," she whispered.

"Meghan with an H. Hannah with an H. This town is so fucking generic."

The breath caught in her throat. "Don't talk like that. The kids could hear you."

"If the worst thing they learn from me is that they come from a shit town and pick up a few curse words, they're getting off easy."

Lindsey narrowed her gaze. She had expected to find that aloof, distant expression she'd come to know well this summer. Instead, she caught a flash of pain in his blue eyes. There was something there. Something dark huddled, frightened and exposed inside, Nick Kincade. But then he blinked, and the depth she had just seen vanished into two pools of empty blue.

"Lindsey, dear," came a voice.

Her godmother, Rosemary Giacopazzi, came bustling up with her camera bag and a small box in tow. "You don't want to forget your camera, honey. And a package just arrived at the house from your mom."

Lindsey collected the items as the preteen campers surrounded Rosemary.

"Mrs. G! Mrs. G!" the children called out, taking turns hugging the tiny woman. Rosemary was the beloved third-grade teacher at Langley Park Elementary. Lindsey noted early on that everywhere they went in town, her godmother was mobbed by excited children and parents spouting warm words and effusive praise.

"All right, boys and girls," Rosemary said, "are you all ready for a grand adventure?"

The children cheered and whooped.

"Remember to listen to your counselors. Have fun and be kind to each other."

All whoops and horseplay disappeared, and the children nodded earnestly.

Mrs. Quigley checked her watch. "Time to load up," she said and ushered the children onto the bus.

Rosemary waved goodbye to the children then turned her attention to Lindsey and Nick. "These five days are as much for you two as they are for the kids. I met my husband when I was a camp counselor at Camp Clemens." She reached out and gave both Lindsey and Nick's hands a squeeze. "It's a special place."

Nick broke the connection and stepped back. He gestured with his chin toward a few stray duffle bags the kids had forgotten to take onto the bus. "I need to get this stuff loaded up." He was already ten feet away scooping up bags before he had even finished the sentence.

Lindsey shrugged her shoulders. "Sorry about him. He's just..."

Rosemary watched Nick toss items into the back of the bus. "He's carrying a lot of pain, that one."

"I wouldn't know. He doesn't really talk to anyone, and when he does, he's usually a creep."

"He's just a prickly pear," Rosemary replied.

"A what?"

"A prickly pear. I've had at least one in my class every year since I started teaching. It's the kind of person who's tough and thorny on the outside but soft and sweet on the inside."

Lindsey eyed Nick as he dragged a bag across the pavement with the delicacy of a caveman. "I don't know, Rosemary. Soft and sweet would not be the first two adjectives I would choose for him."

"Not yet," Rosemary said with a twinkle in her eye. "People can always surprise you."

Mrs. Quigley joined them. "Nick, can you come over here for a moment. I have one more essential item to give to you and Lindsey."

Nick tossed the last bag onto the bus, released an impatient breath, and joined them, his arms crossed tightly against his chest. His fingertips drummed against his biceps.

Mrs. Quigley pulled out a tattered piece of fabric. "This is Langley Park's flag."

Lindsey shared a confused look with Nick. "What are we supposed to do with it?"

"I keep forgetting," Mrs. Quigley replied. "You two aren't from around here."

"Thank Christ," Nick said under his breath so only Lindsey could hear.

"This is the flag you'll be using to represent Langley Park when you play capture the flag at Camp Clem," Rosemary said, reverently touching the faded, yellow fabric.

The flag was about the size of a sports pennant. Sunflowers were embroidered around the edge with a capital L and a capital P stitched into the center.

"This very flag has been part of Langley Park since 1935. It started out in Langley Park's very first school. Then it was given to the Community Center almost forty years ago," Mrs. Quigley said.

"It's a Langley Park rite of passage to bring this flag up to Camp Clemens," Rosemary added.

"Indeed, so please take extra care with it," Mrs. Quigley said, eyes flitting between Lindsey and Nick. Her gaze settled on Lindsey, and she handed over the flag. Her only real choice since Nick's arms were still crossed tightly against his chest.

"Ready to get this show on the road?"

They turned to see the bus driver, Mr. Robbins, wiping his glasses on his Camp Clemens t-shirt.

"I guess the fun starts now," Nick muttered as he boarded the bus.

"Enjoy your time at Camp Clemens, Lindsey," Rosemary said with a warm smile. "And remember what I said about those prickly pears."

Rosemary started toward her car, but Lindsey called her back. She wanted to stop the words from tumbling out, but she couldn't help herself. Her lip trembled. "I talked to my mom last night. She knows all about Camp Clemens." Lindsey paused. "If my dad calls while I'm gone, will you let him know I'm okay, and that I..."

"Of course, dear." Rosemary squeezed her arm, but her signature bright smile had dimmed a fraction.

AT LEAST THEY'D stopped singing, Nick thought to himself.

Lindsey had led the kids in all manner of silly camp songs: "This Land is Your Land," "Do Your Ears Hang Low," "The Hokey Pokey," and that stupid song about eating apples and bananas where you butcher the words by switching the vowel sounds. He hadn't had to deal with that kind of bullshit much this summer. The last thing his twelve-year-old boys wanted to do was sing out loud in front of each other. But something about riding the bus to sleepaway camp made his usually self-conscious campers less inhibited, and they belted out the ridiculous lyrics along with the girls.

He exhaled a sigh of relief. The bus had quieted, and the children hunkered down into the depths of the green, faux leather bus seats. Nick tried to angle his large body into a comfortable position, but it was no use. These seats were made for tiny people who enjoyed sitting at a perfect ninety degree angle. He shifted his knees to the side and wedged his back into the space between the seat and the side of the bus.

Like most shitty camp buses, this one didn't have air conditioning. All the windows were down as low as they could go. Thankfully, the dry Kansas breeze cooled as the bus traveled east into Missouri and toward the Ozarks. He glanced across the bus aisle at Lindsey. She was focused on the Camp Clemens manual. Her lips moved silently as she read. She was pretty. He could admit that much. Chestnut brown hair with hints of red that reminded him of the autumn Kentucky sun streaming through the brown and crimson leaves of the maple tree in his backyard. She was the only girl at Kids' Camp who hadn't thrown herself at him. He couldn't blame the other girls, though. He knew he was easy on the eyes. His features mirrored his dad's, and, from a young age, he had observed how women responded to his father. A prickly sensation of anger tangled with resentment festered deep within his chest.

Looks weren't the only thing he had in common with his father.

Just like dear old dad, he wasn't a good person either. He didn't smile. He didn't socialize. It made his stomach turn to think these girls would still be interested in someone so cruel and unkind.

But not Lindsey.

He had seen her every day at Kids' Camp. She never made excuses to talk to him like the other girls did. He recognized their pathetic attempts at attracting his attention.

"Nick, have you seen my attendance roster?"

"Nick, could you help me carry this heavy cooler?"

"Nick, do you like my new dress?"

No, Lindsey wasn't like the other girls. She kept to her campers. She only communicated with him as a last resort.

The bus hit a pothole, and the vehicle bounced up and down. Lindsey glanced up and caught him staring. He shifted against the sticky seat.

She set the binder on her lap. "Nick?"

He cocked his head in response. He had gotten pretty damn good at not behaving like a human being.

"We should probably look over this together. It's everything we'll be doing at Camp Clem. It may be good to know what we're in for ahead of time."

The way he saw it, he had two choices. He could look at it with Lindsey now, or he'd have to learn it all by himself. The former seemed like less work. He slid across the aisle and sat next to her.

She looked up at him with wide, surprised eyes. He had never noticed the color of her eyes before. They weren't blue or green, but a perfect combination of the two colors like the ocean at dusk. She glanced at her camera bag and the small box and set the items on the floor by her feet, allowing them to sit shoulder to shoulder.

"So," she said, her fingers working in a nervous, disjointed fashion as she flipped pages, "we're here Monday through Friday, but we leave Friday morning after breakfast. That gives us half a day of activities today and then three full days, Tuesday through Thursday."

That much he knew. His lack of response told her that, and she continued.

"Capture the flag is no joke at this place. It looks like we play it almost every day."

He leaned in to see the schedule and was hit with her scent. She didn't smell like most girls her age, drenched in fruity, floral perfume that made his head spin and not in a good way. Lindsey smelled of sweet cream and summer rain, earthy and warm. She tensed as he moved in closer, but she didn't pull away. Instead, she turned and met his eye. But just as their gazes locked, his size thirteen foot bumped into the box on the bus floor.

"Sorry about that," he said, making a clumsy attempt to maneuver his legs to fit into the snug seat.

"It's nothing—just a package from my mom. It's probably filled with gummy bears and graham crackers. She still tries to feed me like I'm a sugar-addicted toddler."

Of course, Lindsey came from a family that sent her care packages. Her bedroom was probably plastered with rainbows and unicorn posters. He would bet her family had "board game night" at least once a week. That prickly sensation in his chest pulsed with resentment. He was just about to make a snide comment about her life filled with picket fences and pony rides when she met his gaze and those blue-green eyes sliced into him with kindness and warmth. He wasn't prepared for it. Girls usually looked at him like he was some shiny, new toy they wanted to show off to their friends.

"That's cool your parents send you snacks," he said. He sounded like a fucking moron, but her eyes and that sweet, delicate scent set him off balance.

"Not my parents, just my mom."

The bus hit another bump, and his shoulder brushed hers. She reached over and gripped his arm and steadied herself. Her fingertips pressed into his skin, and he had the sudden urge to reach his arm around her and draw her into his large frame. He imagined the way her body would feel, cuddled in close to him. All he'd have to do was tilt his head a few inches, and he could press a kiss to her temple. He swallowed hard and pushed the image out of his mind. Lindsey Hanlon was just another girl in this bullshit town, full of bullshit people, in his bullshit world. He stiffened and shifted his body away from her.

Lindsey motioned to the binder. "We should..."

"Yeah, let's just skim over each page."

She nodded.

Nick read through the first half of the binder. Standard camp shit. Daily activity listings. Mealtimes. Health clinic information. He was about to turn the page when Lindsey swayed and leaned against him. Her eyes fluttered closed. How the hell was she falling asleep? He looked back at the campers. At least two-thirds of them had fallen asleep, and the remaining kids were reading quietly.

"Fast car," Lindsey murmured. Her hands went slack, and she released her grip on the binder. Nick caught it before it slid off her lap, but his movement caused her to slide into him.

His chest tightened. "What about a car?"

Her head rested against his shoulder. Wisps of her chestnut-brown hair brushed against his skin and tickled his arm. He inhaled. He couldn't fucking help himself. She smelled like what home was supposed to be, safe and warm, sweet and solid.

Her body relaxed against his. "The song."

He listened. Just below the sound of the breeze passing through the open windows and the bump and grind of the road, "Fast Car" by Tracy Chapman played on the bus driver's radio. Each note, each lyric came to him in gentle drafts of air like an invitation to some-where he had never dreamed of going.

"Yeah, I hear it, Lindsey."

"I love this song," she yawned, slurring her sleepy words together.

Nick trained his gaze on the road. "Me, too," he whispered as his words drifted into the wind.

2

The bus came to a jarring stop, and Lindsey shot up. "I'm awake! I'm awake!"

She wiped her hand across her mouth. Oh, for Pete's sake! Not only did she fall asleep, she drooled.

Nick slid out of the seat. He met her gaze with empty eyes. "Congratulations on waking up. We're here."

She nodded. She always fell asleep during car trips. She thought of her parents drinking coffee in the front seat of their Volvo. The rich aroma filled the car as the sound of the road map crinkling across the dashboard and the hum of the engine made her eyelids feel heavy. The memory washed over her like summer rain until she was hit by the harsh slap of reality.

That life was over.

Lindsey packed the thought away. She stood and turned toward the children at the back of the bus. Some of them must have slept during the drive, too. Several kids had indentation marks pressed into the sides of their faces where they'd rested their cheek against the bus window. At least she wasn't the only one napping. She pressed a self-conscious hand to her cheek, but it was smooth.

If she hadn't slept against the window, she must have...

A hot blush bloomed on her cheeks. But there was no time to worry about falling asleep on Nick Kincade's shoulder.

She raised her hand and made a peace sign which, at the Langley Park Kids' Camp, meant stop talking. The kids quieted. "Okay, guys. We're here!" She tried to inject excitement into her voice. The Langley Park flag was balled up on the seat. She grabbed it and held it up. "Let's have some fun and make everybody back in Langley Park proud!"

The bus was quiet for a beat before the kids broke out into cheers.

Okay. This wasn't going to be too bad.

She looked out the bus window and caught Nick's eye. He gave her a "what the fuck" expression. Forget him. She was here to make sure these kids had fun and stayed safe. She didn't know where that little pep talk came from, but it didn't matter. Nick had ignored her the entire summer. What was another five days?

She was about to toss him a "screw you" look when an older woman in a Camp Clemens t-shirt walked up behind him.

"Welcome, welcome, Langley Park campers! I'm Hannah Harris, the Director of Camp Clem."

Lindsey stepped off the bus and shook the woman's hand. "I'm Lindsey, and this is Nick," she said, hoping Nick would show an ounce of excitement.

"It's nice to meet you, ma'am," he said in his sweetest Kentucky drawl. "Is that Hannah with or without an H?"

Hannah seemed delighted with the question. She pointed to her name tag. "Why, it's with an H!"

What a jerk!

Nick's lips quirked into a cocky smirk. Lindsey threw daggers at him with her eyes, but he met her gaze with one of amusement.

Hannah held up a clipboard. "I was checking our records. I couldn't find either of you on our past camper rosters."

"Nick and I have never been to Camp Clem," Lindsey answered.

"But you're from Langley Park, right?"

"No, I'm from Maine and Nick's from Kentucky."

Hannah put a hand to her chest. "How exciting!"

"You're from Maine?" Nick asked, pinning her with his gaze.

"Yeah, I am." She didn't know what else to say. It was the first real question he had ever asked her.

"Let me share a little 411 on Camp Clem," Hannah said. She was an attractive woman, but she had to be in her late fifties, maybe early sixties. Something about her injecting teen speak into her vocabulary sounded as disjointed as an opera singer opening for a heavy metal band.

"You may not know this, but Camp Clemens is nestled in the Mark Twain National Forest. You may wonder why we're called Camp Clemens?"

"Because Samuel Clemens is Mark Twain's real name," Nick said with enough enthusiasm to fill a thimble.

Hannah beamed, unfazed. "That's right! He's from Missouri. Everything here at Camp Clem is named after him or his works of fiction. Isn't that fun?" She didn't wait for them to answer. "We've got Lake Langhorne." She gestured down the hill toward a giant body of water and a line of canoes lined up against the side of a boathouse. "The Langley Park girls will be staying in Becky Cabin and the boys in Sawyer Cabin." She pointed to two simple rectangular structures separated by a small building made of concrete blocks. "Those cabins are the closest to the bluff. It's a pretty serious drop into the lake and quite shallow at the bottom. You'll need to be mindful not to get too close."

"What's between them?" Lindsey asked. She figured it was a bathroom of sorts, but there was a thick red line spray painted down the middle of the structure. The line progressed onto the grass for several yards in front of the building.

"That's the latrine. Showers and toilets. One side is for the boys, the other for the girls."

"And the red line?" Lindsey asked.

Hannah's expression became serious. "Gleeful glimpses, only."

Lindsey glanced at Nick. He shrugged his shoulders.

"I don't understand," Lindsey said.

"Gleeful. Glimpses. Only." Hannah said each word slowly. "That's

our little motto to help the campers make positive choices." She lowered her voice and glanced over at the Langley Park kids who were milling around the back of the bus. "The boys can't cross over the red line onto the girls' side and the girls can't cross over to the boys' side. This is how we keep all those bubbling, preteen hormones in check."

Lindsey looked at the red line.

"A sound plan," Nick said.

Lindsey could tell he was biting back a laugh. She was having a hard time keeping a straight face, too, but she wasn't about to let Nick know that.

Hannah nodded. "At Camp Clem, we pride ourselves on being a place where preteens make lifelong friendships while building new skills in a safe and nurturing environment." A dreamy look passed over the woman's face, but she startled when two cabin doors creaked open then slammed shut.

A young man and young woman emerged from the two respective cabins: Becky and Sawyer.

"Hi, guys! I'm Meg, and this is Trevor," the young woman said.

They only seemed to be a little older than she and Nick. They were both smiling brightly and wearing the same Camp Clemens t-shirt as Hannah.

"We are so excited you guys made it!" Meg said. She raised her hands into some kind of cheerleader-like pose.

Trevor nodded. He wasn't just a big guy. He was huge. He looked like he could be a linebacker in the NFL.

"Nick and Lindsey, meet Meg and Trevor, two of my finest cabin leaders. They'll fill you in on all the details."

"We sure will," Meg parroted back and again employed cheerleading arms.

"I'll leave you to it," Hannah said and hurried down a path toward another arriving bus.

As soon as Hannah was out of sight, Meg dropped the cheerleader front. Trevor pulled out a ball cap from his back pocket and pulled it low, hiding his eyes from view.

Meg cracked her knuckles. "You know everything Hannah just told you?"

Lindsey and Nick nodded.

"Fucking forget it."

This threw Lindsey for a loop. She wasn't alone. Nick's eyes had widened.

"Trev and I have been here for ten long weeks. That's ten weeks of mosquito bites. Ten weeks of Kumbaya. Ten weeks of bug juice."

Trevor grimaced.

"Bug juice?" Lindsey asked. Jesus, what kind of place was this?

"It's just Kool-Aid, with, like, extra sugar or some shit."

"Oh, I thought it was something awful," Lindsey replied.

"Ten fucking weeks of only bug juice *is* awful," Meg said as Trevor grunted in apparent agreement.

Lindsey met Nick's gaze. He looked just as freaked out as she was.

"Okay," Meg said, pacing a few steps. "We need to regroup."

"Sure," Lindsey said. Talking to Meg was like interacting with a caged animal. "What can Nick and I do to help?"

She caught Nick's gaze again. He nodded in agreement. He also seemed keen on keeping Meg from some kind of camp counselor meltdown.

"I'm so glad you asked," Meg said, then turned to Trevor. "See, we'll be fine. These two have at least half a brain."

Trevor grunted again—clearly his communication modus operandi.

Meg glanced at the preteen campers. The kids were unloading their packs and sleeping bags off the back of the bus. "Trev and I have enough weed to get us through this last week, and we intend on staying high as a mother fucking kite for the next five days. Got any problem with that?"

"No, no problem," Lindsey answered.

Nick nodded. "Whatever you say."

"Perfect. Here's how this week is going to go. You two are going to follow the schedule. If it says to take the campers to the dock, you'll take them to the..."

A beat of silence hung in the humid camp air.

"Dock," Nick offered.

"Yes, the dock!" Meg said, raising her hands to the sky like her prayers had just been answered.

"There's a bluff." Meg continued. "Did Hannah mention it to you guys?"

"Yes," Lindsey answered.

"It's steep and shallow at the bottom. Do you know what happens when a human falls off a high bluff into shallow water?"

Nick clapped his hands together, making a splat sound.

Trevor gave a nod.

"Yes, and don't forget night patrol. Your shift is from two a.m. to three-thirty a.m. every night, morning, whatever the hell you want to call it. *Do not wake us up.* Think of Trev and me like two zombies, minus the brain eating. Our bodies may be in the same cabin with you, but we're going to be totally and completely checked out."

Lindsey nodded. If Meg and Trevor planned on being stoned for five days straight, there wouldn't be much difference between them and a zombie. It was a decent analogy.

"What are we patrolling for?" Nick asked.

Trevor grunted.

"Aren't you sweet!" Meg patted Nick's cheek like he was a toddler. "This is a coed sleepaway camp with twelve and thirteen-year-olds. They sneak out in the middle of the night to make out. Your job is to catch them and send them back to their cabin." Meg raised a hand and paused. "We're okay with them getting to second base, though. Right, Trev?"

Grunt.

Meg nodded. "You can let them hookup. Just don't let them get to third base."

Trevor made another sound and Meg turned her attention to where one of Nick's boys named Rory and one of Lindsey's girls, Rachel, were standing together, heads bent and whispering back and forth.

"Keep an eye on those two. Trev's got great tween hookup radar. He's called every couple we've caught kissing in the bushes."

Lindsey glanced over at Rory and Rachel. They weren't doing anything that seemed out of the ordinary to her.

Meg leaned in and lowered her voice. "And don't mention any of this to Hannah. We'll tell her you guys are lying and then Langley Park will get banned from Camp Clem." She turned to Trevor. "Anything else?"

Trevor pointed to the Langley Park flag balled up in Lindsey's fist.

"Right," Meg said, narrowing her gaze. "You can slack off on almost everything. Don't think you need to master pottery or swim across Lake Langhorne. But, do not fuck with capture the flag. That shit is the real deal here."

Without another word or even a goodbye or a good luck, Meg turned on her heel. Trev followed her into the woods surrounding the camp, and they disappeared into a sea of green.

"Can you believe..." Lindsey started, but Nick was already at the back of the bus grabbing his pack.

Didn't they just have a moment? She would have sworn they connected over that insane exchange with Meg and Trevor.

He's had an entire summer to get to know you. Hell, he didn't even know you were from Maine. Did you think setting foot in Camp Clem would make a difference? The guy's a jerk! He cares for nobody but himself.

Lindsey shook her head and walked to the back of the bus. Her pack and sleeping bag were laying in the dirt next to the wheel. She was the last to collect her personal items. She looked up at the sky and listened to the squeak of the cots and the rise and fall of preteen voices as the boys and girls chose their bunks inside their respective cabins.

"You don't want to forget these," the bus driver said, holding out her camera bag and the package from her mother.

She threw on her pack, nestled the sleeping bag under her arm, and accepted the items.

"Are you ready for the best five days of your life, young lady?" the driver asked.

It hit her like a punch to the gut. In less than a week, she'd be going home—wherever that was.

The sound of Nick's voice caught her attention. She glanced over at the boys' cabin. He was assigning the kids to their cots, calling out their names like a Drill Sergeant. He met her gaze through the cabin's screened windows. No smile. No nod of recognition. He stepped forward and pulled down a window shade, and she was left staring at a tattered, sun-bleached cloth. Was her godmother right? Could Nick just be a prickly pear? Was there kindness inside of him somewhere? She thought she'd glimpsed it, but doubt set in. Who was she to know what was going on inside anyone's head? She thought she knew her father and all that had come crashing down on her.

She swallowed past the lump in her throat and met the bus driver's gaze. "You bet I'm ready."

NICK TOOK one last sip of his bug juice. Meg and Trevor were right. It was fucking awful.

The Langley Park campers were on dining hall cleanup duty. Nick eyed the boys and girls as they went from table to table collecting the abandoned dinner plates. He zeroed in on one of his campers. "Hey, Rory," he called out. "If you keep following Rachel, I'm going to let her pull you around on a leash."

A red blush crept up the boy's neck, but Rory kept his chin up. He gave Rachel a sheepish smile then left to go collect glasses from a table at the opposite side of the room.

Lindsey was back in the kitchen with the campers washing dishes. He could hear her singing with the kids—that stupid fruit song again where you fuck with the vowel sounds.

Ba-na-na

Ba-nu-nu

Ba-ni-ni

His grip tightened on the glass. He hated this place already. It wasn't that the camp was rundown or didn't offer anything interesting to do. As far as camps go, this one was pretty decent. They had completed a scavenger hunt shortly after they arrived, and he had learned the lay of the land.

Most of the cabins were fanned out along the north and east side of the camp, each backing up to the dense forest. But Langley Park's Becky and Sawyer cabins were located higher up, near the west side of the camp, closest to the bluff and set apart from the other cabins. The lodge and health clinic were located at the top of the hill near the camp entrance. The dining hall was at the bottom, perched next to Lake Langhorne. The boathouse was at the far end of the camp tucked between the waterfront and thick Ozark foliage. There were sports fields, tennis courts, a zip line, and a meditation garden— which made him laugh. Lindsey had given him the stink eye for that.

He'd attended summer camps back in Kentucky when he was younger. He knew the drill. He knew the songs. He'd loved those long, carefree summer days. But those memories reminded him of a different time. A life that was light-years away.

Lindsey walked out of the kitchen with a dish towel draped over her shoulder. The kids ran past her in a tangle of whoops and bony elbows. "I told them to go get the flag. They're excited to play capture the flag."

Her cheeks were flushed. She'd arranged her hair in a messy bun, exposing the gentle curve of her neck. Chestnut wisps of hair curled against her skin. A sheen of perspiration on her chest drew his gaze to the neckline of her t-shirt where the subtle hints of virgin white lace peeked out against her tanned skin. His chest tightened. His body ached to have her back asleep on his shoulder. The rhythm of her breath. The soft, endearing words she mumbled as she talked in her sleep. And that scent. He wanted to be encased in it, have it wrapped around him like a blanket.

"Did you say something?" he asked. He had to stop this daydreaming shit.

She removed the dish towel and wiped her hands. "Capture the flag starts in about fifteen minutes. I sent the kids to get the flag." She took a tentative step toward him. "I've never played it before. I read the rules, but—"

"It's not that hard," he cut in. "Hide the flag. Protect the flag. Get the other team's flag."

She looked at the floorboards. "Sure, I'll see you on the field."

Fuck!

He ran his hands through his hair. He'd managed to keep everyone at arm's length this summer. He didn't want to make any friends. He didn't want to fucking be there at all. Spending the summer with his great-aunt in Langley Park was his mother's idea. She had sent him away. She'd wanted him gone. Then his aunt insisted he do something of value with his time. The job as a camp counselor was the icing on the shitstorm of a cake he was forced to live through this summer. Despite behaving like a mute during his interview with the camp director, they still gave him the job. He knew the buckets of money his aunt donated to the Kids' Camp program over the years had everything to do with him getting hired.

The door to the dining hall creaked open. "Mr. Nick, they're going to be ringing the bell for capture the flag. Miss Lindsey sent me down to see if you were coming."

Rory Rogers.

While most of his campers shied away from talking to him, Rory was different. Rory didn't meet his gaze, but at least he had the balls to come and get him. Christ, he probably seemed a lot like Trevor to his campers. Moody. Mute and grunting. "Rory, tell Miss Lindsey I'm coming."

Rory gave a quick nod and was off like a shot, running up the hill.

Nick followed behind, but he didn't run. He was not fucking running to anyone or anything. He didn't care how much this camp loved their capture the flag. At the top of the hill, he saw the Langley Park campers huddled around Lindsey. Across the field, another group of preteens huddled around a male and female counselor. Hannah Harris stood in the middle of the field holding a stopwatch and a cowbell.

Nick walked up to the cluster of Langley Park kids. Lindsey was holding a torn out page of notebook paper. There were notes scribbled all over a hand-drawn diagram of a square.

She glanced up at him. Those blue-green eyes. Jesus, he couldn't let himself fall for her. He turned away and crossed his arms.

"Okay, guys," Lindsey said, turning her attention back to the campers. "The boundaries are marked with red rope. Austin, did you and Andy make the jail?"

"Yeah, Miss Lindsey," two stalky boys called out in unison. "We made sure it wasn't close to the flag."

"Perfect! Everybody knows where the flag is, right?"

Twenty heads nodded in unison.

"Okay, Langley Park," she said in a shaky voice.

Nick could tell she was bullshitting. She kept looking down at the piece of notebook paper, and she wasn't smiling her real smile.

"Lucky for us," Lindsey continued, "this game doesn't count. Whatever happens, we're going to learn something useful, and we'll take all that information into our next game."

"Hands in," she said. The kids made a circle and reached their hands into the center. "Nick?" Her eyes were pleading with him.

He shook his head and took a few steps back.

Lindsey had her fake smile back in place. "Langley Park on three!"

The cowbell rang, and total pandemonium broke out. Langley Park kids went running this way and that. Nobody was guarding the flag. Nobody was on the jail. She didn't even assign offensive or defensive positions. Before he could even blink, Hannah was ringing the cowbell, and the opposing team was high-fiving and fist pumping.

Lindsey called in the Langley Park kids. "Don't give this game a second thought. Remember—it's just practice. Now we'll know what to expect tomorrow."

The kids nodded, but none of them spoke, disappointment etched on each of their faces.

"Let's head back to the cabins," she said, patting kids on the back as they filed past her. She turned and captured him with those blue-green eyes. They cut into him like shards of sea glass, like a thousand tiny slashes into his soul. She didn't have to speak. Her eyes, wide and shining, said everything.

She followed the kids up the hill and faded into the inky twilight. He blinked. His throat tightened. Jesus Christ, was he about to cry? His father would have gotten one hell of a kick out of that. He let out a ragged breath. The image of Lindsey staring at him, her eyes welling with pain and disappointment was too much to bear.

What the hell was happening to him? Why was he feeling like this?

It hit him like a right hook to the jaw.

She was the first person to make him feel anything in a very long time.

3

Tap, tap. Scratch. Tap, tap, tap.

Lindsey yawned. "Five more minutes, Mom. Can you make eggs for breakfast this morning?"

"I'm not your mother, and I'm not making your breakfast."

Lindsey scrambled to sit up. She wasn't at home in Camden, Maine. It took her a moment to orient herself to her surroundings. A chorus of cicada chirps and bullfrog calls hung in the darkness. Her eyes adjusted. She focused on a row of cots lining the opposite side of the room. Camp Clem. Becky Cabin.

"Hey," came a sharp whisper.

She startled again. Nick was on the other side of the window screen.

"What are you doing?" she asked.

"Night patrol. Trevor just got in from fuck knows where and pulled me out of bed."

Lindsey looked over at Meg's cot. "Meg's asleep."

"Yeah, they just got in."

Lindsey yawned again. "Okay, give me a second."

She'd slept in her clothes. It seemed like the most reasonable choice. Swinging her legs to the side of the cot, she pulled on her sneakers.

"Hurry up. I'll be at the door."

Hurry up? Nick Kincade hadn't hurried for anything this summer. He'd barely arrived on time and did nothing to help. She'd let a lot slide. She never bothered him when his campers were out of control. In fact, she had engaged more with those boys than he ever did. After ten weeks, she'd bet he didn't even know all his campers' names.

Lindsey opened the cabin's door and closed it gently. She didn't want to wake the girls. Nick's back was to her. He was looking up at the sky and hadn't noticed her arrival. The moon was full and bright tonight, casting him in a silver hue. He was a work of art. All broad shoulders, toned arms, and muscled legs. If he wasn't such a jerk, she may have asked if she could photograph him. The composition came together in her mind. Strong, clean lines. She pictured a close-up shot of his hands gripping a boat oar or twisting a thick length of rope.

She shook her head and pushed the thought aside. "I'm ready," she whispered.

He turned, and, for a beat, she saw him. The real him. At least, she thought she did. His face wasn't screwed up into yet another insincere smirk. His gaze wasn't empty. She parted her lips to say something. *I see you. I know you're not this asshole you've been pretending to be all summer.* But his next words broke the spell.

"Took you long enough."

Lindsey crossed her arms. "I'm here now. What are we supposed to patrol?

"Trevor said to walk the perimeter."

"He said all that?" Lindsey asked.

An amused look crossed Nick's face. "After he kicked me awake, he made a circular gesture with his hand. I took that to mean that we were supposed to walk around the camp."

At dinner, Lindsey learned that four other groups were attending Camp Clem this week. That made four other cabin areas and eighty preteen, hormone-crazed campers in addition to their own twenty from Langley Park. This could be a long night.

She followed a step behind Nick into the forest. Despite downed limbs, rocks, and no real path, he was walking at a decent clip.

"For Pete's sake, slow down!" she whisper-yelled into the darkness.

"For Pete's sake?" he parroted back, turning to face her. "Is that what they say in fucking Perfectville, USA?"

Lindsey stopped. "Excuse me?"

"You know, where you're from, Perfectville."

"What makes you think I'm from anywhere perfect?"

"Perfect camp counselor. Perfect, perky little smile. Perfect little care package from mommy and daddy straight from your perfect white picket fenced house. Or do you live in a log cabin up in Maine?"

Lindsey clenched her fists. Hot irritation pulsed through her body. "You want to know about my perfect life, Nick?"

He crossed his arms.

She took a sharp breath. "My father left us. It turns out, he's been having an affair with one of his out of town clients. They have a baby together. A child! And he picked them. He moved out in April. He hasn't even tried to contact me. Not once!"

She didn't wait for his reaction. She couldn't. The only people who knew about her father's betrayal were her mother and her godmother, Rosemary. She had never told anyone, and she'd never intended on sharing anything so personal with this jerk.

She stormed past him into the woods. She needed to get away. Her body itched, and it wasn't just a reaction to Nick. The mosquitos loved her. She brushed violently at her limbs, trying to stop them from feasting on her flesh. Nick needling her about having some perfect life and the bugs biting at her skin and buzzing in her ear was too much. She stopped and ran her hands through her hair.

"Hey," Nick said. He rested his hand on her shoulder. "They bite you because you're so sweet."

Lindsey kept her back to him.

Nick released his grip and took a step closer. Twigs and bits of dirt and rock rustled beneath his feet as he slipped something over her shoulders.

"Wear this. At least it'll keep the bugs from going at your arms."

It was the flannel shirt he kept tied around his waist. She stiffened, but not because her body didn't welcome his touch, but because it did. The flannel smelled of him. Not quite a man, but definitely not a boy. Hints of sandalwood, night air and endless sky. His scent was that terrifying intake of breath before jumping off a precipice into the great unknown.

She faced him. "What if you get cold?" she asked. But she was already pulling her arms through the sleeves.

He leaned in and pressed a finger to her lips. They were almost eye to eye, gazes locked. Nick cocked his head to the side, removed his finger, and gestured to his ear.

"Listen," he mouthed.

"What is it?" Lindsey hadn't heard anything. Could it be an animal? She hadn't even considered that they would encounter wildlife prowling around in addition to preteens.

Nick pressed an index finger to his lips. She nodded. His hand fell to his side, but it didn't stay there. The breath caught in her throat as a hand, Nick's hand, solid and warm, wrapped around hers. Without a second thought, she tightened her grip, and their fingers laced together like corset strings pulled tight. He guided her deeper into the woods then stopped and gestured toward his ear again. Lindsey tried to figure out what Nick was hearing.

There was nothing quiet about the Ozarks at night. In the darkness, the forest was alive with activity. Between her heart beating like a drum as a result of Nick's touch and the chatter of nocturnal creatures, she had almost missed it. Voices, low, but clear once she was able to factor out the nightscape of sound.

Lindsey gave Nick's hand a quick squeeze and motioned for him to come close. "I think it's Rachel and Rory."

They followed the voices to a small clearing. They were close to the edge of the bluff. The gentle gurgle and splash of the water down below muffled Rory and Rachel's words, only allowing Lindsey to catch bits of their conversation. The pair sat on a large, flat boulder facing the lake. Her head rested on his shoulder.

Lindsey met Nick's gaze. "It looks like they're just talking."

Nick nodded. "Yeah, but they shouldn't be out here alone, especially this close to the edge."

"I don't want to embarrass them."

"We won't," Nick whispered. He released her hand and retrieved something from the ground.

He held up a stone. "This should spook them enough to send them running back to the cabins."

Nick threw the stone, and it landed with a hard crack against Rachel and Rory's rock. The preteens sprang up, their heads turning back and forth. They slid off the rock and Rory took Rachel's hand as they ran back toward the cabins.

Lindsey watched their clasped hands until the pair faded into the night. She flexed her fingers. They missed Nick's touch. She missed Nick's touch.

Nick shifted his weight from foot to foot. "Sorry about..." His gaze dropped to her hand. "I didn't want you to trip on anything out here. I'm used to running wild in the woods. I used to do it all the time when I was younger."

"It's okay," she said, the buzz of his touch still dancing on her fingertips.

Nick gestured toward Rory and Rachel's rock. "Do you want to sit?"

"You don't think we should make sure they made it back?"

"Nah, Rory's a good kid. He wouldn't let anything happen to Rachel. I'm ninety-nine percent sure they're climbing back into their cots right now."

Lindsey nodded and took Rachel's spot. Nick took Rory's.

Nick rubbed his hands on his thighs then let them rest on his kneecaps. Lindsey gazed out onto the water, but she could still see Nick from the corner of her eye. He rocked forward, fidgeting. She had never seen him like this, edgy, off-kilter. Bathed in moonlight and surrounded by water and wood, his aloof, unconcerned disposition faded.

"I'm sorry," Nick said. His voice was low, gaze trained on the water.

"About what?"

"I shouldn't have come at you like that. I didn't know about your dad."

"It's okay."

Nick shifted on the rock, and his hand rested next to hers. "Did you ever think that your dad's doing you a favor?"

"By cheating on my mom and leaving us?"

Nick angled his body toward her. He rested his hand on top of hers. "No, that part is unforgivable. I just mean, it might be better not to have somebody living with you that would treat you so badly."

She had never thought of her situation like that. Since her father left, she'd been mourning the good times. The trips to Acadia National Park. Watching the windjammers sail into Boothbay Harbor. But those happy memories were from when she was a little girl. The father she had known for the last several years had stopped taking her camping. He didn't ask about her day anymore. He didn't offer to join her in their basement's makeshift darkroom while she processed black and white prints. He wasn't around much at all. She and her mother had settled into a routine that treated her father more like a guest in their lives than a part of it.

"Maybe you're right, but I can't stop wondering why I wasn't enough. Why my mom wasn't enough. What did we do? What didn't we do?" She took a breath. The words were coming faster. "My dad hasn't called me once since he left. My mom sent me to Langley Park for the summer so that she could sell our house in Camden. She wants to start over someplace new."

Nick's hand engulfed hers, and he ran his thumb along her knuckles. The warmth of his touch sent a rush of heat to her core. A tangle of pain and lust welled in her chest. She swallowed, unsure of how to interpret the hot current of emotions coursing through her veins.

He met her gaze. "How do you do it? All that bullshit and you're still singing with the kids, laughing and cheering them on day after day."

He wasn't trying to smooth over her pain or round out its jagged edges. She felt naked, her soul bared to this boy who, only hours ago, she had thought was a selfish prick.

She parted her lips to speak, but the words weren't there. Her entire universe centered around this moment. The ribbons of water caressing the side of the bluff. The hum of insects. And Nick Kincade, looking at her like she made up the entirety of his universe.

"I want to kiss you," he said on an exhale of breath. "Not because you're the prettiest girl I've ever seen, but because, despite all you're going through, you're still such a good, kind person. And your eyes, all I can see in them is strength."

She nodded. It was a subtle movement that would have been lost to anyone else but not Nick. He tightened his hold on her hand and laced their fingers together. She'd held hands with boys back home. Those experiences were clammy, awkward exchanges that never set her body aflame. Nick's solid grip wasn't like anything she'd ever known. It was like being anchored in a safe harbor, tethered together with an unbreakable bond. His other hand found her face, and he drew his thumb back and forth across her jawline as his lips hovered a fraction above hers. The air stilled, and the chorus of lake water and wildlife quieted like nature itself was wrapped in this moment.

"Kiss me, Nick," she whispered.

He released a sound, something between a growl and a sigh of relief, and his lips met hers. Nick's breath was sweet and warm as he pressed a kiss to the corner of her mouth. Lindsey gasped, and he drew the tip of his tongue across the seam of her lips. His hand shifted into her hair, and he captured her mouth, their tongues meeting in a clash of heat and desire.

After what seemed like minutes or maybe hours, Nick pulled

back and ran his finger along her bottom lip. "Lindsey," he sighed. "I never want to stop kissing you."

She smiled and kissed his fingertip. She couldn't answer, not with words. He tangled his hands in her hair and kissed her again. Warm and urgent, his mouth claimed hers, and all she could do was fall deeper and deeper into this forbidden place where only she and Nick existed.

NICK LOOKED across the dining hall and into the kitchen. The second day at Camp Clem was the first day he had known real joy in a very long time. Lindsey had worn his flannel shirt around her waist all day. The red plaid sleeves tied in a knot swayed with her every move, and he'd probably watched every step she'd taken. He couldn't keep his eyes off of her. Her smile was sunshine. Her blue-green eyes were the magical place where the sky met the earth.

It was the same drill as last night. Langley Park did the dinner dishes—which they had learned wasn't a bad gig. One camp group had compost and recycling. Another, latrine duty. Compared to those camp chores, he'd gladly bus tables.

Lindsey's back was to him. Her hair was pulled up into a high ponytail that swished side to side as she sang and dried dishes with the campers. She must have sensed him watching her. She looked over her shoulder and met his gaze.

Holy fuck, he wanted to kiss her again.

They had been together all day, but he couldn't touch her. Not surrounded by twenty bouncing, rambunctious kids. And speaking of campers, his boys seemed to sense the shift in his energy. He'd hardly known a second's peace without one of his campers vying for his attention. But instead of ignoring the boys like he usually did, he laughed with them. He listened to their stories. He guided them attentively through the zip line course. He even sang along with that fucking, stupid fruit song and loved every minute of it.

"We better head up to the field," he called out and gestured to his watch. "It's almost time for capture the flag."

Lindsey nodded and dismissed the campers from dish duty. They joined the others in the dining hall, and twenty Langley Park twelve-year-olds ran out the door and up the hill. Nick waited at the door for Lindsey. His chest tightened just looking at her.

Last night, after their first kiss on the rock, he had walked her back to Becky Cabin, but he was too amped up to go to sleep. He took a few laps around the camp then stopped at the garden. Flowers were never his thing. But the sunflowers, growing in a tangled cluster along the far corner, caught his eye. Even in the dark, he could make out the golden petals—delicate, yet so strong. He found a small one, clipped it with his pocket knife, and left it tucked in the window screen next to where Lindsey's cot was pressed up against the side of the cabin. She had found it, but she hadn't said a word about it. Instead, she'd tucked the stem into her hair near the top of her ponytail. Every time he caught a glimpse of it, he smiled. The yellow blossom was a constant reminder that their kiss had meant as much to her as it did to him.

She met him at the door. "I hope you're better at capture the flag than I am."

"I may have a few tricks up my sleeve," he replied, falling into step with her. He had to be at least a foot taller than she was, but their bodies easily slipped into a comfortable rhythm. He looked down at the sunflower in her hair and let his fingertips glide past the ends of her ponytail. Her soft chestnut-brown hair glowed a subtle auburn hue in the late day summer sun.

The children gathered on the field. Nick whistled and called them over. He knelt down and retrieved a folded piece of paper from his pocket. During his time walking the camp last night, he had paid a special visit to the grounds used for playing capture the flag.

Twenty campers huddled around him. Lindsey stood behind them. He glanced up and met her gaze, and she gave him a little wink as Rory's voice cut into their exchange.

"Mr. Nick, do you have a plan?"

Nick shifted his gaze away from Lindsey and nodded. "I sure do guys. Remember, yesterday didn't count. Put that loss behind you. Today, we are going to rule the field."

The campers were still for a second before a chorus of whoops and cheers broke out.

"Okay! Settle down. It's time to focus." Nick retrieved the folded sheet of paper from his cargo shorts. "We've got offensive and defensive positions. We also need people on the jail, and we need people to guard the flag." He looked around at the group. "On offense: Rory, Rachel, Gavin, Meghan with an H, Hannah with an H, Jacob, and Tyler." He met each child's gaze as he called their name. "Never run in a straight line. Always zigzag back and forth. And no hogging the flag. Pass it off if you've got somebody hot on your tail. We're a team. We play as a team. We win as a team."

The kids nodded.

"Defense: Christine, Justin, Billy, Heather, Alex, and Megan. Spread out. Tag as many of the opposing team's offense as you can." Nick focused on the remaining campers. "Kayla, Joey, and Taylor, you guard the jail. Brandon, Hanna, Heather, and Austin, you guys guard the flag. But don't get too close to it. We don't want to give away the location. I've marked the perfect place for it on the map." He held up the piece of paper, and the kids leaned in to see.

Nick glanced up to see Lindsey's eyebrows raised in amazement.

"Okay, Team Langley Park. Miss Lindsey is going to stick with the defense, and I'm going to stick with the offense. Don't worry if you didn't get the position you wanted. We'll rotate through. Everybody good?"

The kids nodded. Their expressions were as serious as a Seal Team before deployment.

Nick stood and clapped his hands. "Let's go!"

The kids took off, and Nick walked over to Lindsey.

"You didn't think I knew their names, did you?" he asked with a teasing smile.

"My godmother was right."

"Right about what?"

"Nick Kincade really is a prickly pear after all."

He had no idea what she meant, and his expression must have shown it.

Lindsey laughed. "Don't worry. It's a good thing. Now go catch up with the kids! We've got a game of capture the flag to win."

4

―――――

"And then, Mr. Nick, remember when Hannah with an H tossed the flag to Meghan with an H, and she ran it in?"

Nick ruffled his camper's hair playfully. "Dude! Tyler! I was right there. It was awesome!"

"The girls are pretty badass," Tyler said, then turned crimson and gave Nick a panicked look.

"Just don't say badass around your parents and teachers, and you'll be fine—and don't drop the cookies. Come on, fellas, let's bring up the rear," Nick called back to his campers who were carrying an assortment of drinks and snacks.

Team Langley Park cleaned up in capture the flag. They won every game that night and learned winning had its perks. As the top team, they were allowed to pick up snacks from the dining hall to be eaten in their cabins after lights out. His boys' arms were filled with jugs of bug juice, cookies, graham crackers, Chex mix, Hershey bars, and marshmallows. He was in such a good mood he didn't even give Austin shit when the kid grabbed a bag of rice cakes.

"Do we get to eat with the girls?" Rory asked, jogging a few steps to catch up.

"Sorry, buddy. Girls stay in their cabin, and we stay in ours. Camp Clem rules."

The director shared this rule with him not once, but six times, before they'd even filled the pitchers with the super-sweet Kool-Aid concoction.

"I don't mind helping you bring the snacks over to Becky Cabin," Rory added.

"Of course, you don't. Rachel's there," Tyler said, making obnoxious kissing noises.

"Shut up, Tyler. You've been staring at Hannah with an H all day," Rory shot back and added his own barrage of over exaggerated kissing sounds.

"Guys, we're all going to drop off the snacks. But no messing around. You heard the director. We have to stay in our cabins." Nick put a hand on Rory's shoulder and dropped his voice to a whisper. "I'll send you over to Becky Cabin to collect the empty pitchers to bring back to the dining hall."

Rory beamed. "Thanks, Mr. Nick."

The sound of girls singing met them as they made the last turn toward their cluster of cabins.

"Is that..." one of the campers asked but trailed off.

Becky Cabin glowed like a beacon. Girls sang into hairbrushes and danced in groups of three and four to a bubblegum, boy band beat.

Nick and his ten campers stopped, slack-jawed and frozen in place. It was like something from a Disney movie. The girls were twirling and singing their hearts out. Lindsey was in the middle of the pack, standing on a cot, hips swaying, head tossed back, laughing. That's when he felt it. The final click of his heart being set free. He had locked it away behind layer upon layer of anger, powerlessness, and pain. And now it belonged to her.

The music stopped, and the girls of Becky Cabin stared out at the boys.

Lindsey smiled and jumped off the cot. She turned to her campers. "Girls, if there's one thing I want you to remember from our time at Camp

Clem, it's that you never stop dancing. Not for a boy. Not for anyone. And when you meet the right person, they'll love you for just that reason." She pressed a button on the little radio, and a Britney Spears tune filled the night air. The girls stared at the boys and then back at Lindsey, who was already moving to the beat. An invisible rush of energy surged through the cabin, and the preteens threw their hands in the air, twirling and singing at the top of their lungs in a wave of near-tangible girl power.

"Wow," Rory whispered, coming to stand next to Nick. "Miss Lindsey is really..."

"Yeah, buddy," Nick replied and grinned like a sap. "She sure is."

Lindsey met Nick's gaze and cocked her head toward the door.

"Come on, guys," Nick said. He had to shake Tyler and Billy to get them to move. "Let's drop off the girls' snacks."

Lindsey opened the door to Becky Cabin with her gaggle of girl campers crowded in behind her. "We found Meg's CD player. It turns out, she loves cheesy pop music."

Nick took one of the pitchers of bug juice and handed it to Lindsey. "You're amazing."

The girls giggled, and Nick became painfully aware of the twenty pairs of eyes watching him. "Here's Becky Cabin's share of the snacks," he said. He was blushing. He knew it. But he didn't care.

The boys handed Lindsey tins and bags, and she passed them back to the girls. "The ladies of Becky Cabin want to thank the gentlemen of Sawyer Cabin, right girls?"

"You're welcome," Nick said. He wanted to reach out and kiss her, run his fingertips up and down the length of her spine and wrap his arms around her.

Lindsey licked her lips, and Nick swallowed hard. Holy shit. Night patrol couldn't come soon enough.

"Mr. Nick?" one of his campers called out sheepishly.

How long had he been standing there, staring at her like a lovesick puppy? "So, we'll be going back to Sawyer Cabin. Just on the other side of the latrine. I'm sure you know where it is?"

Jesus, what was wrong with his mouth? He sounded like an idiot.

The girls standing behind Lindsey giggled again.

"I'll see you later," she said, adjusting the flower in her hair before shutting the door.

Nick scratched on Lindsey's window screen. But this time, she didn't wake up asking for breakfast.

"Nick," she whispered, opening her eyes in slow, heavy blinks as a broad smile spread across her lips.

He pressed his hand to the screen. Lindsey raised hers and drew her index finger down the length of his palm. She sat up and wound her chestnut hair into a messy bun. "I'll be right out."

He walked to the front of Becky Cabin and waited for the door to open. His breathing kicked up a notch when the old door squeaked, and Lindsey emerged wearing his flannel shirt.

"I've been counting the minutes," he said, gathering her into his arms. But something clunky moved between them before he was able to kiss her. "What's that?"

She took a step back and held up a camera. It was hanging on a strap around her neck. "My camera. It's a perfect night to shoot the clouds."

He took her hand, and they set off down the dirt trail. "Tonight's the perfect night for...photography?"

"And other things," she answered back coyly, shifting her fingers and lacing them with his.

His cock twitched.

They fell into step, and neither spoke as they took a lap around the camp. The chorus of night sounds filled the air. The humid summer breeze softened at night and bathed them in cool, gentle currents of air as the wind came across the lake. Lindsey wrapped both her hands around his and leaned in. His body remembered when she'd fallen asleep on the bus and had rested against him. Jesus, that was barely more than a day ago. A time that now seemed light-years away.

"I don't think any kids are out tonight," he said. "Probably all beat. My boys were asleep before their heads hit the pillow."

"Same with my girls."

They rounded the trail and stood at the top of the hill near the lodge.

Lindsey surveyed the sky. "Let's go down to the boathouse. I think I can get the perfect shot there."

She could have said, let's hop a flight to Vegas or let's get face tattoos. He would have agreed to anything she wanted.

Lindsey stopped short of the water's edge and raised her hands to the sky.

"What are you doing, Linds?"

She dropped her gaze and met his eye. "Framing the clouds."

She sat down and laid back on the grass.

He sat down next to her.

"Lay down," she said. "The whole world changes when you look at it from this perspective."

He leaned back and joined her. The camera rested on her chest as she raised her hands and framed the sky.

She turned and met his gaze. "I think I've got it."

She lifted the camera to her eye. "The trick with night photography is to be very, very still. You need a longer exposure time to let enough light in to capture the image. The moon's bright tonight—which helps—but you have to be so still, you can't even breathe. Any amount of movement can blur the picture."

"Have you always photographed clouds?"

She set the camera back on her chest but didn't pull her gaze away from the night sky. "I've always loved clouds. In school, my art teacher showed us lots of images by Ansel Adams. I'm sure you've heard of him."

"Black and white photos. National Parks. Mountains. That's the guy, right?"

"Yeah, that's him. He took this amazing picture called *Noon Clouds*. It's from Glacier National Park. It's two gorgeous peaks and between them are these clouds. I remember my teacher putting up the slide, and I couldn't look away. The clouds were mesmerizing. The way light danced and played with them. I'm sure five seconds after Ansel Adams took that picture, the light shifted, or the wind blew, and it was a completely different image."

Nick extended his arm and pulled Lindsey in close to him. Her head rested on his chest, and he slid his fingers into her hair.

She sighed. "Clouds are magical, aren't they? You can see them. You know they're there, but you can't hold them or contain them. That's why I want to be a photographer. I get to keep a little piece of every picture I snap."

They watched a swath of thick clouds roll in like nature sensed she was being observed and didn't want to disappoint.

"My teacher says what I like to do is called cloudscape photography," Lindsey continued. "This Belgian guy, Leonard Missone started it back in the 1800s. But I really like the images by this British photographer, Robert Davies. He takes his photographs above the clouds looking down. They're haunting and beautiful."

"Do I need to be worried about this Davies dude?" Nick asked, pressing a kiss to the top of her head.

Lindsey chuckled. "Never. Now be still. I'll tell you when to hold your breath."

Lindsey lifted the camera and peered through the viewfinder. "After our next inhale, we're going to hold our breaths."

He hadn't noticed that their breathing had synced up, slow and steady like a heartbeat. They exhaled. On the inhale, Lindsey stilled. The shutter opened and closed. A mechanical click pierced the air— a foreign sound against the backdrop of water and insects. He liked it. It was comforting. It brought him back to a different time.

She exhaled, and Nick released his breath.

"My mom sent me away for the summer, too," he said, staring up at the sky. "She's leaving my dad this time."

"What do you mean, this time?" Lindsey asked.

He closed his eyes. This wasn't something he discussed. "I knew something was wrong when I was just a kid, seven or eight years old. But I didn't know what it was. My mom would wear dark sunglasses in the house or long sleeved shirts in the middle of the summer. It wasn't until a few years later when I realized that not everybody's dad beat their mom."

He took in a sharp breath as the bands of shame and guilt tightened in his chest. "She's tried to leave him before. We'd go stay with my grandparents for a couple of weeks, but then my dad would promise to change, promise to get help…"

Lindsey set her camera on the ground and cuddled into him, entwining her legs with his and resting her head on his chest. "But he didn't, did he?"

He wrapped his arms around her. "No, he didn't. As I got older and stronger, I'd try to step in and protect her. At first, I thought it worked. The first time I hit my father, he was completely stunned. I was so scared. My dad's a big man. It was like punching a brick wall. He'd left the house, and I thought, that was it. We're going to be okay." Nick swallowed past the lump in his throat. "He came back a few hours later. He was drunk. You'd think that would have made it easier for me to defend my mother, but it didn't. He found us in the kitchen. I was helping her make a pie. He beat her with the rolling pin. I tried to stop him, but he was too strong. He broke my nose with one punch."

"Oh, Nick," Lindsey said, shifting to meet his gaze.

"I couldn't believe it when she told me she was sending me to stay with my great aunt in Kansas for the summer. I've been so angry that she didn't want me there to help her. That she didn't need me there to protect her."

Lindsey pressed a kiss to his lips then tilted her head toward the sky as if waiting for a message. "Our moms," she began and met his gaze. "Our moms are taking this summer to try and make life better for us. I don't think your mom sent you to Langley Park because she doesn't love you or need you. I think she sent you here because she does. It's not your job to protect her from your dad. You're here this summer because this is how she's going to make things right. This is how she's going to protect you."

Nick stared into Lindsey's eyes and cupped her face in his hand.

"She wants to get a little place for us away from my father. She was a teacher. After she had me, my dad wouldn't let her go back to work. She said she wanted to get another teaching job to support us. She said, by next summer, we could take a trip—just the two of us."

"See," Lindsey whispered, emotion lacing the word. "She loves you. Stop being angry with her and give her the credit she deserves. Maybe we'll both be going back to better lives, happier lives, but we were supposed to find each other first, this summer."

"I wasted so much time," he said. He traced the length of her bottom lip with his thumb. "We were together almost every goddamn day this summer, and I pissed it all away being a sullen, angry jerk."

She shook her head. "That doesn't matter. Look where we are. Look what we've found."

Nick sat up and brought Lindsey with him. He had an idea. A million ideas. His mind raced with possibilities.

"What is it?" Lindsey asked.

"I'm going to be a pilot."

Simply saying the words filled him with hope.

She cocked her head to the side.

He smiled. It all made sense. This could work.

"Lindsey, my grandpa used to take me flying in his plane. It was a little Cessna 172 Skyhawk. A four-seater. I used to pretend I was Luke Skywalker flying an X-wing fighter. You know, from *Star Wars*?"

She grinned. "Yeah, I know *Star Wars*."

Excitement thrummed in his chest. "From that minute, I knew I wanted to be a pilot. My grandpa passed away last year, but he left me the plane. It's been sitting in a hangar not far from my house in Kentucky. I'm sixteen. I can get my pilot's license. It doesn't matter that the summer's almost over. I'll be able to visit you, no matter where you move with your mom."

"It doesn't have to end," she said.

Lindsey understood what he was trying to tell her.

"This is just the beginning," he answered.

A flash of lightning tore through the sky. It illuminated Lindsey's face and, in that fraction of a second, Nick saw his future in her blue-green gaze. He saw his mother, safe and sound, teaching at an elementary school. He saw himself, flying above the clouds, calling the tower for landing clearance. He saw Lindsey smiling at him. He saw a life filled with love and laughter and happiness.

Heavy drops of rain began to fall in slow motion before the sky opened up and a rumble of thunder cut through the air.

"Come on, we can wait out the storm in the boathouse," Nick said, scooping up Lindsey's camera and helping her to her feet.

They ran inside the structure. It was open on both ends but provided adequate respite from the rain. It smelled of musty life-jackets and damp wood. Kayaks hanging on the wall tapped together like door chimes every time the breeze picked up, and an old Sunfish sailboat creaked in the darkness as the rain fell steadily, dancing on the lake's surface.

Nick hooked the camera's strap on a bare nail sticking out of the wall then took her hands into his. "Thank you, Linds."

"For what?"

"For making it all so clear. For looking past all the crap and seeing everything at its best. I want to be a better person, and I want to be that person for you."

She smiled up at him. Jesus, with one look, one smile, she could bring him to his knees.

"This is just the beginning," she whispered. Her words hung in the air, buzzing with possibilities.

He lifted their hands and pressed them into the side of the boathouse above Lindsey's head then leaned in and kissed her. Sweet cream and summer rain. Her scent was everywhere. He tasted it on her lips. He felt it warm against her skin. He released her hands and grasped her waist, allowing his palms to move up and down her torso as his fingers pressed into her body. She fit inside his hands perfectly. Every one of her curves was made for his touch.

She released a sweet giggle against his lips.

He pulled back. In the darkness, with her arms above her head, she looked like something out of a fantasy. And then he noticed it. Her watch had gotten tangled in a length of rope that was hanging from a peg high up on the wall. In the darkness, the rope looked like a gnarled, twisted mass someone had carelessly thrown on the hook in a hurry.

"Your hands," he said. He tried to loosen the rope's hold on her wrists.

"Wait, Nick," she whispered. "Leave it."

"Yeah?" A tremor of lust shot down his spine and settled in his belly. His cock strained against his cargo shorts.

"Yeah," she answered, twisting her free hand into the tangle of rope.

He trailed his fingertips from where the rope twisted around her slight wrists and down the length of her arms. She arched forward, her breasts grazing his chest. He drew his fingertips across her collarbone and found the first button. Slowly, he worked his way down, unbuttoning his flannel shirt that looked so damn sexy on her.

"Linds," he whispered, holding the shirt open.

She was wearing a white bra with delicate lace wrapped around each of her perfect breasts. The same virgin lace that peeked out from her shirt that first night in the dining hall. He caressed her breasts, then captured her mouth, kissing her hard. She moaned. Her small, heated gasps sent his body into overdrive. He traced the line down her stomach and popped open the clasp on her shorts. The satiny, smooth fabric of her panties teased his fingertips.

"Is this okay?" he breathed against her lips.

"Yes," she said, drawing him in for another kiss.

He slipped his hand inside her panties and cupped her sex. Lindsey released a moan so primal, so wanton, he nearly came inside his pants. His finger dipped past her entrance, and he rocked his palm, massaging her sweet bud while he pressed one finger inside her body. It was a tight fit, but she was warm and grew slick as he thrust in and out.

She twisted the rope above her head, and her pelvis rocked against his palm as she rode his hand, thrusting and begging him for more. He pushed in a second finger, and she threw her head back. His lips found her neck. He nipped and sucked at the sweet skin, working his way down her jaw. He pressed a kiss to the corner of her mouth as she gasped his name over and over.

"Nick, yes. Nick, please. Nick, don't stop."

Her body tightened. He pressed his thumb against her bud, and Lindsey's body shuddered in his grip, riding out wave after wave of pleasure.

She tilted her head forward. "Wow," she breathed, "I've never done anything like that before."

"Want to do it again?" he asked with a mischievous grin. He could watch her come all night.

"Oh, no," she answered.

"No?" he repeated, confused.

"Nick, look! I can see a flashlight. Someone's coming!"

"Fuck," he whispered, clasping her shorts and fumbling to button up the flannel.

"Hey," called out a voice. "Who's in the boathouse?"

Lindsey released a relieved sigh. "It's just a counselor from one of the other camps. I recognize his voice. He's probably out on patrol."

"That's all good and fine, but we don't want him finding you all..."

"All tied up," she purred.

"Jesus, Linds," he breathed and kissed her hard.

"Is that you, Nick?" came the voice.

"Yeah," Nick called. "Lindsey and I were finishing up patrol when we found this length of rope that wasn't put away correctly. We thought we'd get it all untangled when Lindsey's hands got twisted up in it."

Fucking hell! Who was he trying to fool?

His fingers worked furiously, loosening the rope. After a few tugs, Lindsey's hands broke free. She reached for her camera and held it innocently.

"Looks like we're good," Nick said, pressing a hand to her back and leading Lindsey out of the boathouse.

The counselor flashed a beam of light over them. "Are you sure? You know, your patrol ended like an hour ago."

Nick and Lindsey were halfway up the hill when she started giggling.

"Good to know," Nick called back. "You know Langley Park. We always go the extra mile."

He took Lindsey's hand, and they ran up the hill through the summer rain.

5

"This is it. You've played hard, and all that work has led you to this moment: The Camp Clem Capture the Flag Championship Game."

The kids took a knee and formed a semicircle as they listened to Nick's pep talk.

Their third day at Camp Clem passed in a haze of canoeing, horseback riding, and another night of patrol spent kissing Nick Kincade in the boathouse.

And here they were, the last night at Camp Clem. Tomorrow morning they'd board the bus back to Langley Park. But Lindsey wasn't sad. Sure, she was going to miss this magical place, but the magic with Nick didn't have to end.

This was just the beginning.

She had repeated those five words over and over again like a prayer. The mantra wrapped around her, forming a protective layer. It pieced back together her wounded heart that had been ripped to shreds by her father's betrayal.

"Linds," Nick called and met her gaze with a bright smile.

She joined him.

"Now, for this game, Miss Lindsey and I can't join you on the field.

This is all about you guys. This is all about that great teamwork you've practiced every day at camp."

The campers broke out into nervous chatter.

"Hey," Lindsey said, drawing the group's attention. "Mr. Nick and I know you can do this. Win or lose, you are all coming out of this game as champions."

She met his gaze. His eyes said everything. He adored her. He cared for her. He respected her. He was her prickly pear. Her gorgeous, ripped, blond-haired, blue-eyed prickly pear.

The campers giggled. She and Nick had gotten lost in the moment again. Just that day, Nick had tipped a canoe and almost fallen off a horse—and the kids were starting to catch on. Something was happening between Miss Lindsey and Mr. Nick.

"Right," Nick said and turned back to the campers. "You are all champions in my book. Play hard. Remember: zigzag, stay low, pass off the flag if you've got someone coming in hot."

The camp director rang the cowbell, and the kids sprang into action. Team Langley Park was like a well-oiled machine. The kids sprinted onto the field and took their positions as the defenders ran to hide the flag at the predetermined location. Lindsey and Nick joined the counselors of the opposing team on the sidelines and watched the battle unfold.

Over the week, Rory and Rachel had emerged as the team's power couple. Rory was good at dodging and weaving, and Rachel was the speed. Barely ten minutes had gone by before Rory emerged from a wooded area, flag in hand. He had three guys on him who were closing in fast when Rachel shot in out of nowhere. Rory held out the flag, and Rachel snapped it out of his hand and sprinted across the field and into Langley Park's territory.

"We won?" Nick said, disbelief lacing his words.

"We won!" Lindsey echoed back.

The Langley Park campers raced to the sidelines, screaming and clapping, the level of excitement rivaling that of a Super Bowl win.

"Go shake hands with the other team," Nick said, patting the kids on the back and ruffling heads of sweat soaked hair.

The players met on the field, and the Langley Park kids consoled the losing team, giving them high-fives and hugs.

"They learned that from you, Linds," Nick said with a wide grin.

"Learned what? You're the capture the flag mastermind."

Nick adjusted the sunflower in her hair. Another token left tucked in her window screen. "You taught them kindness. You showed them how to find the best in every situation and in every person, even in a creep like me."

"You didn't turn out to be so bad," she replied with tears in her eyes. She wanted to kiss him. She wanted to cup his beautiful face in her hands and memorize every detail.

"Way to go, guys," came an unfamiliar man's voice.

Trevor?

Lindsey and Nick turned to see Meg and Trevor beaming at them.

"We really pulled it off, didn't we Meg?" Trevor said just as the camp director joined their little foursome.

"Meg, Trevor," the director began, "You've shown incredible leadership this summer. You should both be very proud of yourselves. You, too," she said to Lindsey and Nick like an afterthought.

Lindsey bit back a laugh, and Nick threw her a wink.

"All right, Langley Park!" The director called out. "Gather around! Gather around! We need to take the commemorative picture."

The director placed a gleaming trophy on the ground, and the children huddled up and formed two tiers, their arms wrapped around each other. Nick and Lindsey took their place and stood behind the group. Shielded by the campers' bodies, Nick took a step closer to her. Electricity sparked in her fingertips as Nick hooked his pinky finger with hers. Lindsey turned her head a fraction and met Nick's gaze.

"Three, two, one! Say Camp Clem Champions!"

The director took several shots with a Polaroid camera. The sound of the photos emerging from the device purred mechanically as the group held their smiles.

"Here you go," the director said, passing a photo to Lindsey and then another to Nick.

The Polaroid image came to life. Their twenty campers, red-cheeked and euphoric with Meg and Trevor wedged in on the side, slowly materialized. Her gaze traveled to where she and Nick stood in the back. They were grinning ear to ear, eyes locked on each other.

"Oh, no!" The director said. "You two aren't looking at the camera. Would you like me to take another one?"

Nick drew his index finger across the photo. "No, it's perfect just like this."

LINDSEY COULDN'T SLEEP. After capture the flag, the entire camp celebrated with a bonfire next to the lake. They had eaten s'more after s'more, sang silly songs, and huddled together to watch the sunset. Between their campers and the surprising enthusiasm of Meg and Trevor, she'd hardly had any time with Nick at all. But she didn't mind. They had one more night of patrol, and she wanted to make it special.

Meg had left her trunk open, and Lindsey spotted the small golden packets and pocketed one before she could think twice about what she was doing. She touched the condom tucked into her pocket as if she needed to assure herself it was really there and that she was really going to do this. Nick hadn't pressed, not one bit. He never even brought up sex. But after the last few nights spent kissing Nick and having his body make her feel things she had never felt before, she knew she wanted to sleep with him. She wanted him to be her first time, and she wanted it to be here at Camp Clem.

"You're awake," came Nick's soft voice at her window.

"Couldn't sleep."

"Me either. Come on," he said, pressing his palm against the screen. "I've got something I want to show you."

She tiptoed out of the cabin, untied Nick's flannel from where it hung around her waist and pulled it over her shoulders.

He took her hand. "It looks good on you, you know."

"I should probably keep it."

Nick pressed a kiss to the top of her head as they walked down the path. "Yeah, I think you should."

They usually walked a lap around the camp, fulfilling patrol duties before finding a place all to themselves. But tonight, Nick led her straight to the waterfront.

"We're not patrolling?" she asked.

"Not tonight," he said. "I've got something else planned."

"You do?"

"I do," he said with the hint of a smile in his voice.

They passed the dining hall, and the boathouse came into view.

"Somebody pulled the tarps down," Lindsey said, squinting in the darkness. While the boathouse was open on two sides, thick tarps kept rolled up above the entrances were attached to secure the structure during inclement weather.

Nick pulled back the tarp. A small electric lantern hung off a rusty nail and filled the space with a soft, hazy glow. There were sunflowers everywhere. Nick must have taken all the pitchers from the kitchen and used them as vases for the bright, inviting bunches of flowers.

She went over to one of the bouquets and touched a golden petal. "How did you do all this?"

Nick secured the tarp and joined her. "Turns out, Trevor is quite the romantic. He helped me set this up. I guess he and Meg were really pumped Langley Park won the capture the flag championship. It really is a huge deal here. He and Meg each get a bonus added to their last paycheck."

"And that?" Lindsey asked, gaze drawn to several sleeping bags spread out on the boathouse floor. "Are you getting lucky tonight?"

Nick's eyes widened. "Linds, I don't want you to think that... I'd never ask... That's not what..."

She pressed a finger to his lips. He quieted. She reached into her pocket and pulled out the condom package.

"Lindsey," he said, touching the edge of the foil packet.

Her cheeks felt hot, but she pressed on. "Nick, I've never done this before. But I want to. I really want to." Flashes of his lips pressed to her neck as his hand worked her sex sent a delicious shiver through her spine. "And, I want to do it with you."

He dropped his gaze. "Linds."

"What is it? Do you not want to?" She thought her heart might break right there in the boathouse.

He cupped her face in his hands, and his gaze burned into her. "Linds, I want that more than anything. I want you more than anything. I've never slept with anyone I..."

He broke off. But she wasn't afraid to say it.

"You've never been with someone you've loved before?"

His eyes went glassy, and he nodded. "I've never loved anyone the way I love you. And I know, it hasn't even been a week, but this is the real thing. I've never been more sure of anything in my entire life."

She blinked back tears. "This is just the beginning."

"Just the beginning," he echoed back as his lips crashed against hers.

His hands slid into her hair. He kissed her, and she was home. She was with Nick, flying high above the clouds, safe beyond the horizon, and he loved her. She ran her hands down the hard plane of his stomach, letting her fingers trace the defined V that pointed straight to his cock. She hadn't touched him there, hadn't touched any boy there. But her love for him edged out any trepidation. Her fingers followed the lines of muscle, and she palmed him through his cargo shorts. Nick's body tensed like a coil on the verge of release.

"God, Linds, that feels so good."

She liked setting him on fire. She stroked his length at a slow, leisurely pace, but she wanted to feel him, the real him.

"I want to touch you," she said, breaking their kiss.

"Okay." His chest heaved in short, punctuated breaths.

Nick unfastened his shorts and pulled off his boxers, t-shirt, and shoes. "Now you, Linds."

She didn't even hesitate. She stripped and threw her clothes next to Nick's in a pile on the ground.

They gazed at each other. Lindsey licked her lips. She'd seen him in swim trunks, but this was completely different. She stared at his erect cock and his heavy testicles. She couldn't stop looking. He was glorious, all tan and muscled. A living work of art.

Nick took a step forward and traced a finger around her nipple. It tightened into a sharp peak. He pressed the pads of his thumbs over each peak and massaged her breasts. She arched into him, her body wanting more, and let her hands glide over his cock. She was gentle at first, moving her fingertips over the shaft and tracing the tip. Nick's sighs and deep groans fed her excitement. She grasped his cock firmly, stroking up and down, her pace quickening.

"Maybe we should sit down," Nick said, his voice hoarse.

He led her to the pile of sleeping bags, and she sank down next to him onto the silky surface. Her eyes were drawn to a slim length of rope on the ground. She reached over and pulled the smooth cord through her fingers. The memory of the night she had twisted her wrists into the tangled rope as Nick rocked his hand against her most sensitive place flashed through her mind.

She met Nick's gaze. His eyes were hooded and filled with desire. He was thinking about that night, too. He opened the golden packet and rolled the condom onto his erect penis. She had always thought this would be such a strange thing to witness, but with Nick, it was utterly fascinating.

She laid back on the blankets and extended her hands above her head still holding the rope. Nick's eyes danced over her body and rested on her wrists.

She fingered the edge of the rope. "Can you help me with this?"

Nick slid up her body, his hard, sheathed cock coming to rest at the entrance of her sex. Face to face, Nick pressed up onto his elbows and positioned her arms above her head. He slipped the rope around her wrists and weaved the cord around and around. Lindsey bit down on her lip and released a wanton moan.

"Too tight?" he asked.

She shook her head. She liked this. She liked relinquishing control to Nick. She'd never trusted anyone like this before. Her body tightened with anticipation, and his cock nudged at her entrance.

"Linds," he said, passing his thumb over her bottom lip. They were pressed together, bodies so close. "Are you sure you want to?"

"I'm sure. I love you."

He lowered his head and kissed her. His lips alone made her head spin.

"I love you," he whispered against her cheek as he kissed the corner of her mouth. "I love you so much sometimes I think my chest is going to explode. You're everything to me, Linds. Whatever it takes, I'm never going to lose you. I don't care how far apart we are. We'll always find each other."

She thrust her hips. "This is just the beginning."

Nick let out a low moan as his body tightened. Lindsey could tell he was doing everything he could to hold himself back

"I'm going to go slowly. I don't want to hurt you."

She nodded and relaxed her thighs. Nick positioned himself at her entrance and pushed past her delicate folds. She closed her eyes and opened to him. It wasn't that it didn't hurt, but it was the kind of ache she knew wasn't going to last long. Lindsey concentrated on her breathing as Nick filled her inch by delicious inch.

He stilled. "Linds, are you okay?"

She opened her eyes. She was okay. She was better than okay. She moved her hips, feeling Nick's cock tight inside of her.

Now it was his turn to close his eyes. "Lindsey, you feel so good."

He opened his eyes. Those beautiful blue eyes, blue like the summer sky, gazed upon her with pure adoration.

She moved her wrists against the rope, and Nick's gaze flicked to her hands. He reached up and tightened his grip around her bound wrists. Lindsey's core squeezed around his cock. She liked being tied up, and her body responded to her excitement as she moved her pelvis, feeling the slide of Nick's cock.

With Lindsey grinding into him, Nick wasn't able to hold back. Worry and trepidation drained from his expression and was replaced with unbridled desire. He kept his grip on her wrists and gained leverage with his other arm. He angled his body so that each steady thrust rubbed against her most sensitive parts. The friction, building a wave of pleasure, made her body writhe and pulse until she was flying over the edge, crying out his name in a tangle of breath and moans.

Her body was warm and sated as she watched Nick follow her over the edge and reach orgasm. His body moved over her like a machine, pumping and grinding. His arms flexed and pulsed in a heady beat that had her core tightening with excitement. He tucked his head into the crook of her neck and rode out his pleasure, gasping her name with heated breath. After a beat, he untied the rope and kissed each of her wrists.

Lindsey threaded her fingers into Nick's hair and brushed back a blond curl. "This is just the beginning," she whispered through a lazy grin.

"This is our beginning," he echoed and pressed feather-soft kisses to her smiling lips.

NICK SURVEYED THE CABIN. The plan was to pack up, eat breakfast, and then head back to Langley Park. But after last night, his mind was hardly on camp protocol. He had slept with Lindsey. No, he'd made love to her. All his previous experiences paled in comparison. He had fucked other girls, but he'd only ever loved one.

His mind was whirling with ideas. He would get his pilot's license. Then he could just fly and go visit her. They each had two more years of high school, but they could choose to go to the same college. The world was bright and shining and glowing with possibilities.

This is just the beginning.

That was their mantra. Those five words protected them from the distance that would soon be between them. They'd get back to Langley Park on Friday. His mother wasn't scheduled to be in Langley Park to pick him up until Monday afternoon. Lindsey wasn't scheduled to fly back to Maine until Monday night. They had the entire weekend together. That gave them plenty of time to make a plan and schedule visits.

This is just the beginning.

He just had to keep telling himself that.

The door to the cabin opened, and a terrified Rory met his gaze. "Mr. Nick, I need some help. Rachel fell."

"What do you mean Rachel fell?"

Before Rory could answer, Lindsey was standing outside Sawyer Cabin. "Rory where's Rachel? I thought you guys were just going for a quick walk after breakfast."

"She fell, Miss Lindsey. We were jumping rock to rock, and she landed wrong." The kid looked like he was about to cry.

"It's all right, Rory," Lindsey said, putting a hand on his shoulder. "Just take us to her."

Rory led them to the rock near the bluff. Rachel was still on the ground holding her ankle.

"I'm sorry Mr. Nick and Miss Lindsey. Rory tried to help me, but I just can't put any weight on my ankle," Rachel said, her voice shaky as she wiped away tears.

"Nobody's in any trouble," Lindsey said. "We just want to get you to the clinic."

I'm going to pick you up, Rachel," Nick said, bending over and carefully lifting her into his arms.

They made their way through the forest and over to the clinic. The director was out on the front lawn and came running over.

She ushered them inside. "What happened?"

Nick set Rachel on a cot. "Rachel hurt her ankle. She can't put any weight on it."

The camp nurse rushed over and assessed Rachel's injury. The woman looked up, met the director's gaze, and gave a quick shake of her head. The director motioned for Nick and Lindsey to join her outside the exam room.

She crossed her arms. "This injury happened at a very inopportune time. Lindsey, you're going to need to stay here with Rachel."

"Of course," Lindsey answered.

"Nick," the director continued, "you'll need to chaperone all your campers, boys and girls, back to Langley Park. We'll need to contact

Rachel's parents and have them drive up. I'll have Lindsey driven home after we get Rachel squared away."

He met Lindsey's gaze. "Are you going to be okay?"

"Yeah, I wouldn't want to leave Rachel on her own."

"I could stay," Rory said. "I don't want to leave Rachel either."

"She's in good hands," Nick said, squeezing Rory's shoulder. "Your parents are expecting you back in Langley Park. I'm sure Rachel and Miss Lindsey won't be too far behind us."

Rory nodded but kept his gaze directed at his shoes.

"I'll wait at the Community Center," Nick said, taking Lindsey's hand. Camp was over. That *gleeful glances only* shit was done. He didn't give one single fuck if the director had a problem with him touching his girlfriend.

Girlfriend.

A wave of warmth spread through his body.

"It might be late," Lindsey said, glancing back into the clinic.

"I'd wait all night. I'll be there when you get dropped off. We can go get ice cream or dinner or take pictures of clouds. Whatever you want."

The director cleared her throat and checked her watch. "Nick, you need to get moving. Your bus back to Langley Park leaves in fifteen minutes."

"Rocky road," Lindsey said, giving Nick's hand a squeeze.

"Rocky, what?" he asked.

"Rocky road. It's my favorite flavor of ice cream."

He wanted to kiss her. He wanted to tell her that he loved her.

"Rocky road it is," he said with a smile.

They had all weekend together. Plenty of time.

6

Nick stretched his legs out across the seat and glanced back at the kids, as the bus headed back to Langley Park. Tan cheeks. Tousled hair. Five days of back to back outdoor activities had caught up with them. They'd barely been on the road an hour before the bus quieted and all of the kids fell asleep, lulled by the constant hum of highway and breeze.

They had the same driver, Mr. Robbins, and he'd immediately flipped on his radio after they made the turn onto the interstate. Nick picked up the binder with all the campers' information and took out a blank sheet of paper and envelope. He reached into his backpack and grabbed a pen.

He leaned against the window. Five days ago, Lindsey was sitting with him in this exact seat. Five days ago, he was a different person. An angry person. An unkind person. Five days ago, he was his father. Strike that. He wasn't his father, yet. He'd never raised a hand to anyone in violence. He never purposely terrorized another human, but he was heading down the road of cruelty and self-loathing.

Lindsey had changed all that.

She gave him hope. She gave him her heart. She gave him everything. Her love. Her virginity. She had opened herself up to him in ways he had never imagined knowing another person.

He uncapped the pen.

Dear Linds, I never wanted to fall in love with you.

His eyes were heavy. He blinked them, trying to stay awake.

He never wanted to fall in love. He never expected to fall in love, but he did. He was so happy, so ecstatic. He wasn't even sure how to put it into words. The rhythmic movement of the bus was starting to get to him. He folded up the sheet of paper, slid it inside the envelope, and scribbled Lindsey's name on it. He would finish writing it when he got back to Langley Park.

Nick leaned his head back into the space between the window and the seat. He wished she was with him. It felt foreign not to have her close by. He inhaled. Maybe it was just a trick of his mind, but he caught her scent on the breeze—sweet cream and summer rain. He closed his eyes as the first notes of Tracy Chapman's "Fast Car" floated through the bus. Lindsey had mumbled something about liking this song before falling asleep, her head on his shoulder. Her body, soft and warm. She was his safe place. She was his home. He smiled, and his mind sifted through a jumble of images, all containing Lindsey. He saw her eyes, blue-green and sparkling only for him, before joining the rest of the bus and falling fast asleep.

"Nick, wake up, dear."

Nick tried to stretch out his legs, but his knees bumped into something.

Where the hell was he?

He opened his eyes.

Karen Quigley was standing in the bus aisle, tapping him on the shoulder. "You made it back to Langley Park." Her bright expression dimmed. "I was sorry to hear about Rachel. Luckily, it's not a break, just a bad sprain."

Nick ran the back of his hand across his mouth. Jesus, he had really slept. The drool on his chin was a testament to that. "I'm glad

Rachel's going to be okay," he said, coming to his feet. "Is Lindsey on her way back?"

"Rachel's parents offered to drive her back. I just got off the phone with them. They're leaving the hospital now."

Nick nodded. Just a few hours and he'd have her back.

"There's a little surprise for you," Karen said. "Let me take all that," she said, gesturing to the camp binder.

"What do you mean a surprise?" Nick asked.

"See for yourself! Don't worry about the kids. I'll get them sorted."

Nick grabbed his backpack and got off the bus.

"Nicky! My sweet boy!"

"Mom?" Nick said, not believing his eyes.

"It's good to see you, baby!"

She smiled up at him. He swallowed hard. It wasn't her real smile. She'd also applied makeup, but it didn't entirely cover a narrow slice of skin below her eye. The yellow tinge of a healing bruise glared out at him. She'd done a good job trying to cover it, but Nick had become a master of spotting his father's handiwork.

"Mom," he said. The word fell from his lips in one heartbreaking syllable.

"Look who's with me," she said.

A car door shut, and Nick's father strode up the sidewalk.

"It's good to see you, son. I hope a summer with your great old auntie didn't turn you too soft."

"No, sir," he mumbled.

"What was that, boy?"

"Oh, Cal, don't be like that," his mother said in that placating tone she always used with his father.

With just a flick of his eye, his father silenced his mother.

"Now answer your father like a man. Did a summer away turn you into a pansy?"

Rage coursed through Nick's body. It wasn't supposed to be like this. His father should have been a distant memory. He and his mother should be unpacking their things in a new apartment far away from the tyrannical rule of his father.

Nick squared his jaw. "No, sir, I did not turn into a pansy."

Cal laughed. It was the kind of laugh where you weren't sure if he was laughing at you or with you.

Nick and his mother had learned not to respond and remained silent.

Karen Quigley joined them and put a hand on Nick's forearm. "It was such a pleasure having Nick as a counselor this summer. He's welcome back anytime. I'm just sorry you have to leave so soon."

"Leave?" Nick said, meeting his mother's gaze.

"Daddy got us first class tickets heading back to Louisville today."

"Today?" Nick replied. That didn't give him much time.

"Something wrong with your hearing, son? Now. We need to leave right now. Such a shame we won't get to spend more time in this lovely town," his father said, sharing his million-watt smile with Karen. Always the charmer, his dad.

"We've already been to Aunt Marilyn's to collect your things, sweetheart," his mother added, but Nick couldn't bring himself to meet her gaze. Disappointment coursed through his body, so thick it was like molasses clogging every vein, every artery.

"I won't keep you, folks," Karen said and slipped Nick's camp binder under her arm.

His father pinned him with an icy gaze. "Come on, son. A family belongs together."

LINDSEY CLOSED the door of Rachel's parents' car and waved goodbye. They had insisted on stopping for a late lunch after Rachel was discharged from the hospital with little more than an ace bandage and orders to take ibuprofen for any pain. She was glad Rachel wasn't badly injured, but she was desperate to get back to Langley Park. She needed to see Nick, needed to feel his hands in her hair as he kissed her. She needed every second they had together before she was to head back home—wherever that was going to be.

It was almost seven o'clock, but the summer sky was still bright. She looked around, but she didn't see Nick. He would have beaten her back to Langley Park by at least three or four hours. She knew it was a long time to wait. He'd probably just gone to get something to eat or maybe he went inside the community center to cool off in the air-conditioned building. She set her backpack and sleeping bag on a bench near the entrance and waited.

The doors to the facility opened. Lindsey's head whipped toward them expectantly, but it wasn't Nick. It was Karen Quigley.

"I saw you just got dropped off," the Kids' Camp director said with a smile. "Thanks for calling to let me know how Rachel was doing. It's never easy when a kiddo gets hurt. I'm glad you were able to stay with her."

"Me, too, Mrs. Quigley," Lindsey said, glancing past the director as a couple of teens left the center.

"Are you waiting for someone, Lindsey?"

She bit down on her lip. "I was hoping Nick would still be here."

"Oh, he left hours ago. His parents picked him up right after the bus got here."

His parents?

"Where did they go?" Lindsey asked. Her mouth had gone dry, and her words came out choked and cracked.

"Home," Karen answered. "They had to leave right away to catch their flight."

There wasn't enough air. She couldn't breathe. It just couldn't be true. He wouldn't have left her. He'd beg his parents to stay— only a few hours, just until he could see her one more time.

Karen handed her an envelope. "He did leave this. I found it in his camp binder. It's got your name on it."

She took the envelope.

Karen touched her arm. "Thank you for all your work this summer."

Lindsey nodded, and the woman went back inside the community center.

Her hands shook as she pulled out a single sheet of paper. She unfolded it slowly, her breath ragged and tight.

There was only one sentence. She read it once, then twice.

Dear Linds, I never wanted to fall in love with you.

She held the paper tightly in her hand and started running as tears trailed down her cheeks. She crossed the street and headed into the Langley Park Botanic Gardens. She'd spent many afternoons there, leading her campers on nature walks and geocaching expeditions. There was a spot—a bench hidden behind a tall juniper hedge, secluded and tucked away. Her heart pounded as it came into view.

She sat down and wiped her eyes.

"No," she said, staring at the piece of paper.

She unfolded it and reread Nick's words.

He didn't want to love her?

He didn't want her?

He didn't leave a phone number or an address. He didn't even sign the letter. He was gone. He was just like her father. Nick had made her feel so special, so loved, and then he took all of that happiness and turned it into gut-wrenching pain.

"Why am I not enough?" she whispered into the dense foliage of her hiding place.

She was a fool. She'd never seen it coming with her father, and now, the same thing had happened with Nick.

Lindsey heard something. A pitiful noise that tore through her soul. It was her. She was sobbing. She looked down at Nick's letter as her tears landed on the page with a steady tap, smearing the ink. Erasing the love she thought had just begun. A love she'd dreamed could have lasted a lifetime.

7

PRESENT DAY

Lindsey sank into the diner's upholstered booth. The buzz of conversation calmed her frayed nerves. Noise meant people, and people meant safety. She looked out through the plate glass window into the parking lot. Every car had a Kansas license plate.

She was so close.

Three months of planning.

Three months of living in fear.

She just had to stay strong a little bit longer.

She pulled a map out of her purse and unfolded it. She had made it to Wichita. She was out of Texas. There were six hundred miles between herself and her old life in Houston. She pressed her finger to the map and traced the highlighted line from Wichita to Langley Park, Kansas—her final destination. Her fresh start. *Their* fresh start.

"Can I get you some coffee?"

Lindsey snapped her head up and folded the map into an untidy square.

A waitress. It was just the waitress.

She glanced at the menu. "I'll take some herbal tea and the chicken sandwich, please."

"Sure thing, hun." The waitress's eyes flicked to the map. "Where are you headed?"

"Springfield," Lindsey answered. She hated to lie, but it was the only way to stay safe.

"I know Springfield. I've got a cousin there," the waitress said with a grin. "Is that where your family's from?"

"No, my friend lives there. She just had a baby, and I'm going to visit her."

Provide information that sounds like you're being personable but don't reveal your true destination.

"How nice! Let me get that order in for you."

"Is there a pay phone nearby?" Lindsey asked before the woman turned to go.

"Down the hall by the restrooms."

She slid out of the booth and clutched her purse. She had almost eight thousand dollars in cash and three rolls of quarters. She picked up the receiver and peeled eight quarters off the top of the roll. Three months ago, using a pay phone seemed archaic. But pay phones were hard to track. Pay phones couldn't pinpoint your longitude and latitude the way a cell phone could.

The phone rang once, then twice. "Please, pick up," she whispered into the receiver.

"Hello?"

Lindsey exhaled in relief upon hearing her godmother's voice.

"Rosemary, it's me."

"Is it safe to talk on this line, dear?"

"Yes, I'm on a pay phone. I made it to Wichita. I'm going to spend the night here and drive the rest of the way tomorrow."

"Thank goodness," her godmother said. "Were you able to pick up the car?"

Lindsey had taken the 12:45 a.m. Greyhound from Houston. She transferred to another bus in Dallas and spent the last eight hours making her way to Wichita, Kansas. Rosemary had purchased a car for her a week ago. It was waiting for her at the used car lot.

Lindsey rested her head against the wall. The sting of tears burned her eyes. "Yes, I just picked it up. It's a lovely car. I'm so sorry. I'm so sorry I dragged you into all of this."

"Sweetheart," Rosemary said in a calm, steady voice. "You never have to apologize to me."

When she had arrived at the women's shelter in Houston three months ago, the first thing they told her was that, if possible, she needed to identify a contact person—someone she could trust with every aspect of her life. Her father wasn't an option. They hadn't communicated in years. Her mother had passed away, and her ex-fiancé, Brett Mathews, had made damn sure she didn't have anyone significant in her life besides him. Lindsey hadn't spoken to Rosemary Giacopazzi in well over a decade. But when she phoned her godmother, the woman didn't hesitate to say yes when Lindsey asked for help.

"You have nothing to apologize for, Lindsey. Nothing. I loved your mother. She was one of my dearest friends, and I love you, too. I know your mother would be proud of you."

"But the money," Lindsey said.

"It's your money, sweetheart. You know your mother only left it to me to keep it safe for you. If you ever..."

"If I ever left him."

"Yes," her godmother replied. "She knew you weren't calling the shots. She knew Brett was manipulating you."

"How could I have not have seen it, Rosemary? How did I let it get this bad?"

"You didn't do anything wrong. He abused you. He terrorized you," Rosemary said, her tone firm but even.

"I know but..."

"But nothing. You're Lindsey Davies now. Lindsey Hanlon is gone. Brett doesn't know I'm your godmother. He knows nothing of Langley Park. You're going to be safe here."

Tears rolled down her cheeks. Safe. She couldn't remember the last time she'd felt safe. She reached into her purse and pulled out an envelope with an address and a silver key.

718 Foxglove Lane, Langley Park, Kansas.

"Can I go straight to the house?"

"Yes," Rosemary said. The smile was back in her voice. "It's all ready for you."

"You'll be close by?"

"Less than a five-minute drive," Rosemary answered.

A mechanical voice came on the line. Time was almost up.

Lindsey swiped at a tear. "Thank you, Rosemary."

"This is your fresh start, sweetheart. Get some rest. I'll see you soon."

She was just about to hang the handset back into the cradle when a loud crash ricocheted through the restaurant. Her gaze shot to a man with dark hair and broad shoulders.

She froze like a cornered animal. "He found me."

The man bent down and started picking up pieces of broken glass and plates. Lindsey blinked and stared at him. It wasn't Brett. It wasn't the man who had spent the last three years manipulating her mind, breaking her body, and crushing her soul. She opened her purse, and, with a shaky hand, grabbed the roll of quarters and emptied several into her palm. She tucked the phone between her ear and shoulder, reset the line, and deposited several coins. She didn't count how many went in. The crash of the bus boy's tray had left her mind too frazzled.

The counselors at the shelter said this was common. Battered women often experienced moments where they were entirely positive their abuser was just steps away in a restaurant or walking down the street directly into their path. These faux sightings could happen anywhere, at any time.

Lindsey dialed and waited.

"Is that you, Lindsey?"

"Claire!" The word came out in a tight sob.

"Lindsey, are you all right?"

She nodded, then remembered Claire couldn't see her. "Where is he right now?"

"He's here, in Houston. It's Wednesday. You know he's in surgery."

Lindsey squeezed her eyes shut. The Brett Mathews the world

knew was a talented surgeon. A man dedicated to his work and to his community. His office walls were lined with plaques and diplomas. Patients spoke of him as if he were a god. But Lindsey had known the other side of the good doctor. The dark side. The brutal side. The side that would hold a gun to her head and whisper, "If you ever try to leave me, I'll hunt you down, and I'll kill you."

"Yes, you're right. I just wanted to make sure," Lindsey said in a shaky breath. She opened her eyes and watched the man, who was not her ex-fiancé, pick up the last remaining pieces of glass.

"I wish I could have done more for you, Lindsey—helped you before it came to this. I never imagined my brother-in-law could be so..."

Lindsey pressed a hand to her belly. "He doesn't know about my situation, that's the important thing."

She knew not to mention anything about the baby over the phone.

She had been living underground, in hotels and shelters, and off the grid for the last three months preparing to start a new life. With the help of the shelter's free legal services, she had a new last name and a new social security number. But Claire was the only person, besides Rosemary, who knew she was pregnant.

Claire had been with Brett's younger brother, Mason, since she was fifteen years old and married him when she turned eighteen. Brett, Claire, and Mason were from the same dead end west Texas town and had all bounced around in foster care for the majority of their youth. They escaped their circumstances, studied medicine, and become physicians.

Lindsey was terrified when she ran into Claire at the drugstore just as she was purchasing a home pregnancy test. But Claire had sworn she wouldn't breathe a word of Lindsey's pregnancy to anyone, not even to her husband.

"No, he doesn't know, but...," Claire paused.

"But, what?" Lindsey asked.

Claire let out a breath. "Brett's told people that you pawned all the jewelry he'd given you and stole pain meds from his office. He's making you out to be a junkie who ran out on him."

"It doesn't matter," Lindsey said, shaking her head. "I'm never going to see him again. I'm never going back to Houston. That life is over." She paused. She needed to end the call. "Thank you for being a friend when I needed it most. I'm sorry I can't tell you where I'm going. It's part of my safety plan. I better hang—"

"Were you able to get your camera bag?" Claire asked, sliding in the question.

It was a risk, but last week, Lindsey had left a cryptic message with Claire's office asking if she could retrieve her old Nikon camera bag from Brett's home and send it to a law office that did pro bono work for the shelter. She didn't even know if Claire had gotten the message, but a day before she departed Houston, the camera bag arrived at the shelter.

"I did. Thank you. Brett kept all my camera equipment locked up. How did you get it?"

"Just by luck. Mason and I were over at Brett's last week. He put all your things into boxes. I saw the old Nikon camera bag and tucked it into my purse. There were some old film canisters tucked inside. Did you need those?"

Lindsey swallowed hard. She'd documented each beating with that Nikon. The undeveloped film sat in silent spools. Its secrets locked inside light-sensitive silver halide crystals.

Lindsey glanced down the hall as her waitress placed a mug and a plate with her sandwich on the table. She needed to get off the phone. There was a possibility Brett could get access to his sister-in-law's phone records.

"Claire, I'm sorry. I need to go. I shouldn't have even made this call." She took a steadying breath. "Goodbye, I'll never forget your kindness."

"One last thing," Claire said, urgency coating her words. "Keep the baby safe. That's all that matters."

The breath caught in Lindsey's throat at the mention of her

unborn child. But before she could say another word, the line was dead.

Welcome to Langley Park.

Lindsey tightened her grip on the steering wheel as she passed the welcome sign and entered the town. This place was going to be her home. It all started coming back to her: the streets named after plant life native to the region, the quaint town center, and the surrounding neighborhood of charming Tudor, bungalow, and Federal style homes.

Last time she had been to Langley Park, it was the height of summer. The town was vibrant with color and life. Now it was just waking up from winter's dark slumber. The trees were just beginning to come back to life. Crimson buds lined the spindly branches of the red maples and shoots of green were visible on the bur oaks.

Nature's rebirth. Could it be hers, too?

She headed north onto Aster Road, and the Langley Park Botanic Gardens came into view. The gardens were on the east side of the town center and beyond them, Lake Boley. She pulled over and stared at a large play structure on the grassy lawn. There was a chill in the March air, but a few children were out taking turns crossing the monkey bars as a cluster of men and women chatted nearby sipping coffee.

She bit her lip. It was too soon to think she was in the clear, too early to assume that the safe, quiet life she desperately wanted was just within her grasp. She rubbed her arms and turned up the heater. It was much colder here than it was in Houston.

She thought back to Claire's words and the story Brett was telling to explain her disappearance. He wasn't lying about one aspect of her escape. She had taken the jewelry he'd given her and pawned it. The thought of those diamonds and emeralds turned her stomach. Each gift had come after an assault. Each gift had come with the empty promise that he would never hurt her again, that he couldn't live without her, and that if she would just stop pushing his buttons, he wouldn't have to punish her.

She earned those jewels. She paid for each sparkling gem with blood and tears.

Lindsey shifted the car into gear and glanced at the children. She slowed down as she approached the intersection of Aster and Prairie Rose Street, and the Langley Park Community Recreation Center came into view. It had changed, the entrance looked different, but she had always remembered the giant oaks. They still towered over the building. She bit the inside of her cheek as the memories of her summer spent here as a camp counselor flooded back.

Memories of Nick Kincade. Memories of his kisses. Memories of those blue eyes. Memories of that night in the boathouse. Memories of the sentence that crushed her heart.

I never wanted to fall in love with you.

She blinked back tears. It would be hard coming back to Langley Park, but she needed Rosemary. She had no other family she could depend on. With the baby coming, she needed to be somewhere safe. Langley Park was the best place for her child. And that's what mattered.

She had survived her father's abandonment, Nick's rejection, and Brett's abuse. She would survive the ghosts of Langley Park.

Lindsey dropped a hand to her abdomen. "No man is going to decide our fate. No man is going to dictate our happiness. No man is ever going to hurt us," she whispered as tears rolled down her cheeks. "It's just you and me, little one. Let's go home."

8

"Are you about ready, Nick? We need to head over to Em and Michael's."

Nick ran a hand over his face and pulled on a pair of jeans. He was thirty-two years old and living out of a suitcase in his friend Sam Sinclair's guest room in Langley Park. It could best be described as more of a storage locker than an actual bedroom.

Sam knocked twice and opened the door. He looked Nick up and down. "I can see why you don't have any lady friends. Blond hair, blue eyes, flies airplanes, ripped as fuck. It's got to be hard being you."

Nick shook his head and put on a shirt. "I don't know, buddy," he called back, "I guess they all like the giant, ginger dudes with tats."

Sam ran a hand through his mess of auburn curls. "We're just two bachelors who are unlucky in love, I guess. Would you have pictured us like this back when we were eighteen?"

Nick laughed. "Those were good days."

Nick and Sam had met when they volunteered to go to Honduras and build schools the year after they graduated high school. Sam was a good friend, and he knew a lot about Nick—but not everything.

Sam maneuvered his way into the room. "I have a ton of shit, don't

I?" Sam asked, moving a stack of old comic books off a chair and taking a seat.

"You have lived in this town all your life. I'd imagine accumulating stuff is easy to do."

Sam nodded but didn't give one of his trademark snarky replies.

Nick grabbed a jacket and Sam followed him out of the bungalow.

Sam zipped up his jacket. "You want to walk? You know what they say, 'Walkable and family friendly, everyone's clamoring to move into Langley Park.' "

"That is what they say," Nick echoed.

The men fell into step. Sam lived in a 1930s bungalow on the west side of the town. It was about a fifteen-minute walk to Em and Michael's Foursquare style home on the southside of Langley Park.

"What does Michael need help with?" Nick asked.

Sam let out a breath. "Something in the baby's room. I still can't believe my cousin and Em are expecting a baby. I mean, a baby, dude?"

"They seem pretty happy about it," Nick replied.

"Yeah, they do," Sam conceded.

They walked a few paces in silence.

"Have you ever thought about it?" Sam asked. "You know the whole 'having a family' thing."

A muscle ticked in Nick's cheek. "You know how it was for me growing up with my dad. It's not in the cards for me. I couldn't face myself if I turned out to be like my father."

"Single pilot screwing stewardesses mid-flight doesn't sound like such a bad gig," Sam said.

His friend was trying to lighten the conversation, but Nick had to set him straight. "First of all, they're flight attendants, and second, nobody does any screwing mid-flight—especially not the pilot."

"You're killing my whole Nick Kincade pilot fantasy, man," Sam said as they rounded the corner onto Em and Michael's street, Foxglove Lane.

They stopped in front of the house. The front bedroom window was open, and strange moaning sounds floated out onto the breeze.

Nick bit back a laugh. "Are they..."

"Sweet Jesus," Sam said, covering his ears and shaking his head.

"Maybe we should take a walk around the block?"

"One lap," Sam said, then glanced up at the window. "Maybe two."

Nick threw his friend an amused grin. Sam was a big reason he had decided to make Langley Park his home. Years ago, when the two met in Honduras, he couldn't believe it when Sam said he was from Langley Park, Kansas. Nick had almost told him about the summer he'd spent there, but he wanted to keep his memories of Lindsey all to himself, frozen in time. If he had spoken about her, Sam would have asked what happened. He would have wanted to know why the fairytale didn't come true.

This is just the beginning.

There would be moments when he'd swear he had heard Lindsey's voice whisper those five words, their five words. He would swear he smelled her scent, all sweet cream and summer rain. And when he was flying, he'd swear it was the blue-green of her eyes calling to him in the horizon.

But it wasn't the beginning. It was the end. It ended with his mother taking his father back. It ended with him not getting to say goodbye to Lindsey. It ended with a half-written letter he knew had broken her heart. It also ended with his father who punched him so hard in the gut on the way to the airport that he had three bruised ribs—all because he wanted to make sure Nick hadn't gone soft after a summer living under his aunt's roof.

Nick and Sam finished their second lap around Foxglove Lane and walked back up the path to Michael and Em's place, but the amorous couple wasn't quite finished.

Sam looked at his watch. "I'm knocking. I don't know if they're going to answer, but we can't be huffing it around the block all damn day."

Things inside the Foursquare sounded like they were coming to an end, and Nick gestured for him to go ahead.

Sam knocked and folded his arms. A few minutes later, Michael opened the door.

"What the hell's going on in there?" Sam asked.

Michael joined them on the porch and pulled a ball cap over his tousled auburn hair. He looked like a Hoover had attacked him.

Nick met Michael's gaze and mouthed, "Holy shit, dude."

"Don't let anyone tell you pregnancy is the pits, boys," Michael said, adjusting his hat. "I may be making two a.m. trips to Pete's Organic Grocer for ice cream, bananas, and bacon..."

Nick and Sam grimaced in unison.

"But, it certainly has its perks," Michael said, grinning like an idiot.

Sam gave his cousin a playful shove. "You and Em are the last hope for the ginger race. Science says we're a dying breed. So by all means, go make all the redheaded babies you two possibly can."

Nick smiled as he watched the cousins' exchange. He had grown to care about Michael and Em. They were starting to feel like family. But he sure as hell didn't want to discuss their sex life. He gestured toward the house next door. "Have the new owners moved in yet? You know, into the Foursquare you didn't sell to me."

It was Em's old house, a lovely 1930s Foursquare similar to Michael's. She needed to sell it so her father could purchase an assisted living cottage in the nearby Langley Park Senior Living Campus. He required more intensive medical care for a respiratory ailment, and the campus offered everything he needed to live a more fulfilling life. Mrs. G, a retired teacher who seemed to have been everyone's third-grade teacher in Langley Park, purchased the home for a family member. Nick had only run into Mrs. G a few times, but something about her felt familiar.

"Dude?" Sam said, feigning surprise. "You don't like crashing at my place?"

The last thing Nick wanted to do was hurt Sam's feelings. "You know I appreciate your hospitality, buddy. But now that I'm going to be in Langley Park permanently, I need to find a place that doesn't include waking up to you singing, "Oh, What a Beautiful Mornin!'"

Sam threw him a cheeky grin. "You have something against Rodgers and Hammerstein's *Oklahoma*, Kincade?"

Em joined them on the porch. "You got the job?"

He nodded. "You're looking at the Kansas City Downtown Airport's newest Director of Aviation. I start next week."

Most people had no clue what a director of aviation did—let alone, that the position even existed. When he'd told Sam about getting the job, his friend met him with a blank expression until he explained that he was in charge of all aspects of the airport: flight tracking, aircraft rentals, flight training, maintenance, fueling. The list went on and on. While the airport wasn't as large as Kansas City's main airport, the downtown airport was still an incredibly busy airfield with over seven hundred aircraft, from single-engine, two-seaters to sleek corporate jets, taking off or landing every day.

Sam clapped him on the back. "Hearts are breaking at every port. Airports, that is. Captain Nick is putting down roots."

Em's expression darkened. "Are you going to miss flying?"

"I'll still get to fly," Nick answered. "I'll run the airport, and I may pick up some corporate flights if the opportunity presents itself. Plus, I've always got my little four-seater Cessna Skyhawk I can take up anytime I want. Right now, I need to figure out a more permanent living situation."

"Seriously, man," Sam said, all of his teasing tone gone. "You're always welcome at my place. You know that."

Nick nodded. He never thought he would put down roots anywhere, but Langley Park was the first place that felt like it could be his home.

"Wait a second," Em said. She shared a look with Michael. "Nick, you should move into our carriage house apartment until you find a place in Langley Park."

Nearly all the homes in the town came with freestanding garages or carriage houses. Often, homeowners added a finished second-floor apartment to this space.

"Absolutely," Michael said. "Em and I grew up listening to Sam belt out show tunes. It's a miracle you've survived this long."

Sam chuckled and shook his head.

"What about your mom?" Nick asked. Em's mother was coming in from Australia any day now for a visit. "Won't she need the carriage house?"

Em shook her head. "She can stay in our guest room in the Foursquare."

As much as Nick loved Sam, the thought of having a little privacy and some space to hunker down and prepare for his new position was too good to pass up.

"If you're sure you don't mind, I'd appreciate it. I'm ready to jump when something goes on the market in the area—so I shouldn't be in your hair for too long. I do have an aunt nearby in Mission Springs. She's offered to let me stay with her, but that would involve weekly Euchre games with her Junior League ladies. I politely declined."

"Understandable," Michael said.

"Really, Nick," Em added, "it would be no trouble at all. You can stay as long as you need to."

"Thanks, guys," Nick said. He turned to his longtime friend. "You know I love you, Sam. But with my new job and the crazy hours, it may be good to have a place all to myself."

"Whatever works, bud," Sam said with a grin. "I'm just glad you're making Langley Park your home."

Michael gestured to the door. "Let's head inside. We can hammer out the details while we try to figure out how the hell to put this nursery together. Who writes these directions?"

But just as the group was about to head inside, a sedan turned onto Foxglove Lane.

A tremor shot through his spine.

It couldn't be.

The car passed by the house.

Nick was just about to shake off the strange déjà vu sensation when the car came back down the street and stopped in front of Em's Foursquare. A woman sat in the driver's seat wearing sunglasses and a ball cap. A long cascade of chestnut brown hair fell past her shoulders.

The air left his body like a punch to the gut.

"Do you think that's Mrs. G's goddaughter?" Em asked.

Goddaughter.

Nick knew they'd sold the house to a relative of Mrs. G's, but until this moment, nobody had mentioned it was her goddaughter.

"I'm not sure," Michael answered. "I've never met her. Mrs. G said she spent a summer in Langley Park when she was sixteen. She worked at the Langley Park Community Center's summer camp. Did you ever meet her, Sam? Mrs. G says you guys are the same age."

Sam shook his head. "No, I don't think so."

A muscle ticked in Nick's cheek. "I worked at the Langley Park Community Center's summer camp when I was sixteen."

"You did?" Sam asked. "How the hell did I not know that?"

"My mom sent me to stay with my aunt," Nick answered, but he didn't look at Sam. He couldn't tear his gaze from the mysterious woman in the car.

Things were starting to come together in his mind. It was like staring at one of those pictures where the image is hidden until your eyes fall just out of focus and then the picture jumps out at you, screaming its presence.

Mrs. G's first name was Rosemary. Lindsey's godmother's name was Rosemary. He'd never known her last name.

The woman got out of the car and gazed up at the Foursquare. She hadn't noticed them yet. She was wearing a baggy sweatshirt and worn jeans. Nothing about her said look at me, but Nick couldn't take his eyes off of her. It was like watching a fantasy materialize into a reality right before his eyes.

Em's cheery voice broke his trance.

"Hello," she called out, stepping off the porch and crossing the yard.

Michael and Sam followed, but it took him a second to move. It was her. It was Lindsey. It had to be. Every cell in his body remembered her touch, her scent, her smile.

The woman let out a startled gasp, and her hands went up protectively.

"I'm sorry! We didn't mean to frighten you. I'm Em MacCaslin. This is Michael MacCarron. We're your neighbors. This is Sam Sinclair and Nick Kincade. They're our friends, and they live in Langley Park, too."

Lindsey's hands trembled. She clasped them tightly and gave Em a tight, nervous smile. He had never seen her like this. This wasn't who she was. But he hadn't seen her in more than fifteen years. What the hell could have happened?

"It's nice to meet you all," Lindsey said.

He could hear the shake in her voice. It nearly killed him.

"I'm Lindsey—"

"Lindsey Hanlon," he said. His mouth had gone dry. His words sounded cracked and broken. He had thought of her plenty over the years, but he hadn't spoken her name. Not once. Not to anyone.

She looked away. "It's Lindsey Davies, now."

Nick's gaze shot to her hand. No wedding ring.

"Do you two know each other?" Em asked.

"We worked at the Community Center's summer camp. That summer I was just telling you about," Nick said, his gaze still locked on Lindsey.

Lindsey stilled, and a blush crept up her neck. He knew that blush. She took a step back and glanced at the Foursquare. "I hardly remember that summer. It was such a long time ago. I don't mean to be rude, but I've had a long trip. I'd like to get settled inside."

"Of course," Em said. "Were you able to get the key from Mrs. G? She's your godmother, right?"

Another tight smile. Another quick nod. Lindsey looked ready to bolt.

"Are your things being delivered today?" Michael asked. "If you need any help carrying boxes or moving furniture, just let us know. We're happy to help."

Lindsey took another step back. "There's no moving truck."

The mountain of tension morphed into awkward, pregnant silence.

"Well," Em said. "You know where we'll be. You're welcome at our place anytime."

Same tight smile. Same quick nod. Before Em had finished speaking, Lindsey was halfway up the porch steps.

The door to the Foursquare slammed shut. The sharp click of the deadbolt might as well have been a shot to his heart.

The four of them stared up at the house. Nobody said a word.

Sam put a hand on Nick's shoulder. "Dude, I don't think she remembers you."

Nick's heart was pounding. "No, I know she remembers me. She only wishes she didn't."

"Let's give her some time. Moving is stressful," Michael said, taking Em's hand and heading toward their Foursquare.

Nick was just about to join Sam, Em, and Michael, when he froze. "I'll meet you guys inside. I need to..." He looked at the house that was now Lindsey's home. "I need a minute."

A frown pulled at Em's lips. "Are you sure that's a good idea, Nick?"

"Just a minute," he repeated. The pull of having Lindsey so close was almost too much for him to bear.

He needed to see her.

He needed...

Christ, he didn't know what he needed, but he knew it started with talking to her.

He pounded on the door with the side of his fist. He hadn't meant it to sound so menacing, but adrenaline was coursing through his veins. What had happened to her? Where was the girl who had carried herself with such strength and purpose?

He waited for a beat, then two and knocked again. "Come on, Lindsey! It's me. It's Nick. I only want to talk."

He listened. A muffled sound traveled through the door. A heartbreaking whimper that cut him to the bone.

Nick went to the window, cupped his hands over his eyes, and peered inside the house. Most of the furniture had been sold with the house. Em had only taken her piano and a few other sentimental pieces. The rest of the items in the home now belonged to Lindsey.

He scanned the front living room. Lindsey wasn't there. He ran to the other side of the porch and looked into the adjacent room. He was just about to pound on the door again when he caught sight of her. The Foursquare was essentially a large two-story, square-shaped structure. The first floor consisted of two front rooms and a staircase in the center. A kitchen and a dining area made up the back of the house. From his limited vantage point, he had almost missed her. She was sitting on the staircase, clutching at the banister like it was the only thing keeping her from being blown away.

She was crying. He'd never seen her cry before. The sound tore through him like a million tiny razor blades.

He went back to the door. She was sitting on the steps only a few feet away from him. He crouched down and rested his forehead against the hard wood. "Linds, I know you can hear me. Please, open the door."

A tangle of sobs vibrated through the door. She was there. Only an inch or so separated them. He remembered holding his hand up against the window screen of her cabin and how she would run her finger down the length of his palm. His body had never forgotten her touch. Even through a bolted door, he could feel her. He closed his eyes and listened to the muffled cries of the only girl he had ever loved.

"*Nick.*"

That was her—barely a whisper. He knew it. It wasn't a trick of his mind, or someone else's voice carried from far away on the breeze. She had just said his name. He needed to see her. He needed to look into those blue-green eyes.

He swallowed hard, blinked back tears, and pounded his palm against the door in one last desperate clap. "Please, Linds, open the door."

"Excuse me," came a woman's voice from the street. She didn't sound happy. "What are you doing?"

Nick shot up and spun around. It was Mrs. G.

"Nick, why are you..." She stopped and shook her head. "No, no, no. How could I have not put it together?"

Nick left the porch and joined her on the sidewalk. "Mrs. G, I know Lindsey, I'm—"

"You're the Nick from the summer she stayed with me. I knew you looked familiar. But I couldn't place you—until now."

"I only knew you as Rosemary when Lindsey would talk about you. Nobody calls you that around here. Around here you're—"

"I'm simply Mrs. G," she answered with a sympathetic smile.

Nick ran a hand over his face. "What happened to her? Why is she so scared? I know she remembers me, but she won't open the door."

Mrs. G squeezed his forearm. Her grip was warm and solid, but her words nearly killed him.

"Lindsey's story isn't mine to tell. But the fact that she's made it here, and she's alive is a testament to her strength." She paused and glanced up at the house. "I know you two have history, but I don't know how much more heartache she can take. If there's one piece of advice that I can offer you, it's just to let her be, Nick. Let her heal."

"But—" Nick began when the soft howl of Lindsey's sob carried over the breeze.

"Nick," Mrs. G said, cutting him off. "I need to go to her. I'm all she has. I'm sorry, dear." She released her grip on his arm and hurried past him up the porch steps.

She tapped the door twice. "Lindsey, it's me. It's Rosemary. Can I come in?"

Nick stared at the sidewalk. Guilt wound tight around his heart. He'd never looked for her—never tried to contact her. After his parents had met the bus from Camp Clem and whisked him back to Kentucky, he could have called the community center. He could have tried to see if someone there could put him in touch with her.

But he didn't.

He had sunk back into the routine of living with his father's temper, his mother's empty promises, and the hopelessness he'd known for so very long. The love and happiness he had found with

Lindsey didn't even seem real. That time with her became nothing but a brief respite from a life composed of beatings and disappointment.

Mrs. G tapped lightly on the door again, and the click of the lock disengaging sent a shudder down his spine.

"The deadbolt isn't secure enough," Lindsey said, voice shaking as she opened the door. "And the windows, anyone can see inside."

Nick could hear the tears choking her words.

"Those are all things we can take care of, dear," Mrs. G said. She glanced back at him then closed the door and locked him out.

9

Rosemary led Lindsey into the kitchen. "Let's have some tea. I brought some groceries over a few days ago. I wasn't sure exactly when you'd make it here."

Lindsey sat down on a bar stool and wrapped her arms around her body. "You weren't sure if I'd make it."

Rosemary filled the kettle with water and set it on the stove. "I knew you'd make it. I know you, Lindsey. I know your strength."

"I don't feel very strong." She met her godmother's gaze. "And why didn't you tell me Nick Kincade was here? What's he even doing back in Langley Park?"

"I didn't put it together until just now, dear. I never knew your Nick's last name. I thought Nick Kincade was just an old friend of one of my former students, Sam Sinclair, but it seems he has more of a connection to Langley Park than I ever knew."

"He was never my Nick," Lindsey said, balling her hands into fists, trying to stop them from shaking. She let out a ragged breath. "I'm sorry, Rosemary. You've shown me nothing but kindness. I just never expected to see him again."

Lindsey hadn't told Rosemary about what had happened with

Nick after she had gotten back from Camp Clem. But her perceptive godmother had known something was wrong.

Lindsey had spent her last few days in Langley Park at the botanic gardens near Lake Boley, sitting on the steps of the pavilion, reading the letter from Nick over and over. That's where Rosemary had found her, and she'd shown her the letter. Her godmother hadn't offered any trite words of comfort. She only held her hand and sat with her as she cried.

That was the last time she had spoken his name—until today.

Nick.

Her lips wanted to repeat it. They trembled with the need to whisper the one, single syllable that had crushed her heart sixteen years ago.

The kettle whistled, and Rosemary poured hot water into a mug. "I got you some chamomile tea. It's caffeine-free and safe for..."

Lindsey nodded and dunked the teabag into the steaming cup. Rosemary didn't need to finish her sentence. There were more important things to focus on now. She was going to be a mother, and she needed to do everything in her power to protect herself and her unborn child from the monster she'd been living with for the last three years.

Rosemary took a sip of tea. "I have a few things for you." She reached into her purse and pulled out a checkbook and two credit cards all bearing her new name, Lindsey Davies. "I've added you to my accounts. Everything is under my name as the primary account holder, so it can't be traced to you."

Lindsey picked up the cards and stared down at them.

Mrs. G tapped the checkbook. "The money in the trust is all yours. I may be the executor, but if you decided you wanted to invest it all into a llama farm in Ecuador, I wouldn't stop you."

The hint of a grin appeared on Lindsey's lips. "I don't know anything about farms or llamas, and I don't speak Spanish. It's a pretty safe bet I won't be purchasing anything in Ecuador anytime soon."

"There's that smile," Rosemary said, patting her hand. "Now, let me see, there's more." Her godmother rooted around her purse and placed two business cards on the table. One was for the Rose Brooks Women's Shelter and Counseling Center, and the other was for the Kansas City Chamber of Commerce.

Lindsey picked up the card for the shelter.

"Have I told you about my job working part-time as an office manager for one of my former student's architecture firm?" Rosemary asked, sipping her tea.

Lindsey ran her thumb along the edge of the card. "What does that have to do with the women's shelter?"

"My student's name is Ben Fisher. His wife, Jenna, is very active in supporting the work they do there. It's a good place. They help lots of women and children. I don't think it would hurt to attend one of their support groups."

Lindsey nodded. As grateful as she was for the help she had received from the shelter in Houston, she wanted that part of her life gone, locked away like a bad dream. She pointed to the Chamber of Commerce card. "Another past student?"

Her godmother chuckled. "My goodness, I'm feeling awfully old, but, yes, I taught several current members of the Kansas City Chamber of Commerce."

Lindsey could see why everyone loved her godmother. She had such an open, empathetic way about her that was almost intoxicating.

"I'd mentioned that my photographer goddaughter was moving to the area and learned that the Chamber was looking to hire a full-time photographer. They've got a whole campaign planned. It seems the city is trying to woo families and millennials—whatever millennials are."

Another hint of a smile. Being around Rosemary was the best medicine.

"I showed them your work. It's still online."

Lindsey's expression darkened. "But it's all under Lindsey Hanlon. Won't they wonder why I'm Lindsey Davies now?"

"I just told them you were going back to your maiden name.

Nowadays, you should see what people do with their last names. I just attended a wedding, and the bride had a hyphenated last name and so did the groom. They're now Amanda and Roger Baton-Campbell-Carry-Morgan." Rosemary gave her a mischievous smile. "As long as you don't have four last names, I don't think anyone cares what you would like to be called."

Something warmed inside her heart. That part of her that craved independence. That part that loved exploring the world through a camera lens. Three years ago, she was a successful freelance photographer, photographing nature as well as cityscapes all over the world. She had lived for those moments when the light would shift, and she'd capture an image so unique, so mesmerizing, it would stop you right in your tracks. Her work had been featured in publications all over the world, and, while it was a solitary life, it had been her life to live as she pleased. A shudder passed through her body, thinking of what she'd given up and what she had endured all in the name of what she thought was love.

Rosemary touched her hand. "Don't go there, Lindsey."

Lindsey blinked and met her godmother's gaze. "Go where?"

"To that place where you blame yourself for what happened in Texas."

She nodded, but the echoes of Houston and Brett's abuse followed her like a looming shadow. It haunted her like a ghost. It lurked in the darkest corners of her mind. She'd escaped three months ago, but the nightmares still found her every time she succumbed to sleep.

"One last thing," her godmother said, retrieving a smartphone from her purse, "this is yours, too."

Lindsey picked up the phone. She had only been using pay phones as a precaution for the last three months, and the women's shelter had allowed her to use them as a go-between. Her godmother or attorney could leave messages for her there, and then Lindsey could call in to retrieve the messages.

She tapped the screen and brought the smartphone to life. "Is it safe to use?"

"It is. Just like the credit cards, I'm the primary on the account."

The familiar icons appeared on the screen. Something that had once seemed so mundane now felt extraordinary. "How will I ever repay you, Rosemary?"

"By staying safe. By building a life." Her godmother's gaze went to her stomach. "By caring for your child."

Lindsey hadn't realized her hand had been resting on her belly, rubbing slow, rhythmic circles over the slight bump. She was almost seventeen weeks along, she but was still able to hide the pregnancy with loose clothing.

"You look tired, honey," Rosemary said.

She was tired. Three months living in hiding, going from hotels to shelters was exhausting. She had made the last final push to Langley Park, and it was as if her body knew she could rest. She could close her eyes in a place that was all her own. Lindsey looked around the kitchen. The shock of seeing Nick had kept her from even acknowledging the beauty of her new home.

"The house is perfect," she said, taking in the cozy kitchen. "I haven't even looked around yet."

Her godmother collected their empty mugs and set them in the sink. "I'll go, but I'll come to check on you later. Take some time and explore the house. Langley Park is your home now."

Lindsey walked Rosemary onto the front porch. She scanned the street. There was no sign of Nick, but this didn't make her feel better. She shrugged off the thought. The last thing she needed was another man complicating her life.

"Call if you need anything, dear. All my contact information is on the phone. Do you remember the town much? It's changed a bit since you were last here—more shops, more families, but, all in all, still very much like how it was when you stayed with me all those years ago."

Lindsey nodded. She actually remembered quite a bit about the layout of the town. "Is the hardware store still next to that organic grocer? I wanted to get some more locks installed. I thought I could start there."

"It is," Rosemary said with the hint of a smile. "There's also a very nice camera shop in the town center. Were you able to bring any of your equipment with you?"

"I have my dad's old Nikon. That's all. It's a dinosaur with no digital capabilities. I can't use it for work."

Rosemary squeezed her hand. "Then you've got some shopping to do once you get settled in, don't you?"

Lindsey waved goodbye to her godmother, then closed and locked the door. There was so much to do. She rubbed her eyes. The last twenty-four hours hit her like a ton of bricks. She needed to rest. Step by step, she ascended the staircase and found the master bedroom. Exploring would have to wait. She sank onto the bed, hugged a pillow to her chest, and closed her eyes.

"I SAW you looking at him, you dirty whore. You know how much I love you. Why, Lindsey? Why would you embarrass me like that?"

"I don't know what or who you're talking about."

Brett circled her like an animal. His whiskey-colored eyes matched the liquor in his glass.

"You want to play this game again, do you?" he asked.

She was about to draw a breath, but Brett's hand stopped the air from entering her lungs. He pressed her body against the wall and squeezed her throat.

"You belong to me," he whispered.

Lindsey shot up, gasping for air and scanned the room wildly. Where the hell was she? She sprang off the bed and ran into the hall. The clouds had moved in and the house, once bathed in bright sunlight, looked different in the dim glow of later afternoon.

Langley Park.

Her new home.

Her hands flew to her neck, and she swallowed, testing for pain. A terrible side effect of having your abuser also be a physician meant he knew just how brutal he could be without leaving a mark. But her throat didn't hurt. She took three deep breaths and filled her lungs with even gulps of air. It was just a dream. Brett wasn't here.

Lindsey paced from room to room on the second floor. In addition to the master bedroom with a connecting bath, there were three other bedrooms and a full bathroom situated at the top of the stairs. Two of the rooms were empty, while the one adjacent to the master in the back of the house sat with only a single rocking chair in the far corner of the room. Rosemary must have left this for her. Lindsey ran her hand along the back of the chair and rocked it gently.

She went downstairs and walked a few laps around the Foursquare. The home must have been recently renovated. The smell of fresh paint still lingered, and the appliances in the kitchen gleamed silver and unblemished. There was a back door that led out of the kitchen and into a tidy yard with a freestanding garage in the far corner of the property.

There was no deadbolt on the back door. She jiggled the handle. While it felt secure, she wasn't taking any chances. The digital clock on the microwave read half past three. She had barely slept an hour since Rosemary left, and the hardware store should still be open. She'd never installed a lock, but that didn't mean she couldn't learn. Lindsey took the credit cards and checkbook and put them into her purse.

It was chilly outside but not cold. The fresh air felt good. She had spent much of the last three months cooped up inside hotel rooms or tucked away in women's shelters. She'd escaped from Brett's home, but the prison he had created in her mind reached far beyond his physical grasp.

But not in Langley Park.

She had never mentioned this place to him—not even in the beginning when he'd made her think she was the center of his universe. She'd locked her memories of this place away. As much as Nick had hurt her, she'd never let him go. She took in another breath. Could she handle running into him at the market? Casually passing him in the town square? Then another thought hit her like a punch to the gut.

Was he married?

Did he have a family?

"It doesn't matter," she whispered as she headed north on Foxglove Lane toward the town center. She could have started over anywhere, but she would be doing it all alone. If she wasn't pregnant, she could have lived rough. She had done it not so long ago when she'd photographed native cultures in Peru. But now she was pregnant, and she needed stability. She needed a home. Even if Nick did reside in Langley Park with a perfect wife and 2.5 children, she would learn to live with it. There wasn't any other choice.

She found Pete's Organic Grocer on the corner of Langley Park Boulevard and Mulberry Drive. She headed north on Mulberry and found the tidy little hardware store in a small freestanding brick building next door. She'd only passed by it a few times when she was last here, but it looked almost exactly as she had remembered it.

She opened the door and entered the cozy shop. It was packed with gardening tools, hammers, nails, bolts, and screws separated into what seemed like hundreds of tiny containers along the side wall. There were a few aisles further back, bursting with cans of paint, brushes, and rollers. Buckets and corded rope hung from hooks in the ceiling. The place looked more like a mad scientist's workshop than an actual hardware store, but there was something oddly comforting in the disorganization.

A gentleman with rosy cheeks and a bushy, white beard sat, eyes closed, with his chin propped in his hand. This man would make the perfect Santa Claus. She tried to close the door quietly, but a high-pitched squeak from the door's old hinges sent the man scrambling to his feet.

"Damn door," he murmured, bending his neck from side to side. He looked her over, and the cranky expression disappeared. "Mouse traps?" he said like it was entirely reasonable to guess what customers needed without even asking. He straightened but didn't come out from behind the counter.

"No, I'm looking for door locks, maybe even the kind they have in hotels."

He stroked his beard. "Ah, you want a swing bar lock. Check the first aisle."

Lindsey stepped around a wagon piled high with plungers and found several shelves crammed with all types of door locks. She picked up one of the swing bar locks.

"You don't want one of those."

She whipped her head around and was eye to eye with whiskey-colored eyes. She dropped the piece of metal, and it clanged against the linoleum. She took a step back, but there was nowhere to run. The man with the whiskey eyes bent down to pick up the lock.

Lindsey let out a breath. It wasn't Brett.

The man smiled nervously. He was older than she was. Maybe mid-forties or closer to fifty. He had dark hair like Brett's, but his was disheveled and long around the ears. It looked like it had been a while since he'd had it professionally cut.

He handed her back the swing bar lock. "Those are really easy to jimmy open. You just open the door a crack, slide your finger in, and push the swing bar back. If you want something you know will keep you safe, you would want to go with a Grade One lock like this one." He pointed to a doorknob with a deadbolt and two keys included in the packaging.

"Why this one?"

The man wouldn't meet her gaze. He seemed as skittish as she was.

"It's a double cylinder deadbolt. To open it, you need two keys, one on the inside and one on the outside. Some people don't like them, especially if they have young kids. The kids will take the interior key and hide it somewhere. It drives their parents nuts."

"How do you know so much about locks? Are you a locksmith?"

He shook his head. "I don't have any formal training. I've worked a lot of construction jobs and picked up some skills along the way. I didn't always make the best choices when I was younger. I'm just trying to make an honest living these days and trying to do what I can for my daughter."

"Do you and your daughter live in Langley Park?"

"No, she's in Nebraska with her mother. I send money when I can. I rent a room near Westport."

"Are you working a job in Langley Park? Is that why you're in town?" Lindsey asked.

"Not today. I come here because I don't think the old man who owns this shop has increased his prices since 1985. I can get anything I need for a job real cheap."

Lindsey peered around the corner to see the old man at the counter had fallen back asleep, chin resting back in his palm. She chuckled and set the swing bar lock back on the shelf. "What would you recommend—I'm sorry, I don't even know your name."

"Terrance, but everyone calls me Terry."

"I'm Lindsey. What would you recommend, Terry?"

He scanned the lock display. "If the double cylinder seems like too much, I'd go with this Baldwin single cylinder deadbolt." He pointed to another lock on the shelf. "It's a Grade 2, but it's still better quality than what residential homes require. I've installed several and haven't had any complaints."

"What would you use for your little girl?" Lindsey asked.

"The Baldwin," he said without hesitation.

Lindsey took two off the shelf. "Thank you, Terry."

He nodded and moved on to a collection of tape measures.

She managed to rouse the old man and pay for the locks just as Terry walked out the door. She called after him and met him out on the sidewalk. "Could I hire you, Terry? I just moved into a house in the neighborhood, and I'm looking to add some locks and window coverings. Is that something you could help me with?"

He gave her a shy smile. "Sure thing, miss."

"Do you have a card, or maybe I could get your number?"

Terry pulled a worn slip of paper and pencil from his coveralls and wrote using the palm of his hand. "I'm between jobs. I can start any time, miss."

"Start what?" came a deep voice.

10

———

Nick held a canvas bag with Pete's Organic Market printed across the side. A loaf of French bread poked out as he shifted the groceries from arm to arm. Lindsey met his gaze, flicked her eyes away, but then thought better of it. If this was going to be her home, she had to make peace with the fact that Nick Kincade lived here, too. She lifted her chin and met his eye.

"This doesn't have anything to do with you, Nick," she said, taking the slip of paper from Terry.

Coming face to face with Nick this morning had been a shock. After what seemed like a lifetime of enduring Brett's control and abuse, running into Nick was the final blow.

That's why she had fallen apart.

But that couldn't happen again.

She turned to Terry. "Thanks for your help with the locks. I'll be in touch."

Terry's glance swung between herself and Nick. He gave her a quick nod then headed down the street.

"If you need something done inside your house, I can help you," Nick said. He had taken a step back, adding to the distance between them.

"I can take care of myself," she said with a tight smile.

"Fair enough."

She started off toward Foxglove Lane. Nick's steady footfalls trailed behind. It should've bothered her, having him so close. It should've been unnerving, but it wasn't. For nearly the entire summer she had worked at the camp, Nick was with her, silent and sulking most of the time, but he was there—a presence, an energy, a kindred spirit realized too late.

She retraced her steps home. Nick was still there. Anger coursed through her veins. Was he going to follow her back to her house? Bang on the door and demand she talk to him again?

She stopped and waited for him to catch up. "Why are you here, Nick? Why are you living in Langley Park?"

He took a step closer. "I could ask the same of you? What are you doing here, *Lindsey Davies*? You've got a different last name, but no wedding ring. No moving truck. Not even one stick of furniture. Then you go and lock yourself inside the house. I saw you. You were terrified."

She swallowed past the lump in her throat. "You don't get to ask anything of me!"

She was not going to cry. Her father, Brett, Nick. She was done crying over men.

Lindsey continued down the street.

"I just want to know what happened to you!" he called out.

She spun around and faced him. She bit her lip to stop it from trembling. It didn't matter how much time had passed, Nick's blue eyes were the same eyes she had fallen in love with as a teenager. He was everywhere after their summer ended. The bright blue of a cloudless sky. The muted blue pattern on her mother's favorite mug. The blue trim on a house she would pass on the way to her new high school. He was everywhere, and he was nowhere.

She took in a sharp breath. In her darkest moments, when she was huddled on the floor with the steel toe of Brett's boot pressing down on her throat as she gasped for air, before it would all go black, it would go blue. For that fleeting fraction of a second, she'd be back at Camp Clem, and Nick would be there, smiling with the sun glowing at his back, blond hair like a halo, wild curls falling to brush past those blue eyes.

Nick flinched when she met his eye as if her expression alone had cut him to his core, but he held her gaze.

The front door of the house next door to hers opened and closed, and a woman's melodic voice called out, "Did they have fresh French bread, Nick? I could eat the whole loaf."

It was her neighbor—the woman with the red hair.

"Hey!" she said, standing on the top porch step. "Why don't you two come over. Michael and I are going to sit out on the front porch and have something to eat."

One of the men she'd met earlier, presumably, Michael, joined the woman on the porch. "Come on over. If Em eats all this by herself, we're going to need a forklift to get her inside."

Lindsey's gaze flicked to Nick. "I better not."

"Five minutes," Em said, smiling. "It's such a nice night. I'm also pregnant, so the world basically has to do as I command."

Lindsey stared up at the woman. She didn't look pregnant, but she was wearing a hoodie at least three or four sizes too big.

"Okay," Lindsey said, the words surprising her almost as much as they looked to have surprised Nick. His mouth had fallen open, but he recovered quickly and followed her to sit at a cozy table on Em and Michael's porch.

Em took the grocery bag from Nick. "I know it hasn't even been a day, but are you getting settled in? Mrs. G didn't tell us much about you."

Michael set out a plate with hummus, vegetables, olives, dark chocolate chips, potato chips, and crackers. Lindsey hadn't eaten since she'd grabbed a banana for breakfast hours ago, and the hunger that had been quickly forgotten in the excitement of the day, now made itself known. Her stomach growled and gurgled. A loud, visceral sound that echoed through her body.

Lindsey pressed a hand to her belly. "I'm so embarrassed."

"Don't give it a second thought," Michael said, arranging the food.

"You'll be able to hear Em's stomach rumbling all the way over at your house."

Em threw Michael a playful glare, but he smiled and pressed a kiss to the top of her head, then headed back into the house.

Em spooned hummus onto a small plate. "Pay no attention to Michael. Having some more estrogen around here will be good. With Nick moving into our carriage house, I was going to be outnumbered. Thank goodness you got here when you did."

Lindsey's breath hitched. She stared at Nick. "Where are you living?"

Before Nick could answer, Em swallowed and pointed toward the house. "Our carriage house. There's a studio apartment on the second floor. We've decided to take pity on him and take him in. He's been staying with Michael's cousin, Sam. You met him this morning. Big guy. Red hair."

"You're going to be living next door?"

Nick gave a slight nod. "I'd like to stay in Langley Park. I'm just waiting until I find a place that will work for me. Houses in the neighborhood don't come onto the market too often, and when they do, they sell pretty fast."

"Oh," was all Lindsey could manage. She was going to have to make peace with Nick living in this town. But the idea that he was going to be a stone's throw away in the carriage house next door left her speechless.

Michael was back on the porch, juggling a pitcher of lemonade, four cups, and a six-pack of Boulevard Pale Ale. "I wasn't sure if you wanted a beer or something else," Michael said with a friendly smile.

"Lemonade would be great," Lindsey answered, still trying to process that Nick Kincade was basically her new neighbor along with Michael and Em.

"So, Lindsey, what's your story?" Em asked through another bite of French bread. This time it was topped with chocolate chips and hummus.

"I've lived all over. I'm a photographer." She'd already had her canned 'where are you from' answer ready. It wasn't the whole truth, but it was true enough.

Nick sat up. "You became a photographer?"

"Yeah."

His gaze softened. "I'd always wondered."

"Did you..." She trailed off. She hated how badly she wanted to know if Nick had become a pilot.

He smiled. "Yeah, I did."

"Captain Nick is our pilot in residence," Michael said.

But before Lindsey could ask another question, her stomach growled again.

Em's eyes went wide. "Look at me, stuffing my face while you all sit there with nothing. Let me make you a plate, Lindsey. The men can fend for themselves."

Em put a little bit of everything onto a plate and handed it to her along with a glass of lemonade.

"You'll have to bear with us," Michael said, popping a potato chip into his mouth. "We're on the pregnancy diet around here, which basically consists of—"

"Of whatever I feel like eating," Em said and tossed several chocolate chips and an olive into her mouth."

"How far along are you?" Lindsey asked. A twinge of jealousy pulled at her heart. Rosemary and Claire knew about her pregnancy, but she hadn't mentioned it to anyone, not even the counselors at the shelter. She needed to see a doctor, but it had seemed too risky with Brett being a physician. While Houston was a big city, the medical community was close-knit. She couldn't risk Brett getting even a whiff of her condition. Still, she envied Em, who could share her news happily to the world.

Em popped another olive into her mouth. She shared a smile with Michael. "Almost nineteen weeks."

Lindsey nodded. Their pregnancies weren't that far apart.

"See," Em said, pointing at her. "Our new neighbor likes olives and chocolate, too."

Lindsey looked down. She hadn't even realized she had been eating the strange food combination.

"Have you and Michael lived here long?" she asked, changing the subject. The last thing she needed was for these people to figure out she was pregnant.

"Born and bred," Michael answered. "Em grew up in your house, Lindsey, and I grew up right here. There are many, many happy memories between these two Foursquares. Most of them include Em running around the yard topless."

Em gave Michael a playful punch to the arm. "Number one, I was a toddler at the time; and number two, you ran naked all the way to the town square. That's public nudity, mister. A chargeable offense."

Lindsey smiled. After living in a place filled only with fear and pain, there was something so sweet and so heartwarming knowing the place where she was going to raise her child was steeped in happy memories. She could almost hear the sound of children's laughter floating on the cool Kansas breeze. "It's a beautiful house, Em. I know it's going to be perfect for us," Lindsey said.

Dammit!

"Us? Do you have a partner? Is someone else moving in with you?" Em asked through another bite.

"I meant, me. It's going to be perfect for me," she said, masking the lie with a sip of lemonade.

A pocket of silence closed around the porch, but, before it became awkward, Michael shifted the conversation. "Are you familiar with the American Foursquare style home? Our houses actually came from a Sears catalog back in the 1930s. There are only a handful of them in Langley Park."

Michael described the architectural features of the house with its large front porch, boxy shape, and overhanging, low hipped roof. But she couldn't concentrate on the content of his explanation. Nick was watching her. She could feel his eyes assessing, calculating. Her heart beat a mile a minute. She balled her hands into fists, trying to fight the pull to meet his gaze. She was just about to give in when a truck pulled into Em and Michael's driveway.

Em stood. "What's Sam doing here?"

"Did you smell the hummus, chocolate and olive combo and come to stop such a deliberate culinary atrocity?" Michael called out as Sam cut the engine.

Sam was a big guy. Like Michael and Nick, he was at least 6'3 or 6'4, but Sam had an ominous quality about him, with tattoos running the length of his arms and wild auburn curls. But when he smiled, his open expression dashed any preconceived notions of the man being anything other than a gentle giant.

Sam shut the door to the truck and shook his head. "Em, I don't care what you eat when you're at home, but next time you're at Park Tavern, try not to gross out my staff by ordering a side of pickles with strawberry jelly."

"I don't know what you're complaining about," she answered, going up on tiptoes to press a kiss to his cheek. "It was delicious. You should think about expanding the menu."

"Sam owns Park Tavern," Nick said, leaning in. "It's a local restaurant and bar in the town center."

"I saw it when I got into town," Lindsey answered, running her thumb nervously over the rim of her glass. Michael and Em left the porch to talk with Sam, and, with their departure, the air became heavy, filled with ghosts of their shared past and so many unspoken questions.

"Kincade," Sam called out. "I'm making a house call."

"We should..." Nick said, getting up from the table.

"Of course." Lindsey stood and followed him off the porch.

Sam extended his hand and gave Lindsey an easy smile. "I'm Sam Sinclair. We met earlier today."

"I remember," Lindsey said. "It's nice to see you again."

"Is that my stuff—in garbage bags?" Nick asked.

"That's all your shit, dude," Sam replied. "I was a good friend and packed it up for you. I had some time before I needed to get to the tavern, and I thought I'd help you out."

Nick opened one of the trash bags. "Why are there a bunch of bananas in with all my aviation manuals?"

"I didn't say I did a good job packing your shit, only that I did it," Sam answered with a cheeky grin.

Michael held up a pilot's hat filled with tortilla chips. "Okay, boys, I don't think this will take us too long to unload. Lucky for us, Captain Nick travels light. Sam, pull your truck back to the carriage house. It'll be easier to unload it there."

The men sprang into action, laughing and dishing out plenty of good-natured ribbing as they carried Nick's uniquely packed belongings into the carriage house. Lindsey watched Nick. He had seemed to have found his place in this world.

"They're quite a little trio," Em said with a chuckle.

Lost in her thoughts, Lindsey hadn't noticed her come up.

"There's some history between you and Nick, isn't there?" Em asked.

Lindsey glanced over at Em and tried to be nonchalant. "We both spent a summer in Langley Park. We were camp counselors together when we were sixteen."

Em narrowed her gaze. "I haven't known Nick all that long, but I've never seen him look at anybody the way he was looking at you."

"I...it's..." Lindsey began, but the words wouldn't come.

"Complicated?" Em supplied with a knowing look in her eye.

Lindsey nodded.

"Langley Park has its fair share of complicated. Had you asked me six months ago about this place, I would have told you wild horses couldn't have dragged my ass back to this town. But here I am, pregnant and the happiest I've ever been." Em paused. "Sweet Jesus, being pregnant has me talking like I'm some kind of cheesy greeting card."

Lindsey chuckled. It was easy being around Em.

"I should get your number," Em said, pulling a phone from her pocket. "I know we live right next door to each other, but in a few months when I'm as big as a house, I may need you to help get my ass off the couch. And you're a photographer, right?"

"Yes," Lindsey answered.

"Have you ever done any portraits?"

"I've done everything from photographing indigenous tribes in

Central America to aerial shots of major cities. Why do you ask? Are you looking to have your portrait taken?"

"Hell no! You've seen the way I eat. I expect to be Stay Puft Marshmallow-size soon—and I'm enjoying every minute of it." Em pulled a potato chip out of her pocket and popped it into her mouth. "But my friend, Jenna Fisher, is involved with a women's shelter in the area. It's called Rose Brooks—you may not have heard of it."

Lindsey froze. Rosemary had given her a business card for Rose Brooks.

"They've been looking for a photographer for a project. I'll introduce you to her. I think you'd be perfect for it. Do you have any jobs lined up?"

"Rosemary or Mrs. G, that's what you all call her, right? She tells me the Chamber of Commerce may be hiring a full-time photographer."

"If Mrs. G's recommending you, there's like a ninety-nine percent chance you've already got the job. Mrs. G walks on water in this town."

"That's it," Michael called, grabbing the women's attention as he walked up the driveway. "Nick's all moved in."

Nick and Sam joined the group.

"All that's left to say is, welcome home, Nick," Em said smiling. "And, Lindsey," Em squeezed her hand. "You're home, too!"

11

Nick couldn't sleep. His thoughts whipped around wildly like a propeller on the brink of flying loose. Around and around, and with every rotation, Lindsey's face flashed before his eyes. He narrowed his gaze and focused on Michael's worn punching bag hanging in the corner of the first-floor garage of the carriage house.

Jab, hook. Jab, hook.

He repeated the movement but couldn't settle into a rhythm.

He punched harder, faster. Sweat trailed down his chest. His breath came in short, heated gasps.

His pulse raced. He wanted to go to her. He wanted to know everything—every single detail of what her life had been like since their last day at Camp Clem.

He could have stared at Lindsey all night. He could tell by the way her eyes darted back and forth, she was nervous. But she'd relaxed a bit, sitting there on the porch with Michael and Em. Whispers of that teenage girl he had fallen in love with sixteen years ago were there. The gentle, upturned curve of her lower lip as she smiled. The way she had focused her attention like she was framing a photograph in her head while she listened to Michael describe the Foursquare's architecture.

She was just as beautiful as the last time he had seen her. Maybe more so, if that were even possible. She'd been wearing a bulky sweatshirt, but when she'd pushed up the sleeves, revealing her slender wrists, the image of her delicate hands twisted and entwined in rope made him hard like a teenager unable to control his primal urges.

He continued to pummel the punching bag. Tight uppercuts mixed with quick jabs. His vision went hazy, and his father's face, angry and snarling, manifested in front of him. Nick punched harder. Regret and frustration fueled his assault. His muscles quivered with exertion, and after what seemed like an eternity, he fell forward, holding onto the bag, cheek pressed to the worn leather.

He stayed like that for a long time, swaying as the chain holding the bag suspended from the ceiling creaked out a weary tune. The bag stilled, and he closed his eyes. His body started to relax when he heard a sound. He'd propped the door to the carriage house open to let in the fresh night air, but all had been quiet on Foxglove Lane until now. The noise was a muffled cry. He knew immediately that it was Lindsey. She was calling out. She needed help.

He ran outside. He was only wearing mesh athletic shorts and running shoes, but the cold March air was the last thing on his mind. He ran to the back of Lindsey's Foursquare. She was whimpering, begging for her life between sobs. He tried to open the back door. It was locked. Adrenaline coursing through his body, he reared back then thrust his shoulder into the door. The weak lock buckled, and the door swung open. He ran through the kitchen, past the family room, and into the foyer. He scanned for any intruders. There wasn't anyone on the first floor. The front door was closed and locked. No sign of forced entry. He hit the stairs, taking them three at a time.

"Please, stop. Please!"

Christ, he had to get to her. He checked each bedroom and found her in Em's old room. She was alone. He didn't dare turn on a light. If there was an intruder, he wanted to catch the bastard off guard. But after a few seconds, Lindsey called out again, her face contorting in the moonlight. He checked all the rooms one more time. There was no one else in the house.

"Lindsey," he whispered. He fell to his knees next to her bed. "Lindsey, wake up."

Wisps of hair clung to her sweat soaked forehead, and he brushed a few strands from her face.

She opened her eyes. "Nick, you're here. You're really here. It's you."

She blinked slowly, hovering in that space between sleep and wakefulness. Her eyes, glassy with tears, stared up at him in awe. She touched his face as if she wasn't sure if he were real.

"How did you know I needed you?"

He swallowed hard. No one was in the house. She wasn't in any danger. "I heard you, Linds. I heard you calling out."

She cupped his face in her hands and pulled him close. Her breath was warm against his lips. "Nick," she breathed, letting her fingers trace the shell of his ear.

What the hell was going on?

She had been traumatized by the mere sight of him when she'd arrived at the house. The next time he saw her outside the hardware shop, she had made it quite clear she didn't want anything to do with him. But now, with her so close and looking at him just like she did when they were teenagers, he couldn't stop his body from responding to her touch. He had never found that level of connection with anyone besides her. The closest he'd ever come to that feeling of all-encompassing joy were those moments when he was flying, that split-second during takeoff right before the aircraft took flight. But having Lindsey right here, lips millimeters from his, the flying sensation became a far second in comparison to being close to her.

"Linds, what's wrong? Why were you calling out?"

"Aren't you going to kiss me?" she asked, her words a dreamy, sing-songy whisper.

He hadn't kissed anyone in ages. He had tried to have girlfriends after their summer, but nothing clicked. He'd had the real thing, but life had fucked all that up. He had spent the last decade having meaningless sex, and he hadn't kissed a woman—properly kissed a woman— in over a decade.

His body tensed. A tremor of excitement ran down his spine. Every part of him wanted her. Christ, he wanted to climb into bed with her, crash his lips into hers, and sink his throbbing cock, hard and pulsing with desire, into her sweet center. He wanted to run his hands up the length of her arms and wrap his fingers around her delicate wrists. He wanted her blue-green eyes locked on his. He wanted to disappear into the safety of her world just as he had that summer.

"Nick," she breathed, the word infused with sunshine and wild-flowers. It was an invitation, but to what?

She inched forward, and her lips grazed his. As gentle as a lullaby, but as ominous as a low rumble of thunder, every memory of their time together came flooding back. A torrent of sensations raining down on him like a hail storm. His breath came faster. His body tightened. Despite her crazy mixed signals, despite knowing that something in her past was haunting her, and despite knowing he would hate himself in the morning if she rejected him, he laced his fingers into her hair and leaned in closer.

His lips pressed against hers, and he was home. He rested her head back onto the pillow and hovered above her. She sighed and gave him the opening he needed to claim her mouth. Their tongues remembered the slow, sensual rhythm of their kisses.

"I never wanted it to end," he whispered, his words hot and breathy between kisses.

Lindsey trailed her fingertips along his bare back. The sensation sent a sharp pulse to his cock, and he groaned as his body came to life under her touch. He inhaled. She was warm and smelled of sweet cream and summer rain. It was all so right, so familiar, so perfect.

He shifted his body on top of her. Her lower half was tangled in the sheets, and he reached a hand down to loosen the bedding. His hand grazed her stomach, and everything changed. The air shifted like something dangerous had just entered the room. Lindsey stilled and shook her head. A quick, tiny motion that broke their kiss.

"No," she murmured. She sounded confused, disoriented.

He pulled back. "Linds?"

"No!" she said, more forcefully.

She was wide awake now. The slow, dreamy movements had stopped, and she pushed his chest, wriggling out from under him to get away.

"What are you doing here, Nick?" she said, sheets pulled up to cover her body.

He edged off the bed and took a few steps back. "I heard you. I thought someone was hurting you. I broke down the back door. I was trying to help you."

She took in a sharp breath. "By forcing yourself on me?"

"I didn't force myself on you. You asked me to kiss you. You told me you needed me."

Her mouth fell open, but nothing came out.

"I'd never hurt you, Linds." The second the words left his mouth, he knew he'd just lied. He had hurt her. It had been years ago, but the pain reflected in her eyes proved without a shadow of a doubt, he'd hurt her badly, and that hurt still lived in her heart.

"Get out!" she said, throwing her legs over the side of the bed and pulling down the sweatshirt she'd been sleeping in.

"Lindsey, please, tell me what happened. Tell me why you're having nightmares where you're begging for your life."

She crossed her arms. "Did you say you broke down my door?"

"It was locked," he replied.

She pushed past him. "You had no right."

She hurried down the stairs, and her light footfalls tapped an angry rhythm.

He met her in the kitchen. She examined the broken door, wearing only a sweatshirt and a pair of tiny boy short panties. Despite her angry outburst, the image of her sweet ass encased in white cotton sent a jolt of desire straight to his cock. He tried to shift his stance and hide the evidence of his arousal, but he'd timed it all wrong. Lindsey turned her attention away from the door just as he adjusted his rock-hard cock.

Her eyes darted from his crotch to his face. "Is that all you want?"

He started to answer, but she stopped him.

"I know it was a long time ago, but I thought you cared for me. I thought you loved me. I gave you my..." She lifted her chin and shook her head. "You could have called the community center. You could have left a message. I didn't even know what town you lived in. I didn't know your aunt's name. You knew I'd be in Langley Park for that last weekend. You could have tried!" She raised her gaze to the ceiling and ran her hands through her hair. "Forget it. Forget it all. Just go, Nick. Leave!"

"No," he said, holding his ground. "Do you know what it was like getting off that bus, thinking I was going to get to see you in a few hours only to find my mom nursing a black eye and my father standing by her side? My mom caved again to my father's demands. Believed his lies, again. The kindest thing that man ever did for us was to die young of a heart attack. You have to know, Lindsey, I didn't want to leave you."

"But you did, and you could've tried to contact me, but you didn't. Did you?"

His mouth went dry. She was right. He hadn't tried.

How could he make her understand that before that week with her at Camp Clem, he was on track to become just like his dad. That summer, he'd slipped into the same patterns as his father—the cruelty, the aloofness. He hadn't physically abused anyone, but that darkness was inside him, entwined with his DNA like a ticking time bomb. He hadn't believed that his mother was going to leave his father until Lindsey helped him see a better life was possible, an alternate route that didn't end with him turning out like his father. She made him believe he could be a better person. But when he had gotten off that bus and seen his parents, all the light and love Lindsey had infused into his soul was overshadowed by the darkness of a future that included a life with his father.

"No." The word tasted bitter and charred. "I didn't try to contact you."

Lindsey gave him a barely perceptible nod. She was bathed in moonlight, and his heart clenched. That's how he'd fallen in love with her, wrapped in the humid summer air, the sounds of the night all around them. And the moonlight. Illuminating her smile, sending silver streaks in her dark hair. And her eyes. Even in the darkness they entranced him, owned him, haunted him.

She moved past him and held the door open. Her lip quivered.

"Lindsey," he tried, but even to his ear he sounded defeated.

"Go," she breathed. The cold night air clung to the word with an icy grip.

He flinched. Her whispered command sliced through him like an ice pick.

His feet moved, but the rest of his body screamed for him to stay. It wanted her lips, her sweet scent, her delicate touch. But his feet won, and the cold March breeze whipped through him as he walked the short distance to the carriage house. He had left the door open. It swung gently, tapping the frame with each gust of air. He stopped short of entering and rested his head against the door frame. His body ached, but it wasn't from the cold air. Lindsey's soft sobs had followed him outside. Each whimper cut into his heart like a thousand shards of glass.

12

Lindsey clasped and unclasped her hands. After a moment, she crossed and then uncrossed her legs.

Settle down.

She glanced around the sitting area of Hangar 12, the main building that housed the offices and pilots' lounge for the Kansas City Downtown Airport. An impressive glass window spanning two-stories looked out onto one of the airport's runways. A small single-engine plane taxied by the window, light reflecting off the tail. She liked these smaller, regional airports. While they were always busy with flight training and corporate jets coming and going, the proximity to the action was what she loved best. Planes and helicopters were parked so close, you could reach out and run your fingers down their sleek surfaces.

She let out a breath. Even after sixteen years apart, airplanes always reminded her of Nick.

After her encounter with him last night, she had woken early. There was no time to dwell on the past. She had to start creating a future for herself and her child. She called Terry and scheduled a time for him to repair the door and upgrade all the locks. Then, she followed her godmother's advice and visited the camera shop in the town center.

It had been such a long time since she had talked shop, but as she handled the different Nikons and Canons, her life as a professional photographer came back to her. She chatted with the shop owner for more than an hour. Focal range and ISO performance. Using a crop camera versus a full frame. A spark she hadn't known in years lit a fire of excitement that pulsed through her veins.

Lindsey settled on a Canon. Her potential job was working for the local Chamber of Commerce. Several cities and Chambers had contracted with her over the years, and she had a good idea of what they would be asking her to do in Kansas City. This kind of photography called for equipment that could capture the vastness of a cityscape as well as the intricacy of a ladybug resting on a blade of grass.

Along with the Canon Digital SLR camera, she purchased several lenses and filters along with other accessories she would need. The owner kindly threw in a camera bag which was helpful because starting from scratch didn't come cheap. She had spent nearly ten thousand dollars. But these were the tools of her trade. As the shopkeeper swiped her new credit card belonging to Lindsey Davies, she said a silent prayer of thanks to her mother for leaving her the means to start over. She had met many women at the shelter who, after being saddled with children and no way of providing for them, were often forced to return to the home of their abuser.

Two pilots strode past her, and each gave her a polite nod. Her equipment sat neatly in the camera bag on the small side table of the airport's seating area. She ran her hand across the bag's strap but shot to attention when the sliding glass doors of the building opened, and a man with whiskey-colored eyes and dark hair entered the lobby.

"It's not him. It's not Brett," she whispered.

The man walked by and gave her a curt nod.

A slight woman dressed sharply in a midnight blue pantsuit entered the lobby and met her gaze. "Miss Davies?"

Lindsey blinked once, then twice. This was the first time anyone had addressed her this way. "Yes, that's me."

"I'm Brenda Chen," the woman said.

After stepping out of the camera shop, Lindsey had received a call from Ms. Chen, the Vice Chair of the Chamber of Commerce's Board of Directors. Rosemary had undoubtedly sung Lindsey's praises to her and the other board members, and Brenda had suggested they meet that day at the Downtown Airport.

"Thanks for meeting me on such short notice," the woman offered with a warm smile.

A plane came in for a landing, and the women turned to watch.

"It's a beautiful airport and quite busy," Lindsey said.

"It's the second busiest airport in the state," Brenda replied. She settled into a chair and gestured for Lindsey to do the same. "I wanted to meet here because this is where the board would like you to start."

"I've got the job?" Lindsey asked. She heard the note of excitement in her voice and tried to tamp it down by keeping her face neutral.

"Mrs. G shared your work with the board. Everyone loved it. Those aerial shots of Charlotte and Omaha were breathtaking. We would like you to do for us, what you did for them. Plus, we'd like to expand the campaign. In addition to the aerial work, we wanted to highlight some of the local attractions in the area that people don't know about like the Langley Park Botanic Gardens."

"Wow," Lindsey said.

Brenda pulled an envelope from her tote and handed it to Lindsey. "Half of the board had your godmother as their third-grade teacher. While we know she loves all her students, a recommendation from her is quite another thing. It says something to have an endorsement from Rosemary Giacopazzi."

Lindsey straightened. It was an offer of employment complete with benefits and a generous salary. She read the letter three times before it sank in. In a matter of hours, she had found a new home and a new job. She swallowed past the lump in her throat. "I accept your terms and truly appreciate this opportunity."

Brenda smiled and handed her a business card. "Excellent! Call Kellen in Human Resources. She'll get you squared away with our healthcare plan, 401K plans, and all the employment forms." She paused. "If you've got some time today, I was hoping to introduce you to the airport's Aviation Director. He's retiring in a few days. You won't be working with him for very long. But I thought he'd be the best person to help get the ball rolling."

"My entire day is free. I'm happy to be at your disposal," Lindsey said, making a mental note to thank her godmother. None of this would have been possible without her.

She followed Brenda up a staircase to the second floor. They paused and looked out the window as a sleek corporate jet taxied to a stop.

"Mrs. G said you'd spent a summer here when you were a teenager."

Lindsey shifted her stance. "Yes, I did. I worked at the Community Center's Kids' Camp."

"My boys went to camp there last summer. It's still one of the best programs in the state. I'm sure you have a lot of good memories of your time here."

Lindsey nodded. All those memories contained Nick. But he wasn't just a memory anymore. He lived here, too. For Christ's sake, he lived in her backyard. But it wasn't permanent. He would find a place and move out of Em and Michael's carriage house. She would focus on work and...

Her baby.

It was the first time the thought of the tiny human growing in her belly didn't send a pang of fear spasming through her chest.

"I'm glad to be back and living in Langley Park permanently," she said, finding her voice.

"Brenda! It's good to see you."

A gentleman with a broad smile and cropped silver hair shook Brenda's hand.

"Are you sure you're ready to retire Artie?" Brenda asked.

"Oh, yes! The missus and I have been planning on starting a vegetable stand the minute the ink is fresh on my retirement papers."

"Lindsey," Brenda said, "this is Artie Bartnik. He's been the Aviation Director for..."

"For a very long time. Almost twenty-nine years," the man said, finishing Brenda's sentence.

Lindsey shook his hand. "That's quite an achievement."

"This airport has grown and changed so much since I've been here," Artie said, gazing out at the runway. "But the energy, the people, the love of aviation, that's what keeps this place so special." He shifted his gaze from the runway and gave Lindsey an appraising look. "You must be the new photographer."

"Yes, I'm Lindsey Davies."

There, she had said it. Maybe soon, she would believe it.

"Nice to make your acquaintance, Ms. Davies. Are you pretty well versed in aerial photography?"

A tingle of excitement cartwheeled down her spine. This was the real interview. "I've shot Las Vegas, Chicago, Rome, Cairo, and London. In those locations, I was wearing a harness and hung out of a chopper to get the best images. In Miami, Austin, Omaha, Charlotte, and Atlanta, I opted for an aircraft. I like the Cessna Skyhawks. Four seats. Plenty of room for gear."

"Things ever get dicey?" Artie asked, his expression carefully neutral.

Lindsey knew what he was asking. There are photographers out there who ask pilots to push the limits and break the rules to get a shot. She wasn't one of them. "No, anytime weather rolled in, or the aircraft was due back, I always deferred to the pilot's judgment."

"No hot dogging it when you're at three thousand feet?"

"No, sir," she answered. "As I said, the pilot's in charge. I'll always defer to his or her call."

Artie looked over her shoulder. "That should be music to your ears, Nick. Come and meet Lindsey Davies. You two are going to be working together."

. . .

NICK COULDN'T MOVE.

What was Lindsey doing here? And why the hell would he be working with her?

He composed himself and joined the group. He recognized Brenda Chen from the Board of Directors of the Chamber of Commerce. Artie had introduced him to her after he was hired to take over as Aviation Director. They had discussed a multifaceted campaign to promote the Kansas City area nationally and globally. They wanted to highlight the Downtown Airport as well as other places that weren't as well known. There had been talk of some aerial photography work, but Nick wasn't aware the Chamber had hired Lindsey.

Artie waved him over. "Brenda, Lindsey, this is Nick Kincade. He's going to be taking over as Director of Aviation."

"Yes," Brenda said, shaking his hand. "We've met. It's nice to see you again, Nick."

He exchanged pleasantries with Ms. Chen but kept Lindsey in the corner of his eye. The color had drained from her cheeks.

He reached out to shake her hand like they were strangers. "Miss Davies, it's nice to meet you."

She stared at it, and her eyes flicked to his. He tried to read her. She had wanted him last night. In that intangible place between sleep and wakefulness where only unfiltered honesty dwelled, she'd revealed that she needed him.

Aren't you going to kiss me?

Those words. Lindsey's words clouded his mind before he fell into a fitful sleep. But he couldn't escape her. He dreamed of her. A twisted, disjointed jumble of Lindsey smiling in the glow of the lantern light that morphed and contorted into her sprawled out on the Foursquare's kitchen floor, sobbing as darkness pooled around her, flooding the room and drowning out her sobs.

She shook his hand but didn't meet his eye. "Likewise."

"Are you sure you're the right person for this job, Ms. Davies?" he asked.

She flicked her gaze up to meet his. The color returned to her cheeks, and an angry slash of crimson peeked out above her collarbone. "Why wouldn't I be the right person?" Her words were as sharp as a knife's edge.

"Do you know Kansas City well?"

She gave him a tight smile. "I spent some time here when I was younger."

"You don't think it would make more sense to hire a photographer who's more familiar with the area?"

"Are you from around here, Mr. Kincade?"

She was playing the game.

"I spent some time here when I was a teenager, too."

She cocked her head to the side. A slight movement, but he'd noticed it. "So, it's your expertise and understanding of aviation and how airports function all over the country that made you a top candidate for the position of Director of Aviation here in Kansas City?"

He nodded. She was laying a trap. He could feel it, and he liked it. He saw the spark in her eye. The same spark she'd had when she was sixteen. She wasn't scared of him. The woman he was face-to-face with now wasn't the person who'd arrived in Langley Park, timid and frightened like a cornered animal.

"I've done aerial photography projects in cities all over Europe, North America, South America, Australia, and Asia. I've shot the indigenous Maori people of New Zealand and the Pech in Honduras —and that's just the tip of the iceberg, Mr. Kincade. So while I may not have lived in this area long, it's safe to say, I know cities, and I know people. I know their energy, and I know how to capture that on film." She let out a breath. "I bet it's kind of like how you know all the intricacies of airports, just not this one in particular."

No one said a word as the muffled sound of a helicopter flying overhead filled the void.

After it passed, Artie let out a full belly laugh. "Brenda, I think you and the board have picked the perfect photographer to capture our fair city. You've certainly got my support, Ms. Davies. It's comforting to know there will be someone willing to go toe-to-toe with the airport's new Aviation Director."

Lindsey smiled. "I'm just here to do my job."

Artie clapped his hands. "Let's get Lindsey up in the air. It's a beautiful day. I'm sure one of our flight instructors can take you up for a little loop around the city."

"I'll take Ms. Davies. In fact, I insist on it," Nick said. There was no way in hell she was going up with anyone but him.

Brenda's face lit up. "I think that's a great idea, Lindsey. We can meet later in the week to go over the campaign in more detail."

Lindsey's expression went deceptively neutral. "I'd hate to inconvenience Mr. Kincade."

He pinned her with his gaze. "It's no trouble, Ms. Davies."

"I'll see Brenda out and let the boys know to gas up your Skyhawk, Nick," Artie said, gesturing for Brenda to go ahead of him.

Brenda shook Nick's hand then turned to Lindsey. "Enjoy the flight. I'll be in touch. Don't forget to get everything squared away with Human Resources. Your healthcare and other benefits begin today." She paused, and a satisfied smile stretched across her lips. "And I agree with Artie. We couldn't have picked a better photographer for the job."

"Please give my thanks to the board. I won't let you down," Lindsey said, but Nick could feel her watching him from the corner of his eye.

The air grew heavy after Brenda and Artie's departure. After a long beat, Lindsey met his gaze. He was sure she was going to give him a piece of her mind, but her blue-green eyes softened.

"Skyhawk?"

She remembered.

"It's not my grandfather's. That one was pretty old and had seen better days. I sold her for scrap and parts a few years ago. I picked up this Skyhawk last year."

"You don't have to take me up, Nick. I can wait until one of the flight instructors has time."

His phone pinged. "That's the ground guys. We should go."

Her gaze danced between him and the staircase like she was contemplating making a run for it. What had made her this wary of people? The answer hit him like a slap across the face. He had. He didn't know what had happened to her since he'd last seen her. All he knew for sure was that he had hurt her, and she still carried that pain.

He gestured toward the stairs. Lindsey retrieved a large camera bag and walked a half step ahead of him. The clouds shifted and caught her hair in a stream of sunlight. The chestnut-brown, red, and gold strands called to him. He wanted to weave his fingers through each gentle wave.

Christ! What was he doing? One minute he was kissing her, the next, he was gunning to get her fired on her first day. He wasn't thinking clearly. She had cracked open the memories he'd locked away deep in his heart with one kiss and had changed everything.

He had lived a very uncomplicated life, these last sixteen years. He had finished high school, went to college and studied aviation. He was a pilot—and a damn good one at that. It had not only been his life's work. It had been his entire life. His pilot stripes were all he had to show for his time on this planet. While that once was enough, seeing those blue-green eyes again chipped away at the façade he had mistaken for a life.

"Is that yours?" Lindsey asked, pulling him from his thoughts.

He looked up. There she was: his Cessna 172 Skyhawk. Callsign Lima six, four, two, three. Pearl white and just as shiny as the day she had come off the line. Two racing stripes, one sky blue and one forest green, cut a clean edge along her body and arched artfully near the nose just shy of the propeller. The breath caught in his throat. Jesus, her eyes. He had known the minute he'd seen this plane that she was the one for him. But he'd never understood the lightning-fast connection—until now.

"Yeah, that's her." He crossed in front of Lindsey and helped her into the cabin of the plane.

"She's good to go, boss," one of the crew called from behind.

Boss.

On top of having Lindsey crash into his life, in a few days, he would be in charge of this facility. But contending with fuel costs, mechanical issues, weather delays, and novice pilots seemed like a breeze compared to living only a few feet away from the woman he had locked away in his past, like a child's treasure, hidden in a dented metal tin far away from prying eyes.

He settled into the cockpit. Lindsey buckled up and put on her headset. She stared out the window. She wasn't tense. Her shoulders weren't up by her ears, tight and anxious like they had been when she'd first arrived. Any fool could tell, she had done this before.

Most people have flown commercial, herded like cattle into a 747 or an Airbus, but it's quite a different story to hop into a two or four-seat prop engine plane. It's the proximity that gets the novices. The cockpit is tight. The controls are only inches away. Gauges, switches, and screens blink and beckon to be touched. You see exactly what's controlling your fate. There's no buffer of folding trays or flight attendants. Visceral and breathtaking, this kind of flying was the real deal.

Man. Air. Machine.

He gave Lindsey another glance before pulling on his headset and taking his kneeboard out of the side pocket. He pressed a button on the panel and the sound of a woman reading off the most recent weather report cut into his headset.

Winds variable at four miles per hour. Good visibility. Temperature at seven degrees Celsius, about forty-five degrees Fahrenheit.

He continued listening and scribbled the information down onto his board. That spark he hadn't felt since the first time his grandpa had taken him up flared to life.

It was a good day to fly.

He entered the flight plan into the computer. "Do you have any questions?" he asked, going into default instructor mode.

"I'm not going to pretend I understand everything you're doing, but I know enough to keep out of the pilot's way until after we've been cleared by the tower."

"Roger, that," he replied.

She was sticking to business.

He went through the preflight checklist, and the familiar routine centered him. He contacted ground control and was cleared to taxi out onto the runway.

"Kansas City Downtown Ground, Cessna six-four-two-three Lima is taxiing to runway one-niner for departure to the south. KC Downtown Ground."

"Cessna six-four-two-three Lima, KC Downtown Ground. You are cleared for take-off, heading south on runway one-niner. KC Downtown Ground."

Nick taxied to the runway and lined up the nose of the Skyhawk with the yellow center line. Follow the yellow brick road. That's what his grandfather had told him the first time he had taken the yoke with his other hand steady on the throttle. He got the final clearance and, in the time it took most people to tie their shoes, the Skyhawk was airborne, climbing to a comfortable cruising altitude.

The downtown airport is situated at the confluence of the Kansas and Missouri Rivers. Nick followed the majestic body of water as they left the airport's airspace and began a lazy loop around the city.

"Is there anything in particular you want to make sure we pass by?"

"No, I just want to take it all in," she answered, her voice sounding neutral and mechanical through the headset.

He liked talking to her this way. Eyes on the sky. Her voice merely words coming through the headset. If it wasn't for her scent, she could have been just a voice over the radio. Not a real flesh and blood woman, sitting inches away.

He followed the outline of the Kansas River and continued south toward Langley Park.

She leaned forward. "Is that Lake Boley and the Langley Park Botanic Gardens?"

"It is."

She was quiet as they passed overhead. Though it was nearing the end of March, winter hadn't entirely released its grip, and the gardens still looked spindly and sparse from eighteen-hundred feet.

"When did your dad pass away?"

He wasn't expecting that. "My father?"

"Yes, last night you said the kindest thing he did for you and your mother was to die young."

Last night. Christ! He did tell her that. He swallowed hard. "My freshman year of college. He died of a heart attack. He was with some woman he was having an affair with. My mom and I didn't know he had died until a couple of days later."

They passed through a crosswind, and Lindsey put a hand on the console to steady herself as he found a smoother patch of air.

"I'm sorry, Nick."

He didn't answer. He hated that phrase. It made him think of his mother.

I'm sorry, Nick. I can't leave your father.

I'm sorry, Nick. He promised he wouldn't hurt us again.

Nick never had a real relationship with a woman because he never wanted to hear those words. There was no need to apologize when nothing was expected. He had been with plenty of women, but he'd always steered clear of commitment.

He glanced over. Lindsey rested her left hand on top of the control panel as she gazed out the window. Something angry stirred inside him. Her ring finger was bare, but she had married someone else. Maybe it was the mention of his father or his disappointment with his mother, but agitation flooded his system.

"You married the cloud guy, didn't you?" he said. The mechanical bite of the headset couldn't hide the bitterness in his voice.

He felt her eyes on him. "Who?"

"The big cloud photographer guy, Robert Davies. You mentioned him at Camp Clem. You liked his work."

A beat of silence and then a rush of laughter filled his headset.

13

Lindsey couldn't help herself. After all she had been through, Nick just assumed she'd run off and married some photographer she had admired as a teenager. It was so simple, and so completely off the mark, it left her laughing like a lunatic. Davies was also her maternal grandmother's maiden name. She hadn't even considered choosing Davies because of the photographer.

She took a breath, stopped another convulsion of laughter from breaking loose, and focused on a stretch of wispy clouds far off in the distance. She exhaled. There were no more giggles to suppress as she fixed her gaze on the clouds, pink, yellow, and silvery-blue in the late afternoon sun. There was something beautiful though, that the name she had chosen connected both her mother's heritage and her love of photography.

She caught Nick out of the corner of her eye. He had gone rigid. His knuckles on his hand holding the throttle had gone white. This was no joke to him. It also presented a problem she hadn't anticipated.

Why was her last name Davies?

She hadn't expected anyone besides her godmother to know her in Langley Park. She'd had no reason to expect this question. But now that Nick was in her life again, she needed to come up with something.

"It's complicated," she said into the headset mic, not answering his question.

A muscle ticked in his jaw. "You're either married, or you're not married, Lindsey. There's nothing complicated about that."

"I'm not married." She hoped he would hear the finality in her tone. She was done with answering his question. He was digging, and digging was dangerous for someone who was trying to live under the radar.

Her stomach flipped, and a wave of hot nausea forced her to brace herself on the console and drop her head between her arms.

"Linds, are you okay? Are you going to be sick?" The anger had drained from his voice and was replaced with concern.

She started to shake her head, but the motion only made the dizziness worse. "This doesn't usually happen. It's been a while since I've been up in a prop plane. It's probably just that."

All true, but she'd never flown pregnant. She broke out into a cold sweat. She hadn't even seen an obstetrician. There were restrictions on flying for women in their third trimester. She knew that. But she didn't know much else about pregnancy and flying. She couldn't be hurting the baby, could she? Anxiety ripped through her chest. She needed Nick to land the plane.

He read her mind. "Linds, can you hold on? I can have us on the ground in less than ten minutes."

"Yeah," she breathed. She lifted her gaze and focused on the Kansas City skyline. "I can make it."

"Do you want an ambulance to meet the plane? I can call it in."

She turned her head a fraction and met his gaze. She didn't see the person who'd just interrogated her over her last name. No, that man was gone. All she saw now was the boy who had told her he loved her. She focused on the horizon. "No, I'll be okay. Let's just land."

. . .

NICK KEPT HIS WORD. He didn't have an ambulance waiting when the plane landed, but he did insist on taking her straight to the emergency room. Lindsey dangled her feet off the side of the examination table as a shiver spider-crawled its way up her spine. She didn't like hospitals. Hospitals were full of doctors. The fact that Brett was a doctor was one of the qualities that intrigued her in the beginning. There's something intoxicating about someone skilled in the art of healing. It pulled her in. It blinded her.

The door to the exam room opened, and a woman with dark hair fashioned into a loose twist entered the room. Ebony tendrils framed her face as she paged through a chart. "Ms. Davies, I'm Dr. Samira Al-Amin. It looks like you're experiencing some nausea from a plane ride. How are you feeling now?"

She released a shaky breath. "Better, the nausea's gone."

Dr. Al-Amin wrote something on the chart then gave her a warm smile. "You're new to Langley Park?"

"Yes, I've only been here a couple of days."

Dr. Al-Amin scanned the chart. Her brown eyes softened. "You remember giving the nurse a blood and urine sample before she took your vitals?"

Lindsey dropped her gaze to the floor. "I know I'm pregnant. What I don't know is if going up in that plane did something to the baby."

"We can certainly check and see how the baby's doing. Do you have an obstetrician in Langley Park yet?"

Lindsey shook her head and blinked back tears. "I haven't seen a doctor about the baby at all."

Dr. Al-Amin patted Lindsey's hand. Her touch was soft and reassuring. "Let's take a look. Your blood and urine both looked good. You could do with some more iron, but that's common for many pregnant women. I'm going to do a quick physical exam, and then we'll see about the baby."

A tiny drop then another made small circular dots on her skirt. Tears. Tears trailed down her cheeks and fell in slow, steady droplets as Dr. Al-Amin pressed and palpated.

Breathe in. Breathe out. Does this hurt? Follow the light with your eyes.

The doctor's rich, honeyed voice put her in an almost meditative trance, and the tears stopped.

"Why don't you lie back," Dr. Al-Amin said, adjusting the table into a reclining position. "Let's say hello to your baby."

Lindsey sat back and looked down at her abdomen. Hardly a bump at all.

"When was your last period, dear?"

She didn't know the exact date of her last period. What she did know, with exact precision, was the date she had gotten pregnant. She hadn't been with Brett in months which had been a relief. She knew he had to be screwing someone else, but she didn't care. Brett used sex to humiliate and defile her. That's how they would *make up* after a disagreement. Her, bruised and battered. Him, holding her by the back of the neck as he forced himself on her from behind.

She let out a breath. "The date of conception was in mid-November."

The doctor made a note in the chart then rolled a portable ultrasound from the corner of the room. "That puts you at around seventeen weeks." She motioned for Lindsey to lift her blouse and squeezed a generous amount of a jelly-like substance on her belly. "The gel will be a bit chilly, but it has an important job. It provides a bond between the skin and transducer."

"Transducer?"

"This," Dr. Al-Amin held up a device. It looked almost like an electric razor except that the end of the instrument was smooth. "It works kind of like SONAR or how bats use echolocation. Sound waves are aimed toward a structure, in this case, your baby, and as they bounce back and forth, you get a picture. Rest assured, it does no harm to you or the baby."

Lindsey nodded.

"Here we go," Dr. Al-Amin said, pressing the transducer onto her slick belly.

Lindsey stared at the screen. Fuzzy black and white bands spasmed back and forth.

"There you are," the doctor said, angling the implement.

It was just like in the movies. A grainy black and white image appeared of the profile of a head attached to a tiny body and a steady flicker of movement pulsed in the baby's chest.

"Is that the heart?"

The doctor nodded. "It is indeed. I'm going to take a few measurements and then we'll take a listen."

Dr. Al-Amin moved the transducer around her abdomen, and the grainy picture of the baby went in and out of focus.

"Your baby is measuring a little small, but still within the normal range. Structures and organs look good. Your baby could fit into the palm of your hand like a little banana, Ms. Davies."

"So small," Lindsey whispered.

"But strong, take a listen."

The doctor pressed a button. A fast whooshing sound filled the air.

"The heartbeat is one hundred forty-two beats per minute."

"That's okay?"

"It's perfect," Dr. Al-Amin answered.

Lindsey exhaled. She had been holding her breath.

The doctor lifted the transducer and the rhythmic sound faded. "You can clean off with these," she said, passing Lindsey some tissues.

Dr. Al-Amin glanced toward the door. "Ms. Davies, do you feel safe in your home?"

Lindsey deposited the tissues into a small trash receptacle and adjusted her blouse. Did the doctor know Nick was a few feet away waiting for her? Did she think Nick might be hurting her?

She met the woman's gaze. "I'm safe now. I'm safe in Langley Park."

"I'm very glad, Ms. Davies." She reached into the breast pocket of her lab coat. "Here's my card. I'm just on call at Midwest Medical today, but my practice is close by in the medical wing of the hospital. If you'd like, I can see you through this pregnancy."

Lindsey took the card. "I'd like that very much."

"And don't forget these," the doctor said, passing her three, index card sized pieces of smooth photo paper. "These are a few pictures of your baby."

Lindsey stared down at the grainy images. She ran her finger along the curve of the baby's profile. "Thank you, Dr. Al-Amin."

The doctor pushed the ultrasound machine back into the corner. "I look forward to seeing you, Ms. Davies."

The doctor left the exam room. Lindsey fastened her boots and smoothed her blouse and skirt. She put the ultrasound photos into her purse and walked out into the ER's waiting area. Nick must have been watching the glass doors. Before it even closed behind her, he was there.

He took her purse. "Let me carry this." A frown line creased his brow. "I asked the nurses how you were doing, but all they said was that you were with the doctor."

"I'm all right. I've got low iron."

It wasn't a lie, just another half-truth.

He nodded. "Should we stop at the pharmacy? We can get some iron tablets."

"I can do it tomorrow. I just want to go get my car and head home."

A sheepish expression crossed his face. "I took your keys out of your purse and asked a couple of my ground crew guys to drive your car back to the house. I should have asked you, but you looked terrible. I just wanted to try and make things easier for you."

"Okay," she said. She didn't have it in her to fight. Seeing her baby for the first time and hearing the heartbeat had left her in a fog.

Surprise flashed in his eyes. He wasn't expecting to get off so easily. "I'll take you home."

It was dark out as Nick settled her into his car. Lindsey stared out the window, watching the street lamps cast pools of soft light onto the ground. He could have gone home a different way—a shorter way. The hospital was off Langley Park Boulevard. The boulevard was the main artery that bordered the south side of the Langley Park's town center. Foxglove Lane ran perpendicular to it. But Nick had left the hospital and headed north, and that meant passing by the community center.

"It looks different now," she said. The front of the building had changed. Graceful arching, wooden beams gave the structure's entrance a modern, barn-like quality.

Nick didn't answer. But from the corner of her eye, he gave her a tight nod.

They headed south and weaved their way through the rows of Tudors and bungalows to 718 Foxglove Lane. Neither said another word.

She unbuckled her seatbelt and reached for her purse when a pang of anxiety flared hot in her chest. "Nick, I don't know where I left my camera bag! It contained everything. My new camera, the lenses—"

He put his hand on top of hers. "It's okay. I told the guys to lock it in your trunk. See, there's your car." He pointed to the gravel driveway that ran parallel to Em and Michael's.

She let out a breath. "Where are my keys?"

"Behind the flower pot."

Lindsey hadn't noticed a flower pot. "Where?"

"On the porch, there's an empty flower pot in the far corner."

She got out of the car and hurried up the porch steps. There was a flower pot, but no keys.

The floorboards creaked behind her. "Did you find them?"

"No," she said, looking around.

Nick went to the window and peered inside her house. "Did you leave a light on?"

He jiggled the doorknob, and the front door clicked open.

"Would your guys have gone into my house?"

"No, I've known Edgar and Silas for as long as I've been flying into the Downtown Airport. I trust them." His expression darkened as a clank came from the back of the Foursquare. He handed her his car keys. "Go get in my car and lock the doors."

She did as he said. Her heart pounded, the beat echoing and

pulsing like a fire alarm. Had Brett found her? Did she need to run? Then she remembered Terry.

He was supposed to come over and fix her back door. She had told him she'd meet him here this afternoon. Jesus, he probably knocked on the door, and when she wasn't there, he assumed the keys hidden behind the planter were for him. It was an honest mistake. Lindsey burst out of the car and ran into the house.

Nick was holding Terry by his coveralls.

"Nick, it's okay. I know him. It's Terry, from the hardware store."

Nick kept hold of Terry. "Who?"

"Terry, the handyman. He was going to come over this afternoon to fix the door and install new locks."

Terry stuttered a few times before the words came out fast and shaky. "When nobody answered the door, I figured you had left the keys for me to get started, miss."

"Nick, it's okay," she said, taking a step closer. "I just forgot Terry was coming over with everything that happened today."

Nick released Terry's straps, but his hardened expression didn't change.

Terry picked up his toolbox. "I was just finishing up. I changed out the locks and fixed the back door. Did somebody break in here?"

Lindsey gave Terry a tight smile. The adrenaline rush receded, but her limbs still trembled with that fight or flight response. "Let me walk you out, Terry."

"Keys," Nick said, voice low and deadly.

"Right, right." Terry patted his pockets until he found the right one and produced her set of car keys and two new silver door keys.

"Thanks, I'll take those," Lindsey said, ushering Terry to the front door.

"I'm really sorry, miss," he said.

"It was just a misunderstanding, Terry. I'm the one who should be sorry."

"Nah," Terry answered, kicking a few stones on the sidewalk. "I'd have done the same if some guy I didn't know was in my girl's house."

Lindsey nodded. "Thank you for fixing the door."

Terry lifted his chin and briefly met her eye. "I can start installing the window coverings as soon as you decide what kind you want."

"That would be wonderful. I'll be in touch."

Terry nodded then headed up Foxglove Lane toward the town center. He didn't have a car. He must have ridden the bus into town.

Terry's form disappeared into the darkness, and Lindsey went back inside the house. She closed and locked the front door, satisfied with the sturdy click of the new deadbolt. She rested her head against the door when a sound from the kitchen caught her attention.

Nick was still there. His heavy footfalls moved methodically back and forth but stopped when she entered.

A muscle ticked in his jaw. "I don't like him, and I don't want him in your house."

"You're the one who broke down my door," she countered.

But before she could tell him to leave, her mind went fuzzy. A lightheaded fog passed over her. She reached out, knocked her purse onto the floor, and braced herself on the table.

Nick swooped in, taking her forearms into his hands. "Linds?" he breathed, craning his head to meet her gaze.

They stared at each other. A beat passed, then two, before she leaned forward and pressed her lips to his. Kissing Nick Kincade in her kitchen was the last thing she thought she would be doing today, but at that moment, it was the only thing that made sense.

Her escape from Brett, her new home, her new job, her baby's heartbeat, and the run-in with Terry had pushed her over the edge. She trembled, exposed and raw. Her nerves popped and writhed like live wires frayed into a million stripped threads. She needed something to ground her, something solid and true.

She needed Nick.

His body tensed, but he didn't break the kiss.

She pulled back a fraction. "Please, Nick."

Her barely breathed words were all the confirmation he needed. His hands flew from her arms, and he weaved them into her hair, changing the angle of their connection and deepening the kiss.

Last night, she had been caught in that place between sleep and wakefulness when he had kissed her. She thought she was dreaming, the sounds of Camp Clem at night were so clear until Nick tried to touch her abdomen. Like the piercing ring of a fire alarm, that slight touch instantly roused her. She and Nick weren't two teenagers kissing under the Ozark stars. He had gotten into her house and was inches away from caressing her pregnant belly. But now, she was fully awake, and, baby or not, she needed him.

His thumbs made tiny circles along her jawline as his fingers cradled the back of her head. His hot breath danced with hers. And his lips. She hadn't kissed many men since Nick, but none of them ignited the heat in her core the way Nick's kisses did. The rhythm, the pressure, the slow licks of his tongue across her bottom lip had her wet and ready. She wanted him hard between her legs, cock pulsing, twitching to be inside of her. She wanted to feel the delicious weight of him as he pinned her down and claimed her body.

But she couldn't let him touch her. How would she explain the baby? She wasn't showing, not really, but she couldn't take the chance. She broke the kiss and glanced around the kitchen.

Two aprons hung off a hook on the back of the pantry door.

"Sit," she commanded, pulling out a kitchen chair.

He complied and met her gaze with hooded eyes.

She grabbed the aprons and fell to her knees next to the chair.

"Linds, what are you doing?"

She gripped his wrist. "Do you trust me, Nick?"

He held her gaze a beat. "Yes."

"It has to be like this," she said, tying his wrist to the leg of the chair. She'd done a sloppy job. She was never good with knots. All she could hope was that Nick would understand what she needed.

She inhaled sharply and waited.

He let his free arm fall to the side and held his wrist near the other chair leg.

He understood.

Lindsey released a relieved breath and secured his wrist with the second apron.

He could have freed himself. But he didn't. He sat still. He sat waiting. Hooded blue eyes watching her, drinking her in.

She stood in front of him and flicked off the kitchen light. The glow from Em and Michael's outdoor lighting warmed the room in a haze of silver. Lindsey blinked and let her eyes adjust. Nick hadn't moved, hadn't tried to free himself. His broad shoulders heaved up and down in the dim light with each breath.

She pulled down her panties and left them in a tiny pile on the floor. She started to unzip her boots when Nick spoke.

"Leave them on." His voice was a low, hoarse growl.

She released the zipper and stood between his legs. Her fingertips trailed along his thighs. She worked her way to his cock and palmed him. He took in a sharp breath. Lindsey licked her lips. She unbuckled his belt, undid the button, and unzipped his trousers. His cock strained against his boxer briefs. He shifted his body, and Lindsey pulled down his pants and underwear. Using her thumb and index finger, she played with the head of his cock. Rubbing it gently between her fingers. Exploring. Remembering. Outlining the shaft before wrapping her fingers around him and stroking up and down.

Nick groaned as the taut muscles of his abdomen flexed and tightened with each stroke. She dipped her head and kissed him, and he captured her mouth with a growl as she climbed onto his lap. She released his cock and unbuttoned his shirt, pulling it open and allowing her fingers to follow the lines carved by hard muscle. She traced each line before working her way to the hard V that led to his cock. She wrapped her fingers around his thick shaft.

"Do your wrists hurt?" she breathed as his cock jumped in her hand.

He took her earlobe into his mouth. "I don't give a fuck about my wrists right now."

She rolled her hips and pressed his cock to her entrance.

He let out a deep moan. "Do we need to use protection?"

She shook her head, and he thrust his hips up to meet her. "You're so wet for me."

She positioned his cock and sank down, taking in every inch. She cupped his face and kissed him then let her hands explore. His torso, his neck, his jaw—they were stronger, more defined than she had remembered. But she would have known his body anywhere. It was as familiar to her at this moment as it was sixteen years ago.

"Nick," she gasped, her breath hot against his cheek.

"I know, Linds. I know," he answered, emotion lacing his words.

She held onto his shoulders and rolled her hips, back and forth in a slow, steady rhythm. The primal slap of flesh intertwined with the sounds of their gasping breaths and wet, hot kisses. She dug her fingertips into his shoulder blades and increased her pace. Her thighs trembled with need as she pumped harder and faster, riding his cock. The wooden chair rocked and creaked beneath them.

"I never wanted to leave you," Nick whispered, thrusting hard. "I've never stopped loving you. It's always been you, Lindsey."

She twisted her fingers into his hair, arching into him, tears trailing down her cheeks as his beautiful cock pumped inside her tight, slick core.

She teetered on the edge of pleasure—so powerful, so perfect, she couldn't form another coherent thought. Her orgasm ripped through her. Her center pulsed and gripped his length as their mouths met in a tangle of lips and teeth and breath.

The chair's legs clawed against the hardwood floor in a feverish, frenzied scrape. He followed her, calling out into the darkness, his deep thrusts stretching and filling her completely.

She rested her head on his shoulder and let out a ragged breath.

He pressed a kiss to her neck. "Can I touch you?"

She reached down to release the apron strings, but only felt his wrist. The apron restraints hadn't held. But his hands remained at his sides, unbound, gripping the chair legs.

She traced his naked wrist with her index finger. "It came loose. When did that happen?"

"About a minute after you tied them."

She heard the smile in his voice.

"Why did you keep them there?"

"Because that's what you asked me to do."

She let out a pained breath and dropped her head to the crook of his neck.

He bent his head. "Please, let me touch you."

She nodded, and his arms wrapped around her. It was like falling back in time. It was like finding the space where every part of you fit. It was everything she had never thought she'd know again.

He smoothed back her hair and brushed a tear from her cheek. "Don't cry, Linds. Please, don't cry."

She raised her head and met his gaze in the silver light. Where was she supposed to start? What was she supposed to say to this man? She'd never stopped loving him either? She wanted nothing more than to erase the past and pretend the world started at that moment?

"Cody, boy!" came a deep voice from outside.

Lindsey stiffened. "Who's that?"

Nick cupped her cheek. "It's just Michael out with his dog, Cody."

She let out a relieved sigh.

"Can we talk, Linds?" he asked, his words looming in the darkness.

She nodded and climbed off his lap. Smoothing her skirt, she picked up her panties and turned on a small lamp. A golden pool of light warmed the room. She kept her back to Nick, giving him time to right his own clothing.

"What the hell is this, Linds?" His tone was sharp.

She turned as Nick retrieved something from the ground. The contents of her purse had spilled onto the floor. Wallet, cell phone, lip balm, and two small, rectangular ultrasound photos. Nick raised the third photo, holding it out like it was radioactive.

14

"Is this your baby?"

Nick almost didn't want Lindsey to answer. Maybe she had found these ultrasound pictures outside. Em and Michael must have dropped them. She'd put them in her purse and was going to return them the next time she ran into them. But the look on Lindsey's face told him that the fantasy he had concocted was utter bullshit. He took a closer look at the picture. Today's date along with Davies, Lindsey was in bold capital letters at the top of the photo.

"Who the hell is the father, Linds?"

She stared at the floor and shook her head.

He stood up and gestured to the chair. "We just fucked in your kitchen. I think you owe me some answers."

"I can't," she said, still shaking her head. "I thought..."

"You thought, what? That I'd be fine sleeping with you while you're pregnant, fucking pregnant, with someone's baby?"

"It's not that simple, Nick."

He barked out a laugh. Her head shot up, and she met his gaze. He nearly crumbled. If anything was going to break him, it was those damn blue-green eyes. They owned him, haunted him. But this—a baby. This was huge. This was life altering. This deserved an explanation.

He crossed his arms. "Either you start talking, or I'm leaving."

"I'm about seventeen weeks pregnant."

"And?"

He heard his father's cruelty infused into the word. If he looked into a mirror right now, he would see his father's empty eyes, the strong jawline, tight and rigid. And fists, ready to inflict pain. The darkness would rule him just as it had ruled his father.

She rubbed her hands together before placing them on her belly then lifted her chin and met his hollow gaze. "And that's all I can tell you."

"This is not how it works, Lindsey. You don't get to play with people's hearts and minds." The callousness in his voice. The notes of contempt and disdain. He sounded like his father berating his mother.

He should have known better. He knew there was something wrong the minute she got out of her car yesterday. Something that went beyond the heartbreak of their shared past. *But a baby?* Christ, he didn't even know where to start.

He had decided long ago that he couldn't be a father. He'd never even imagined becoming a husband. He couldn't take the chance. He was too much like his father. If he put himself into a situation where he could hurt a wife or a child, genetics would take over. He was sure of it. That internal programming would call the shots, and he wasn't about to let anyone tempt him into becoming his father.

Not even Lindsey.

"I'm—" she began.

He stopped her. "Don't you dare say you're sorry."

Nick wasn't sure who he was looking at, Lindsey or his mother. His vision had gone red. This is why he didn't have relationships. This is why he'd never allowed himself to love again. With trembling hands, he crammed the ultrasound photo into his pocket and opened the back door.

He looked at the new, shiny deadbolt. "I'm glad you've got new locks." The words tasted acrid, like biting into charcoal. "Because I certainly won't be breaking down your door to try and save you again."

Her mouth fell open, and he slammed the door behind him.

"Everything okay?" came a voice in the dark.

It was Michael. He had Cody on a leash. The old golden retriever nosed Nick's hand, looking for affection.

"Yeah, everything's fine," he said, scratching between Cody's ears.

"Is Lindsey all right?" Michael's gaze flicked to the Foursquare.

"She's a big girl. She can take care of herself."

He didn't mean for the words to come out so harshly. He just needed to be alone and try to work through what had just happened.

"Nick, I don't want to overstep, but anyone could tell there's some history between the two of you."

He looked at the house. Lindsey was still in the kitchen. She sat at the small table, head bent over, staring at the ultrasound photos.

"That's all it is. Just history."

She wasn't his problem. She wasn't his concern.

He hated himself for thinking that. But that was who he was. Thanks to his father, the capacity for cruelty was woven into his DNA. For one reckless, fleeting moment, lost in her touch and sweet scent, he thought they could be together. He hadn't lied. He loved her. He always would. But when he saw that ultrasound photograph, the realization ripped through him like a jagged knife. They couldn't be together. Not now. Not ever.

"Life's not always black and white," Michael said.

Nick was glad of the darkness. It hid the angry blush heating his skin. "Unfortunately, it is for me."

"HERE'S the list of prenatal vitamins Dr. Al-Amin recommends."

Lindsey glanced up and finished zipping her boots as Dr. Al-Amin's nurse cracked open the exam room door. It had been a week since she'd seen the doctor in the ER. She had taken her advice and made a regular prenatal appointment with her office. They had gone over all the things most pregnant women did during the first trimester, and Dr. Al-Amin assured her the baby was doing fine.

The nurse gave her a warm smile. "We've got a bunch of samples I could send home with you today. When you're finished in here, I'll meet you at the scheduling desk. We can get your next appointment on the books, and I'll have those goodies ready for you to take home." She closed the door, and the clap of her footsteps disappeared down the hall.

Lindsey fastened the last button of her blouse but paused before leaving the room. Pictures of Dr. Al-Amin smiling next to women in hospital beds holding tiny bundles lined the walls. She studied each picture. Mothers and fathers beamed at her from the past. She tried to find a picture with just a mother. There were a few, but even those women seemed to have someone with them.

"We can do this," she whispered to the tiny human, barely the size of a small banana, living in her belly. She'd laughed earlier when the doctor made the comparison, but now, Lindsey blinked back tears. There was no reason to cry. She wasn't going to be alone. Rosemary would insist on staying by her side during the delivery. Again, she thanked the universe for her godmother's kindness.

She had her hand on the doorknob when one of the pictures caught her eye. She stared at the family. The husband, blond and smiling. The mother, petite with dark hair almost the same shade as hers. Lindsey closed her eyes and imagined Nick, leaning in, his arm wrapped around her shoulders as he gazed down at their baby.

But it wasn't their baby. It would never be their baby.

The look on his face when he saw the ultrasound photo told her everything she needed to know.

She patted her belly. "It's just you and me, little banana."

She wasn't quite showing, not even at nearly eighteen weeks. A slight sway to her stomach was the only visible evidence of her pregnancy.

She met the nurse at the scheduling desk. The woman's hands were filled with pamphlets and sample packets. "I've got all your appointments here," she said, handing Lindsey a printout. "We make the appointments up through forty weeks. If you deliver sooner, the hospital will let us know, and we'll take care of canceling them."

Lindsey nodded, a bit bleary-eyed. It was a lot to take in. Exam room doors opened and closed behind her. The chatter of nurses fielding calls and the click of their typing buzzed through the office.

The nurse retrieved a small reusable tote from under the desk and filled it with more papers and pamphlets. "Here's some information on birthing classes and diet and nutrition. I'll put all the vitamin samples in here for you as well." She paused when another nurse handed her a piece of paper. "Looks like your iron is still a little low, but the doctor hopes with the prenatal vitamins that will improve. Don't you worry, we'll keep an eye on it, and if anything comes up, don't hesitate to call."

"Thank you."

She handed Lindsey the tote then hurried down the hall. "We'll see you soon, Ms. Davies."

"Lindsey, is that you?"

The voice sounded familiar. Lindsey turned and found herself face-to-face with her neighbors, Em and Michael.

What now?

"I had no idea," Em said, taking a step closer and glancing at Lindsey's belly.

"I hadn't..." Lindsey began. "I didn't..."

Michael patted her arm. "Why don't you join us for an early dinner. It's always easier to talk over a meal. Did you drive here?"

Lindsey nodded.

"Let's drop our cars off at home, and you can ride with us to Park Tavern," Em added.

"Okay," Lindsey said, still a little off-kilter.

She made the walk to her car and drove home on autopilot. Her body did all the right things, but her mind was elsewhere. There was no way to completely hide a pregnancy unless she lived in a cabin in the middle of nowhere. She had known people would take notice, but she wasn't prepared for what to say, or how to explain the lack of a husband or father.

They found a table near the back of the restaurant. At four o'clock, it wasn't busy. Park Tavern's long Cherrywood bar gleamed red-gold in the late afternoon light. Bottles of spirits lined the shelves, giving the place a golden glow. Lindsey's eye caught three bottles of Teeling's Irish whiskey, sunlight dancing and glinting off the amber liquid, and framed the shot in her head.

"I know that look," Michael said with a knowing grin.

"Sorry," Lindsey answered, turning her attention to Michael and Em. "This place has such character. I can see a hundred ways to photograph it."

Michael shared a glance with Em. "Em's a musician. I'd know that 'artist at work' look anywhere."

They chuckled politely, but after a beat, Em leaned in, brows knit together. "How far along are you, Lindsey? I hope you don't mind me asking. Feel free to tell me to shut up and mind my own business."

Something inside her loosened. A tenseness she had lived with since falling under Brett's control relaxed a fraction. "I'm almost eighteen weeks. How about you?"

Em threaded her arm with Michael's. "Almost twenty. My mom was supposed to come into town for the big gender reveal today, but she had to present at a conference. She's an educational researcher in Australia. So we did the whole thing over video chat."

"You know what you're having?" Lindsey asked.

Em's blue eyes shined with emotion. "A little boy."

"A ginger boy, right?" came a booming voice.

"They weren't able to confirm hair color on the ultrasound," Michael said, standing to shake Sam Sinclair's hand. "But Dr. Al-Amin assures us there's a high probability."

Sam bent down and kissed Em on the cheek. "Congratulations, sweetheart! Zoe's already forwarded all the pictures you sent her from the ultrasound. In another fifteen minutes, the entire Kansas City metro area will know you're having a boy."

A woman with a wide grin and sparkling gray eyes approached their table carrying a massive monstrosity of a cake. "I'm just excited for my best friend. What's wrong with that?"

"What are you doing here, Zoe? And what the heck is that?" Em asked, looking down at the blue lumps of cake interspersed with lopsided clumps of icing.

"This is what happens when I try to bake," Zoe answered with a playful glint in her eye. "I've got a pink one, too. I left it at my parents' house. I could go get it?"

"No!" Michael, Em, and Sam said in unison.

Lindsey watched the exchange with a grin. She could see why Nick had chosen to live in Langley Park.

Zoe feigned offense but only held the expression for a few seconds before breaking into laughter. "I know it's awful, but I promised your mom we'd have a little surprise celebration. So, when Sam texted me that you guys were here, I threw the cake in my car and headed over."

"That would certainly explain the shape," Michael said, swiping some icing onto his finger then grimacing as he tasted it.

Zoe set the cake on the table and extended her hand. "You must be Lindsey. I'm Zoe Stein."

"It's nice to meet you," Lindsey replied. "Are you from Langley Park, too?"

"I am. I have a place up in Lawrence near my work at Kansas Public Radio, but I've got so many friends and family in town, I'm either crashing at my parents' place or Sam's bungalow more often than not."

Lindsey nodded. In thirty seconds, she already felt like part of the gang. After all that time of being isolated by Brett, it was almost intoxicating to be surrounded by such life and vitality.

Zoe narrowed her gaze. "You're Mrs. G's goddaughter, the photographer for the Kansas City Chamber of Commerce living in Em's old house, right?"

This girl didn't beat around the bush.

"That's me," Lindsey answered as a sliver of panic wove its way through her chest.

Zoe sat down. "Mrs. G is the office manager for my brother's architecture firm. She mentioned you're working on the publicity campaign for the city."

Lindsey's anxiety dialed down a notch. She knew her godmother would be careful with the things she shared with others. Of course, people would be curious about the new girl in town.

Zoe picked up a morsel of cake and popped it into her mouth, grimaced the same way Michael did, then swallowed hard. "My mom and sister-in-law want to meet you. They've got a couple of projects going that the Chamber's agreed to highlight."

"Yes," Lindsey answered, grateful the conversation had veered to work. "I think I might know what you're talking about. Brenda Chen emailed me this morning regarding the Rose Brooks Women's Shelter fundraiser and a series of free women's self-defense courses being offered at different yoga studios around the area."

"Yep, those are the projects. My mother and sister-in-law are very civic minded."

"I'll be shooting a self-defense class at the yoga studio in the Langley Park town center tomorrow morning."

Zoe's expression brightened. "I'll be there. That's my mom's studio. It's right up the street from here, off Mulberry Drive just past the coffee shop." She leaned in. "There are a few things you need to know about my mother and sister-in-law. My mom, Kathy, has a crazy, unhealthy obsession with Buddha statues. And my sister-in-law, Jenna, you'll initially want to hate her because she looks like a better version of Barbie, but then she'll open her damn mouth, and you won't be able to help but love her."

Em nodded, fashioning her thick auburn hair into a bun. "That's a pretty spot-on description."

"And it might be the nicest thing you've ever said about me, Zoe," a lovely woman who did look like a better version of Barbie, said with an amused expression. "Hi there, I'm Jenna Fisher."

"Lindsey Davies," she replied and shook the woman's hand.

"I'm Kathy Stein, Zoe's mother. It's nice to meet you, Lindsey," said the petite woman with salt and pepper hair standing next to Jenna. "And I'm not hoarding Buddha statues."

Jenna, Em, and Zoe shared an amused look.

"Mom," Zoe lamented, "last I checked, there were like thirty-eight of them. And don't think I didn't see the two you've got hidden underneath the couch in the living room." She threw the group a conspiratorial glance. "You know it's bad when she's resorted to hiding them at the house."

"All right, folks," Sam said, cutting in. "How about I get some appetizers out. I'll send a waitress over to bring everyone some water and take drink orders. The good news is...we've got plenty of food, and we don't have to eat Zoe's cake."

Everyone let out a whoop of delight as Jenna and Kathy sat down, one on each side of Lindsey.

Jenna gave her a warm smile. "I'm so glad to get some time to chat with you. You're the new photographer with the Kansas City Chamber of Commerce?"

"I am," Lindsey answered.

Jenna leaned in. "Has anyone mentioned anything to you about the Rose Brooks Women's Shelter fundraiser?"

Lindsey took a breath. It wasn't that long ago when she'd relied on the lifesaving services of the Houston Women's Shelter. But this was no time to let her past interfere or cloud her judgment. This was work. This was her career. Behind the camera, she called the shots.

"Yes," Lindsey said, slipping into professional mode. "Em mentioned it to me last week, and just today, I received an email from Brenda Chen that the Chamber of Commerce is onboard. I'm happy to help in whatever capacity suits your needs."

"Oh, I'm glad you're able to help," Jenna replied with a relieved sigh, "because there's not much time. The fundraiser is right around the corner, and I was hoping to get something pulled together in the next few weeks." Her expression darkened. "I've volunteered to oversee this project, but I don't know quite where to start."

Lindsey drummed her fingers on the table. What she loved about photography was the way it allowed her to capture and alter perspectives and to tell a story from a unique point of view. "What do you think about getting some of the shelter's staff and maybe even some past or current residents behind the camera? I can teach them the basics of photography, and this approach would allow the people who know Rose Brooks best to capture its essence."

Jenna nodded. "I like that idea. And I'm sure the local camera shop would be happy to lend us some cameras. The owner has been a longtime supporter of the shelter."

"Are you two done talking shop?" Zoe asked. The waitress delivered several plates of appetizers, and Zoe popped a stuffed mushroom into her mouth then turned her gaze toward the entrance and shared a look with Em and Jenna. "Ben, Kate, Clay, and Nick just got here. Jenna, you're in charge of squashing any *Star Wars* debate. Tonight is all about my shitty cake and Em's sweet baby boy."

Em added a dollop of strawberry jam to a mozzarella stick. "You were the one who mentioned Jar Jar whatever last time we were here, Z."

Jenna stood. "Let's make some time to chat about the fundraiser. Will you be at the self-defense class tomorrow at the yoga studio? I've heard the Chamber's involved in that project, too."

"Yes, I'll be there taking photos for the campaign."

"Wonderful! We'll talk more then."

Jenna patted her shoulder and made her way through the restaurant. When she stopped next to a tall man with dark hair, Lindsey's breath caught in her throat.

That's not Brett. Brett doesn't know anything about Langley Park. He can't find you.

Lindsey silently repeated the mantra.

"So," Zoe said, drumming her hands on the table and pulling Lindsey out of her panicked state. "Are you ready for the rundown?"

"Rundown?" Lindsey asked.

"Oh, Zoe," Em sighed. "Lindsey has barely been here a week. Don't go freaking her out with all our crazy."

"Everybody's got some crazy, don't they?" Zoe asked and met Lindsey's gaze.

Lindsey nodded, noticing Zoe's expression had lost that wicked sparkle.

Zoe rebounded. "The sweet little monster is my niece, Kate. She's seven going on seventeen."

Kate smiled up at Jenna who was tucking wild strands of the little girl's wavy locks behind her ears.

"They're a crazy adorable family—think, Mayberry-perfect, version 2.0. Moving on," Zoe continued, "the guy with the buzz cut who looks like he could be cast into any cop movie as a cop *is* a Langley cop. That's Detective Clay Stevens."

Lindsey nodded and tried to keep all the names straight.

Zoe lowered her voice. "Now those three," Zoe said and pointed to Jenna, Nick, and Jenna's husband. "That's my brother, Ben. Your godmother is the office manager of his architecture firm."

"Right," Lindsey said, remembering that tidbit.

"Here's the juicy part. Captain Nick and Jenna used to date, but that all ended when she came back to Langley Park and reconnected with my brother. She and my brother met in high school and had some instant love connection that never faded."

"Nick dated Jenna?" Lindsey bit down hard on the inside of her mouth.

"Yeah, but it wasn't any real kind of relationship. My brother is a giant hardass and could win a gold medal in holding grudges. If he can be friends with Nick, anything is possible. Plus, a blind man could see the way Jenna looks at my brother. They're all friends now. It is super-mature adult of them. Plus, Ben and Nick are both *Star Wars* geeks. That seems to supersede any issue of who dated who. And don't get them started on anything *Star Wars*. The discussion will go on for hours."

Lindsey gave a tight nod. She knew she couldn't have Nick. He made that crystal clear. But a wave of relief washed over her as she watched Jenna Fisher gaze lovingly at her husband.

"Zoe Christine Stein," Kathy said with a mother's warning tone.

Zoe shrugged her shoulders. "Fine, mother. I'll lay off the Langley Park 411."

Lindsey looked at Nick. He was laughing at something Ben was saying but must have sensed her watching and turned her way.

"Now, there's a look I've never seen from Captain Nick," Zoe said, eyes dancing.

Lindsey tried to muster a smile. "I've had a long day. It's been wonderful meeting everyone, but I think I'm going to head home."

"Would you like me to drive you?" Michael asked, starting to stand.

Lindsey waved him back. "No, I think a little walk and some fresh air would be good."

"Are you sure?" Em asked. Concern clouded her eyes. "You know, you can count on Michael and me. We're always here to help."

"I'll be fine. Thank you, Em."

Something passed between them. She had felt this same connection with Em the night on the porch. A kindred spirit, a female connectedness. Maybe it was just that they were both pregnant, but it seemed like more than that. She sensed Em felt it, too.

Em nodded. "I'll see you soon." But her gaze said more. It said, I'm here for you. You're not alone.

Lindsey turned. She was on the verge of tears and took a slow breath to settle her nerves. Kate had run over and was sitting on Zoe's lap, but Jenna, Ben, Clay, and Nick were still chatting by the entrance. Lindsey ducked her head and tried to pass by unnoticed. But Jenna stopped her.

"Lindsey, this is my husband, Ben, and our friends Clay Stevens and Nick Kincade."

Lindsey nodded to the men.

Jenna narrowed her gaze. "Are you leaving so soon?"

"Yes, it's been a long day." She didn't dare meet Nick's gaze.

"Your car is at the house," Nick said, cutting in with a disapproving air.

"I'm going to walk home," she answered, still not meeting his gaze.

Nick crossed his arms. "Would you guys mind telling Michael and Em congratulations for me, and that I'll catch up with them later on tonight? I need to check on something at the carriage house. I can walk Lindsey back."

That got her attention. "I'm fine on my own."

"I have to go that way. It's no trouble," Nick countered.

Lindsey caught the little glance Jenna shared with her husband. Everyone in this town seemed to sense she and Nick had something strained between them.

"All right," Lindsey agreed, trying not to make a scene.

What was Nick doing, anyway? He was the one who walked out. Granted, he'd just learned of her pregnancy in the worst way possible. But he had made his feelings known, loud and clear.

Twilight had melted into a moonless evening as he followed her out of Park Tavern. It reminded her of their night walks together through Camp Clem. He was so much bigger than she was, but their bodies always moved together in a seamless harmony. After a few paces, her chest tightened with emotion. Their steps *still* fit together. She wanted to alter her gait, take a misstep, anything that would tell her the opposite of what her heart knew to be true—Nick Kincade would always be the one for her, even if they couldn't be together.

They had only gone half a block when a couple emerged from a bookstore. Lindsey caught a glimpse of the women, and a strange spark of recognition passed through her. She stopped and turned just as the woman did the same.

"Miss Lindsey," the woman asked. "Is that you?"

15

Nick would have known these two people anywhere.

The woman clutched the arm of the man at her side. "Oh my gosh, Rory! I knew it!"

"Rachel?" Lindsey asked. Nick heard the tenderness in her voice.

"Oh my gosh! Oh my gosh!" Rachel cried. Her gaze bounced from Nick to Lindsey. "I knew you two would end up together. Didn't I, Rory? I always told Rory, if any two people were perfect for each other, it was Miss Lindsey and Mr. Nick."

"You did, babe," he said, smiling down at Rachel. He extended his hand to Nick. "It's good to see you. I hope I can just call you Nick."

Nick shook his hand. "Absolutely!"

"It's so good to see you, Mr. Nick," Rachel said, pushing up on her toes and planting a kiss on his cheek. She stood back and opened her arms. "Miss Lindsey!"

The women embraced.

Lindsey wiped a tear from her cheek. "You're all grown up."

"You are, too," Rachel said, eyes shining with emotion.

"Are you two visiting Langley Park?" Rory asked.

"No," Nick answered stealing a quick glance at Lindsey. "We just moved here permanently."

Rachel shook her head. "Of course, you guys live here now that we've moved to San Francisco."

"Our flight back leaves in a few hours. Rachel just got a position as COO for a big up-and-coming tech company," Rory said, beaming at Rachel. "Rachel's parents are watching our boys. This is our last night in Langley Park."

"Boys," Lindsey said. "Congratulations!"

"Twins," Rory said. "Eighteen months old. We're flying by the seat of our pants, but I wouldn't trade it for the world."

"It's all thanks to you two, Nick and Lindsey," Rachel said.

Rory wrapped his arm around Rachel's shoulders. "Yeah, just watching the two of you made us understand what it meant to care for someone. Rach and I have been together ever since that summer at Camp Clem."

Nick stole a glance at Lindsey. She was smiling, but it wasn't her real smile.

Rachel and Rory didn't seem to notice.

"The camp closed a few years ago. Such a shame," Rachel said, shaking her head. "Someone bought it, but last I heard, they're not doing anything with it. They did put in a runway. Isn't that odd?"

"A runway?" Nick cut in. "For a plane?"

"Yeah," Rory answered. "We flew into the Ozarks last summer and saw it when we passed over the camp."

"Speaking of camp," Rachel said, "guess who we ran into in San Francisco?"

"Who?" Lindsey asked.

"Meg and Trevor. Remember them?"

Nick glanced at Lindsey. Her real smile was back. "Oh, yeah, Lindsey and I remember Meg and Trevor."

Rachel clapped her hands. "They're married and living outside the city. Trevor's a motivational speaker and—"

"Hold on," Nick said, sharing another side glance with Lindsey. She was biting back a laugh. "Trevor, the same Trevor who slept in Sawyer Cabin with us at Camp Clem? He's a motivational speaker?"

"Yeah," Rory answered. "I guess he's a pretty good one, too."

"We're meeting them for dinner next week," Rachel added.

"Wow, that's great! You'll have to tell them hello for us," Lindsey said, barely keeping her voice steady.

The campers must have never caught on that Meg and Trevor were stoned ninety percent of the time. He was surprised Meg and Trevor even recognized Rachel and Rory, let alone remembered them.

Nick copied Lindsey and bit down on his lip. He had only heard Trevor speak a full sentence on their last day of camp. To think of him addressing crowds of people was just too funny.

Rachel's phone pinged. "Darn it! That's my mom and dad. We better get back and pick up the twins, Ror."

"It's so good to see you both," Lindsey said, embracing Rachel and then Rory.

"It is," Nick said, hugging Rachel and slapping Rory on the shoulder.

They parted ways, Rory and Rachel heading west on Bellflower Street as he and Lindsey headed east. After half a block, Lindsey stopped, held onto a bench, and bent over.

He crouched down next to her. "Linds, are you in pain?"

Lindsey shook her head and burst into laughter. "Trevor is a motivational speaker."

Her laughter was contagious, and he joined in. "I'd have to see it to believe it."

"Me, too," she replied. Her giggles subsided, and her expression grew thoughtful. "I'm glad we ran into Rachel and Rory. I'd always hoped they'd end up together."

Nick nodded. "They were good kids. It looks like they've turned into good adults."

"We should probably get going," Lindsey said.

"Yeah," Nick agreed, falling into step beside her.

"You know they thought we were..." Lindsey didn't finish the sentence.

His chest tightened. "I know."

If life were perfect, if happy endings truly existed, he and Lindsey would be together. But it's not. Life is messy and tangled and complicated.

Complicated.

That was the word Lindsey used when he had demanded an explanation.

They walked in silence the rest of the way home which was a godsend. Nick bristled, but it wasn't from the cool night air. What was he supposed to say? What was he supposed to do? He loved her. He always would. Except, they could never be together.

He had barely been able to focus on anything that week. Everything from his job to his damn temporary home reminded him of her.

This week had been hell. They had celebrated Artie's retirement Tuesday night. By Wednesday, Nick was in charge of the downtown airport. They'd had an emergency landing that morning after one of the flight training planes experienced a hydraulics malfunction, and he had gotten an earful from a group of self-righteous medical professionals who had to endure a whopping ten-minute departure delay due to the emergency.

He glanced at Lindsey. She seemed lost in thought, eyes trained forward. His gaze slid down to her abdomen. She was pregnant. His gut gave a sick twist. Was he mad she was pregnant or was he upset that the baby growing inside her wasn't his? He released a frustrated breath.

Her house came into view, and Nick wracked his brain. What was he supposed to say to her? But Lindsey broke the silence.

"What's that?" she asked in a frightened whisper.

Nick tensed and looked from side to side. "Did you see someone?"

"No, on my porch. There's a package."

He squinted his eyes. In the dim glow of the porch light, he could make out a box sitting propped up against the front door.

"Oh, no. No, no, no." Lindsey was shaking. Her hand gripped his forearm and squeezed.

"I don't understand what the problem is, Lindsey. It probably got delivered today. Did you order something?"

She met his gaze with wide, terrified eyes. "I have a post office box. Nobody's supposed to know my mailing address."

"Why do you need a post office box?"

She shook her head like she had done when he questioned her about her past. Had she not been so frightened, he might have laughed. He'd spent the majority of his career flying for UPS. Packages, like the one on Lindsey's doorstep, had been a daily part of his life for years.

"Come on," he said, resting his hand over where she was clutching his arm. "We'll look together. It may be a package that was delivered to the wrong address. Em and Michael order things all the time. It could be for them."

Lindsey's trembling grip relaxed a fraction.

They ascended the steps and stopped. There weren't any postage markings on the package. No return address. And an envelope was taped to the top of the box.

Lindsey's grip tightened, and she let out a shaky breath. "I did everything right, Nick. I did everything they told me to do. They said I'd be safe. Only Rosemary knows, and she would never tell anyone."

Lindsey wasn't making any sense, and her tone was growing more hysterical by the second.

He took her hand into his. "Slow down, Linds. I'm going to open the envelope."

She turned her head from side to side like she was expecting somebody to jump out of the bushes.

"Lindsey," he said, cupping her face. "I'm going to open the envelope. Let's see if there's a note or something inside before you get upset."

She blinked, and her eyes focused on his. In the porch light, they called to him, blue-green like a turbulent sea desperate for peace. He bent down and plucked the envelope off the box. There was a white folded sheet of paper inside. He pulled it out and unfolded it. Fisher Designs was printed at the top of the page along with the address of his friend, Ben Fisher's architecture firm. He scanned the page and released a relieved breath.

"It's a note from your godmother, Linds." He held out the paper. "See, she used the stationary from the office she works at."

Lindsey stared at the paper for a beat. "She found some things I left at her house back when I'd spent the summer with her."

Nick nodded. "Yeah, that's all it is, Linds."

She reached into her purse, pulled out a set of keys, but her trembling hands dropped them on the porch.

Nick scooped them up. "Let me help."

He unlocked the door, picked up the package, and followed her inside. She made her way into the kitchen. Her movements were slow and dreamy as if she wasn't sure this was all real. She filled the kettle with water and placed it on the stove.

Jesus! What just happened?

She was terrified of something or someone—he knew that for sure.

"Lindsey, sit," he said, pressing a hand to her back and guiding her over to the kitchen table. "I'll take care of this."

She nodded, almost childlike in her compliance, and sat at the table.

He went to the pantry to look for the tea and honey when he heard her draw in a sharp breath.

He spun around, ready to react. Her panicked state had left him all keyed up. But all he saw was the opened box, and Lindsey holding a red, plaid piece of fabric. It was a long sleeved flannel shirt. She ran her fingers down the cotton fabric, following the line of buttons, then looked up and met his gaze. In her eyes, he saw her wearing that flannel shirt. His flannel shirt. He'd draped it over her shoulders on their first night of patrol at Camp Clemens. The mosquitos had been attacking her, and she had brushed and slapped at her skin.

They bite you because you're so sweet.

That's what he'd said to her. The memory passed through him like a ghost.

He tugged at the sleeve. "You kept it."

"Rosemary kept it," she said, staring at the buttons.

He dropped the flannel. "What else is in there?"

A surprised look crossed her face as if she hadn't even thought there would be more. She pushed back the box flaps, reached inside, and pulled out a handful of photographs and a few letters.

The color had returned to her cheeks. "I guess I took a lot of pictures that summer."

Black and white photographs of the Langley Park Botanic Gardens and shots of the town center littered the table.

"You could say that," Nick said, fingering the edge of a picture of the Langley Park fire station.

"Do you remember this?" Lindsey held up a picture of Langley Park's tattered flag with the embroidered sunflowers.

A smile pulled at his lips. "How could I forget?"

"I wonder if they still have it? It was barely more than a rag sixteen years ago."

"They do," he answered. "It's framed and hanging inside the Langley Park Community Center." The sight of it had stopped him in his tracks the first time he'd gone there to workout.

Lindsey pulled out another photo, but this one wasn't black and white. It was an old, Polaroid picture. She traced its edges with her fingertip. It was the photo they'd taken after winning the capture the flag championship game. Like a moment trapped in time, the campers were cheering, mouths open in mid-whoop, arms wrapped around each other's shoulders while he and Lindsey smiled, gazes locked on each other.

"That was a good day," he said, voice tight.

But he wasn't thinking about capture the flag.

He was thinking about their night in the boathouse. He sat down in the chair next to her and leaned in to take a closer look. He inhaled her heady scent of sweet cream and summer rain, and images of her wrists, slight and delicate, twisted and tangled in the rope as he buried himself deep inside of her flashed through his mind. Her lips, her breasts, the feel of her breath against his neck. He remembered everything. Each kiss. Each caress. Each thrust of his cock. Her memory lived in every cell of his body.

She set the picture down and fingered an envelope. It was crin-

kled and creased like it had been balled up and smoothed out repeat-
edly. Yellowed with age, but unmistakable with her name written in
his hand.

He rested his hand on top of hers. "I know what you must have
thought when you read that. It killed me to know Mrs. Quigley was
probably going to find that letter in my camp binder and give it to
you."

She looked away, but her fingers shifted like her body couldn't
help but lace them with his. Her body remembered his, too.

"What was I supposed to think?"

"I never got to finish the letter. I fell asleep on the damn bus."

She met his gaze. "What would it have said if you had gotten to
finish it?"

He stared into those blue-green eyes and tightened his grip on
her hand. He couldn't answer. Instead, he leaned in and pressed a
kiss to her lips and then another.

"Lindsey," he whispered between kisses.

It was all he could say. He knew he couldn't have her, but his heart
wanted her. For sixteen long years, he had starved it. Kept it cut off
from any real nourishment. He'd known love—her love. From that
moment on, his heart knew it was that real love or nothing. There
had been placeholders—women he had slept with, women he'd been
fond of, even cared about. But he never loved any of them.

Lindsey sighed as he ran the tip of his tongue across the gentle arc
of her lip. He weaved his hand into her hair and pulled her in closer.
In the space of a breath, she was straddling him. His hands clenched
around her ass while her arms wrapped around his neck. She rocked
into him, grinding down, and his cock came to life. He dug his fingertips into the soft flesh and guided her up and down. They dry-
humped like teenagers, and her breath, ragged and laced with sweet
moans and soft gasps, kicked his desire into overdrive.

He kept one hand clenched around her ass as the other moved to
her breast. Through the thin fabric of her blouse and bra, her body
responded. He drew his thumb and index finger around the pearl of
her breast's tight peak, and she took his bottom lip between her teeth.

It was the perfect combination of pleasure and pain, and his hips bucked to increase the friction between their bodies.

"Jesus, this is so fucking right," he said, massaging her breast.

She unbuttoned his pants just as the high-pitched whistle of the kettle tore through the room. It might as well have been a freight train, loud and monstrous, barreling down the track. Lindsey broke their kiss and stared down at the space between them. His hands shifted. He had clasped her waist, and his thumbs made tiny circles against her abdomen where...

The kettle screamed, and he lifted her off his lap and set her back on her chair. He flexed and clenched his hands. Only seconds ago, he had massaged the skin millimeters above the child growing inside of her. He went to quiet the boiling kettle, staring down at it as if the answers to what the hell he was supposed to do would somehow materialize in the puffs of steam.

"I know what scares you," she said after a long beat of silence.

He didn't turn around. He couldn't. If he looked into her eyes, he'd be a goner.

"It's your father. You've been running from him your entire life, haven't you?"

His chest tightened as he turned to face her. The taste of bile flooded his mouth. "How about we talk about what scares you? You broke down at the sight of a package on your doorstep. You were near hysterical. Do you want to explain that reaction to me?"

"I can't."

Nick shook his head and narrowed his eyes. "Just like you can't tell me who the hell the father of your child is or why you whimper and call out in your sleep like a beaten dog."

"I need you to go, Nick," she said, lip trembling. "I thought—"

"You thought what? A little walk down memory lane and I would forget that you won't tell me anything. And if that wasn't enough, Lindsey, I could never be what you need. I can't give that to you."

"You're not your father," she said in a hoarse whisper.

"You don't know what I am, and you don't know what I'm capable of."

She gazed up at him. Christ, those eyes. When he looked at her, a tiny part of him wanted to believe her, wanted to believe he wasn't like his father. He had to go. He had to get away from her. He opened the back door and stood, caught between two worlds.

"Nick, wait," she said.

He didn't turn around. "Lock the door behind me, Lindsey. I won't be coming back."

16

Lindsey crouched down, focused the lens, and framed the shot. A man in a thickly padded suit and a helmet was lying on the floor. A petite woman twisted his arm and administered a swift blow to his groin then to his knee. The studio erupted into cheers.

The self-defense instructor patted the woman on the back and rose to his feet. "Thanks for taking part in our class. Feel free to grab a flyer to share with a friend or loved one. All the self-defense workshops are being taught by retired law enforcement officers, and all of them are excellent teachers. If you want a refresher course or would like more practice working on skills, don't hesitate to come to our next free training."

Lindsey framed another shot. She was in her element, moving seamlessly around the yoga studio as the instructor addressed the participants. That was Photography 101: get the shot, but don't disrupt the organic flow of the situation.

"Remember, self-defense isn't just the physical act of punching or kicking. There's a huge mental component, and the mantra for this mental side of surviving an attack is—"

The instructor paused, and the room erupted. "Never stop fighting."

The instructor clapped his padded hands together. "That's right! Never stop fighting. Today we practiced several self-defense moves and simulated possible attack scenarios. But none of that matters unless you can turn that adrenaline rush into action instead of fear. With fear, we freeze. With action—"

"We fight!" the women called out.

The instructor gave another motivational clap. "Use everything in your arsenal: Be aware of your surroundings, be assertive, carry pepper spray, even ballpoint pens and car keys can serve as a weapon. I have one more thing I'd like to show you before we bring the class to a close. I'll need another volunteer."

Zoe Stein raised her hand, and the instructor motioned for her to come forward. He pulled a roll of duct tape from his bag.

"Zoe and I are going to show you how to free yourself if your wrists are duct taped together."

Zoe's eyes went wide.

"If you don't mind, Zoe. Please press your hands together."

Zoe complied, and the instructor wrapped her wrists with five layers of duct tape.

"Try to pull that apart."

Zoe's expression grew serious as she struggled, pulling and twisting her wrists. No matter how much she tried, the tape remained intact and her wrists tightly bound.

Lindsey stood behind the instructor and continued shooting. A mother and her teenage daughter caught her attention. The daughter's eyes were trained on the instructor as the mother gazed down at her daughter, face solemn and serious. This mother had clearly endured something—possibly an attack or an assault—and wanted her daughter to be prepared if she were trapped in a dangerous or threatening situation. It was something Lindsey sensed. This was the shot she'd been waiting for. All the participants were red-faced and sweaty from practicing the self-defense moves, but this shot of mother and daughter embodied the essence of the free self-defense trainings.

"Duct tape is extremely strong," the instructor began. "But you can break free. Now, Zoe, I want you to hold your wrists as high above your head as you can."

Zoe lifted her arms.

"Now bring them down against your legs with as much force as you can."

Zoe eyed the man skeptically. "Here goes."

She took a breath and slammed her arms against her legs in a fluid gust of force. A sound, like someone had ripped a strip of fabric into two pieces, cut through the air.

"Holy shit. It worked!" Zoe said, rubbing her wrists.

"Language, Zoe Christine Stein," Kathy and Rosemary said in unison.

"And that's our class," the instructor said. "Thank you for coming out and thank you to Kathy Stein for hosting. Remember, always choose action. Always choose to fight."

The instructor dismissed the participants, and Lindsey scrolled through the shots on her camera's display. She looked up when Em tapped her shoulder.

Em glanced at the display. "Did you get what you needed?"

"I did. There was a great turnout," Lindsey answered, removing the camera's lens.

"There sure was," Rosemary said. "And a range of ages from high schoolers to seniors from the Langley Park Senior Living Campus."

"And I have all the consent to be photographed forms for you in the back, Lindsey," Kathy Stein said, joining them.

Zoe bounced back and forth like a prizefighter. "Sweet baby, Jesus! I am pumped. Come at me, Jenna! All six feet of you! I'd prefer Em, she's smaller, but you know, she's all knocked up. So it's up to you, Super Barbie."

Jenna laughed. "I'm hardly six feet tall, and I don't think anyone in this room would bet against you in a fight."

Zoe turned her attention to the instructor. He was still wearing the padded suit as he waved goodbye to the last of the participants.

"Mr. Self-Defense," Zoe called out. "One more time, come at me."

"I'm with Jenna," the instructor answered. "I've seen many hardened criminals in my days on the force. I think the sight of you would terrify all of them, Zoe. But you," he said, turning his attention to Lindsey. "You didn't get to practice. Let's run through a few scenarios."

Lindsey shook her head. "Oh, no! I'm just here to take some pictures for the Kansas City Chamber of Commerce."

"I'm well aware of that, Miss Davies. But I wouldn't be doing my job if I wasn't sure everyone who attended the self-defense workshop didn't come away with some of the skills."

Lindsey glanced around the studio. Only Kathy, Rosemary, Jenna, Zoe, and Em remained. All the other participants had left. She turned to the instructor. Her heart rate kicked up a notch. She hadn't noticed his eyes. He had been wearing that hockey-like helmet contraption, and the bars had obscured them. But now he'd taken it off. Dark hair matted against his forehead. An errant curl brushed past his eyebrow, and below it, whiskey brown eyes.

Lindsey shifted her stance. "I learned quite a bit just by watching."

The instructor fitted the helmet back on his head. "Five minutes. It'll give me peace of mind."

"Wait," Em said. "Lindsey's—"

But Lindsey cut in before Em could finish. "Sure, let's do it. Five minutes can't hurt." She met Em's gaze. Her friend's eyes were wide and blue and questioning. Em had taken part in a few of the self-defense role-play scenarios but mostly watched.

"Go easy," Rosemary said. She was still her tranquil self, but she had crossed her arms.

"Okay, Miss Davies, let's have you start with your back to the wall."

Lindsey handed her camera to Em. "All right, whatever you say." She was trying to keep it breezy and light, but the instructor's eyes, so much like Brett's, sent a jolt of panic down her spine.

She pressed her back against the wall and gazed past the instructor's shoulder at one of the Buddhas on the floor of Kathy's yoga studio.

"Don't forget to shout," he said, giving her a reassuring nod. "You have a voice. Don't be afraid to use it."

He leaned in and simulated grabbing her by the neck. Lindsey's vision grew hazy, and her gaze locked on the man's whiskey brown eyes. He had perfected the art of playing the attacker. He'd role-played different attack scenarios with all the participants. Each time, he had morphed from encouraging teacher to heartless attacker.

She knew that look.

She froze just as she had been conditioned to do under Brett's control.

The instructor softened his expression. "Fight, Lindsey. Fight back."

She blinked. She couldn't fight for herself, but she could fight for the life of the child growing inside her belly. She balled up her hands into tight fists and went for his throat, his nose, his groin.

Someone was yelling. A piercing primal sound that resonated as loud as if she were standing inside a bell tower.

"You did not break me! You did not break me! You did not break me!"

"I got away! I got away! I got away!"

"Lindsey! Lindsey! It's okay. You're okay."

She scratched and kicked, arms flailing. All she saw were those whiskey eyes, and something snapped. Something inside her that had been crammed down deep in her chest burst forth. That innately human drive to live exploded within her like a gladiator ready to conquer whatever atrocity was about to be unleashed into the ring.

She couldn't stop screaming, couldn't stop fighting. Her entire world centered on fighting off Brett, and there was nothing else. No yoga studio. No people standing by. No instructor, shielding himself from her attack.

"Lindsey Anne Hanlon," came her godmother's voice. "Sweetheart, you need to stop. You're safe. You're not in any danger."

At the sound of her name, her real name, Lindsey took in a sharp breath and gazed around the room. She wasn't in Houston. She wasn't at Brett's house. She looked down at her hands. Her fingernails were ragged as if she had clawed at the bark of a tree.

She met her godmother's gaze. "Oh, no!" Hot tears burning with humiliation spilled down her cheeks. She ran to the back of the studio and curled into the corner.

Em got to her first and sat down next to her on the floor. Moments later, the other women surrounded her.

Her godmother took her hand. "It's all right. You're safe in Langley Park."

Lindsey nodded then gazed around the circle. "The instructor?"

"He's gone," Kathy answered. "I thought it would be better if he left. I told him we would take care of you."

Tears streamed down Lindsey's cheeks. "I'm so sorry. I'm so embarrassed."

Kathy Stein shook her head and put her hand on Lindsey's knee. Her warm gray eyes were peaceful and open. Lindsey took her first full breath and let it out in a shaky exhale all while holding Kathy's gaze.

"This is a safe place to talk, Lindsey," Kathy said, sharing a look with Rosemary. "No one here would betray your trust. I love and trust these women with my life. I want you to know, you can, too."

"I think it would help to talk about it," Rosemary said, gently. "You've been holding so much inside, sweetheart. You don't have to do this alone."

Lindsey wiped the tears away and looked at the women. There was no judgment in their eyes, no pinched expressions. Only kindness.

Lindsey took another breath, still a bit shaky, but a fraction smoother than before. "I don't know where to start."

"Start where it feels comfortable. There's no right or wrong way to begin," Kathy replied.

Lindsey took another breath. "I met Brett about three years ago when I was hired to photograph the Houston Arboretum and Nature Center. It's a beautiful place. My images were being used to spearhead a fundraising effort for the center, and the director had asked me to stay for the first fundraising event. Brett was there." She shook her head. "I didn't see it then. I didn't see the monster. He was so charming, so chivalrous. He swept me off my feet, made me feel like the most interesting person in the room." She buried her face in her hands.

The shame. The humiliation. It cut bone deep.

"Lindsey, I want you to listen to me when I tell you this," Kathy said.

Lindsey dropped her hands.

Kathy's gray eyes were still warm, but her expression was serious. "I was a social worker for many, many years. I worked directly with women and families in crisis. I can tell you from all my time in the field and from all the research I've read, domestic abuse happens to women of all races, all creeds, and all colors. It happens to women with Ivy League degrees and blossoming careers. Abuse knows no bounds. You do not carry any blame for what Brett did to you."

"Kathy's right," Rosemary said, giving her hand a gentle squeeze.

"Batterers charm you, isolate you, and after you're alone and often dependent, that's when the violence begins."

Lindsey nodded. "After a month, I'd moved in with Brett. I lived out of a suitcase back then. My life was my job. But Brett enchanted me. He was a surgeon and a philanthropist. He lived in a beautiful home. He seemed like the perfect man. I was about to leave for New Zealand for a shoot, when my mother was killed in a hit and run accident." She squeezed Rosemary's hand. Grief and heartache flooded her chest, tight and thick, like drowning in quicksand. "After I got the call that she'd been killed, I broke down. My father walked out on us when I was sixteen. My mom was all I had. She was the one who insisted I follow my dreams and become a photographer. I could barely cope, but Brett was there. He insisted I take medication to calm down, but when I finally emerged from the fog, it had been more than a week. She'd already been laid to rest, and I wasn't there."

"Oh, Lindsey, that's awful," Em said, eyes shining with emotion.

"It spiraled down from there," Lindsey continued. "I wouldn't take any more medicine, but I'd fallen into depression. I canceled the remaining jobs I had booked and let Brett take care of me. At first, I couldn't get over how kind and how patient he was. But then, I started to feel better. I wanted to get back to work. This threw him into a rage like nothing I had ever seen. He broke one of my cameras and threatened to smash all my equipment. He said he'd taken care of me, and I was a thankless, heartless bitch who wanted to leave him. That was the first night he hit me. He threw me up against the wall and slapped me so hard the blood vessels in my eye ruptured. After that, he held a loaded gun to my head and told me if I ever tried to leave him, he'd hunt me down and he'd kill anyone who tried to stop him."

Lindsey paused. For a moment, the scent of rosewater, her mother's scent, hung sweet and fragrant in the air as if her spirit was there, offering strength. Lindsey closed her eyes and focused on her mother's face.

"I'm not sure how I allowed myself to settle into a life with him. It just happened. I hadn't worked in over a year and a half. Brett had damaged most of my equipment. But he didn't break my old Nikon. I couldn't use it for work. Maybe he had just assumed it was worthless. It didn't have any of the bells and whistles of today's cameras. I started using it to document the abuse. When he was at work, I would photograph my black eyes, my bruised ribs, the gashes, the scrapes. Somehow, that became my normal."

Zoe wiped a tear from her cheek. "You didn't think the police could help?"

"I was worried that if I called them, Brett would hurt them, shoot them just like he'd threatened. I just figured, if I could contain his rage and limit it to me, I'd be protecting other people. I know it makes no sense..."

"Many women have felt the way you did, Lindsey," Kathy said with a solemn expression. "It's a common response not to want others to have to endure abuse."

"But that all changed when I found out I was pregnant," Lindsey continued. "I'd had a gash on my scalp that wasn't healing. I had started taking antibiotics without telling Brett. The last few months we were together, he'd mostly left me alone in the bedroom. He was preoccupied with some issue regarding his brother. They're both surgeons. I'm not sure if it had to do with their practice. He didn't share that kind of information with me. But one night, he came home late. He was terribly angry and agitated—more than usual. I was already in bed. I tried to pretend to be asleep, but he woke me, and he..."

"He forced himself on you," Rosemary said, giving her the words.

Lindsey nodded. "I knew I was in danger of becoming pregnant. I prayed I wouldn't. But..." She pressed her hand to her belly and met each woman's gaze. "I'm eighteen weeks pregnant. I left Brett the moment I found out. I was able to pawn some of the jewelry he'd given me to get by. I also stayed at women's shelters. They helped me change my last name. And then there's Rosemary." She met her godmother's gaze. "If it weren't for you, I wouldn't have a home or a job or..." Lindsey looked around the circle.

"Friends," Em said, placing her hand on Lindsey's leg next to where Kathy's hand rested.

Lindsey nodded, blinking back the tears.

Jenna added her hand to where the other women's hands rested on Lindsey's leg. "You've got us now."

Zoe added her hand to the pile. "And there's no way we're going to let any dick whistle of a douche canoe like your ex do anything to hurt you or your baby."

The air stilled. For a beat, no one moved a muscle until Em broke out into a giggle. "Zoe Stein, where do you come up with those words?"

The room erupted into laughter. Lindsey couldn't help herself. A bubbly, blissful laugh she hadn't heard in years echoed in the small space as tears of relief and gratitude rolled down her cheeks. But a twinge in her stomach silenced her.

She pressed her hands to her stomach. "I think I felt something."

Kathy's brow furrowed. "What is it, dear? Are you in pain?"

"No, I think the baby's doing something." Lindsey stilled. There it was again, that little flutter like being tickled from the inside. "I'm okay," she said, concentrating on the sensation.

"I think your baby needs ice cream," Zoe said through a teary smile.

"I think we all could use some ice cream," Jenna said.

Em pressed her hand to her belly. "I need ice cream and rotisserie chicken."

"Let's head over to The Scoop," Rosemary said. "If there's one thing that can make anything better, it's ice cream."

"Topped with bacon and rainbow sprinkles," Em added with a teary smile as the women laughed.

They came to their feet and filed out of the back office, but Em reached out and took Lindsey's hand before she could follow the women out of the yoga studio. "I'm glad you're in Langley Park, and I'm glad you're living next door in my old house. We're all here for you. Remember that. Michael, too. You need anything—anchovies, mayonnaise, pineapple pizza. He'll already be going to the store to pick up God knows what for me."

Lindsey squeezed her hand. "Thank you."

"Girls," Kathy called. "Ice cream awaits."

17

Nick reclined in his chair and skimmed through one of the many Special Airworthiness Information Bulletins from the FAA. He couldn't fault the Federal Aviation Administration. Air safety was a huge undertaking. An aviation director could spend days on end reading service bulletins, information bulletins, aircraft safety alerts, and the airworthy directives. He glanced up when two knocks on his office door pulled him away from his papers.

Michael MacCarron opened the door a crack. "Hey! Getting in a little light reading before our jaunt into Kansas City's airspace?"

Nick held up the bulletin. "The FAA doesn't do anything lightly. This directive is a riveting tale about a helicopter part that was incorrectly identified in a catalog, and this one," he held up another piece of paper, "is all about the failure of a connecting rod on a glider."

"Sounds as interesting as reading page after page of civil procedure or worse—the six hours I spent with a ninety-nine-year-old woman who wanted to cut her great-grandson out of her will because he gave her a box of milk chocolate buttercreams instead of her favorite, milk chocolate maple fudge."

Nick ran his hand down his face. "Who knew the law and aviation would be so riveting?"

"Right!" Michael agreed. "They both look so cool on television. Think, *Top Gun* and *Law and Order*."

Nick craned his head. "Are Sam and Ben going to join us? My Skyhawk seats four."

"Sam had something come up with his brother."

"His brother?"

"Yeah, they don't talk all that much. Gabe's my cousin, and I hardly ever hear from him. Family, nobody gets to pick theirs, huh?" Michael added.

Nick placed the aviation paperwork in his desk drawer. He wasn't about to touch that family comment. "And Ben?"

"Jenna had a self-defense thing to go to at Kathy Stein's yoga studio, so Ben's on daddy duty today with Kate."

Nick smiled. He had known Jenna for nearly a decade. They had met after he started flying for UPS and she was setting up an elementary reading program in Louisville. For a time, they were exactly what the other needed. Sex with no strings attached. Contact but no connection. A chance encounter with Jenna and Ben in Langley Park had flipped a switch inside of him. He and Jenna had been the same—loners who didn't open their hearts to anyone or anything. But after seeing Jenna with Ben, it kindled a spark of hope that maybe he could build a life somewhere. But Lindsey's tumultuous entrance back into his life had thrown all that for a loop.

"You get me all to yourself," Michael said with a teasing grin. "I left Em with a truckload of Wheat Thins, gummy bears, and pineapple. She should be okay for the next couple of hours."

Nick grimaced. "The craving du jour?"

Michael nodded, and a wide grin spread across his face.

Christ, what he wouldn't give to have even a fraction of what Michael and Em had. Nick let out a breath and pushed the thought from his mind. He couldn't have that. The only woman he had even remotely considered that with was living less than fifty feet away from him and was pregnant with someone else's baby.

"Let's head down. The ground guys should have my Cessna ready to go," Nick said, leading Michael out of the Hangar 12 building and over to the apron where a smaller Cessna was being unloaded.

Michael buckled his seatbelt. "The perks of knowing a pilot. What do you have planned for today? A few loops around the city?"

"I was thinking something else," Nick answered, pulling on his headset and gesturing for Michael to do the same.

Last time he was in the Skyhawk, Lindsey was sitting next to him. A few hours after that, they had made love in her kitchen. He needed to get into the sky. He needed to be thousands of feet above Langley Park.

Nick went through the preflight checklist and entered his flight plan into the computer. Christ, they should just do a few loops around the city—check out the stadiums, fly over Langley Park and let Michael see his Foursquare from two thousand feet. But that's not what he entered into the computer.

"How about a trip to the Ozarks and back? It takes about an hour to fly there and then an hour to get back depending on the winds," Nick said as nonchalantly as he could manage.

"That would be great. Do we need to stop and refuel?"

"No, we've got a full tank, and we're flying light. It's only a little over three hundred miles round trip. I could get at least another two hundred if I had to."

Michael slapped his hands on his thighs. "Let's do it!"

Nick contacted the tower. Within minutes, they were airborne, heading southeast toward the Missouri Ozarks.

"I think I know what you and Lindsey were arguing about the other night," Michael said after they left Kansas City's airspace.

"Lindsey and I knew each other a long time ago. That's all there is to it."

"Bullshit, dude. Em and I know about her condition."

A muscle ticked in Nick's cheek, and he tightened his grip on the yoke. "Did she tell you guys?"

"No, we ran into her after one of Em's ultrasounds. Em and Lindsey have the same obstetrician. I don't think Lindsey wanted anyone to know about her pregnancy."

"She definitely has her secrets," Nick answered.

"Nick, any idiot can see the way you look at her. She's not just some random girl from your past."

Nick settled his gaze on the horizon. "No, she's not."

"Then what's going on? You were really letting her have it, the other night."

The muscle in Nick's cheek ticked again. "She's pregnant. She won't tell me anything more than that. She's got a different last name but says she's never been married. And if that wasn't enough, my father thoroughly fucked me up. I'm not going to risk doing that to some kid."

"I can sympathize. If things were reversed and Em came back to Langley Park pregnant and tight-lipped, I'd be pissed as hell, too. But, you can't let having a shitty childhood affect your happiness."

"You never met my father," Nick said. His mouth had gone dry.

"Before my dad was diagnosed with Alzheimer's and had to go into assisted living," Michael began, "he was no picnic of a father either. He did his best, but he never supported my interest in music. I had no path other than to become an attorney and continue on the family business."

"I thought you were happy with your set up. You get to practice law, and you and Em work on music together."

"I am. But I'm happy because I have Em. I have a full life. I may not have had the best relationship with my father, but I sure as shit am going to learn from that and do better—at least fucking try."

"It's not my child growing inside Lindsey's belly," Nick said and hated himself for it the moment the words left his lips.

"Biology doesn't mean you're going to be a good parent or even that you're going to be a bad parent. What matters is what you do. Look at Jenna. She's not Kate's biological mother, but Kate is just as much her daughter as she is Ben's."

"It's complicated," Nick said, using Lindsey's words.

Michael chuckled. "Everything is fucking complicated, dude. Welcome to Langley Park."

Nick shook his head. *Fuck.* He didn't know what to do or what to think when it came to Lindsey. He checked his instruments. They were getting close to Camp Clem.

Michael leaned forward. "No way! I know that place."

The boathouse and dining hall came into view as they flew over Lake Langhorne. The water shimmered and kissed the side of the bluff.

"That's Camp Clem. You and Lindsey went there, right?"

"Yeah," Nick said, but his attention was drawn toward a ribbon of dirt that started at the bluff's edge and went inland.

"Is that some kind of runway?" Michael asked. He saw it, too.

"It looks like a pretty crude one. It's not very long. I could land my Cessna, but you wouldn't be able to land anything much bigger."

They circled the camp. The cabins were just as Nick remembered them, wrapped around the periphery with the lodge at the center. It still looked the same, if not a little worse for wear.

"Camp Clem closed a few years ago. We heard there were new owners, but nobody knows who it is," Michael said as they made another pass.

Rory and Rachel had told them the same thing the other night.

Nick checked his instruments. "We better head back to Kansas City. The winds are picking up. It looks like some weather may be blowing in."

"Are you worried?" Michael asked.

"Nah, we should just head back," he answered, swallowing hard and taking one last look at the boathouse.

NICK TAXIED down the runway and parked his plane in the airport's apron.

"That was great, Nick. Going up with you never gets old," Michael said, unbuckling his seatbelt and slipping off the headset.

Nick nodded to his friend, but his attention was drawn to the tarmac. One of the pilots who flew private chartered flights was having an animated discussion with two men.

"Hey, Michael," Nick said, gaze trained on the men. "It looks like there's a situation I may need to weigh in on. Can I catch up with you later?"

They deplaned, and the ground crew arrived to tow his Skyhawk back to the hangar.

"Sure, is there anything I can do to help?"

"No, I think this is a job for the Director of Aviation. I know the pilot. He's a good guy. If anyone's laying into him, it's because they want him to do something shady or bend the rules."

Michael gave him a nod and headed toward the Hangar 12 building, while Nick assessed the situation. The two men, both around his age, maybe a few years older, had the same dark hair and were of average height and build. One of the men was gesticulating wildly, while the pilot kept shaking his head apologetically.

Nick approached the trio. "Zach," he said, addressing the pilot, "is there anything I can help with?"

Zach gave him a wary look.

"Who the hell are you?" the angry man asked.

"I'm the airport's director of aviation."

Now that he was closer, he was able to take a better look at the men. They must have been related—maybe brothers or cousins. The older of the two had a dark glint to his brown eyes, something hollow and sinister Nick couldn't put his finger on. The man seemed unaffected by his companion's outburst and hung back, indifferent eyes flicking between his phone and the heated discussion on the tarmac.

"Mister..." Nick met the angry man's gaze and put his hand out despite every cell in his body telling him this guy was bad news.

"Doctor," the man said with a sneer. "I'm a fucking doctor, and this idiot," he gestured toward Zach, "won't fly us where we paid him to take us."

"Nick," Zach said with pleading eyes, "they want to go to an uncharted airfield, which would be fine, but I can't find anyone to give me approval."

Nick put a hand on Zach's shoulder and eyed the irate man. "I'm sorry, doctor," he said, emphasizing the word, "but it's trespassing to land on private property without permission."

The doctor took a step closer. "I have the GPS coordinates. It's not that difficult. A goddamn monkey could do it."

"You can't just change your destination last minute and expect us to accommodate it without question, sir. That stipulation is in the contract you signed," Zach said.

The doctor took a step toward Zach. "You have one job, and it's not even that hard. Get in plane. Fly plane. Do what you've been paid to do."

"Hold on a second," Nick said, inserting himself between the men. He was done fucking around with this asshole. "Part 157 of the federal aviation regulations specifically states any alteration, activation, or deactivation of airfield must be registered. To the best of your knowledge, doctor, is this airstrip registered?"

The doctor shifted his stance. "This is fucking bullshit."

Nick crossed his arms. "It's unsafe to try and land anywhere where conditions are unknown. This is no longer Zach declining to fly you to your location. As the director of aviation and the individual in charge of the operations of this facility, I'm telling you, no. You're welcome to be taken to any FAA registered airfield, but you're asking one of my pilots to do something potentially illegal, and I won't allow that."

"You're making a scene," the doctor's companion said, glancing up from his phone.

The angry man shook his head and trained his gaze on Zach. "We're going back to Houston. Can you manage that? Just fly the plane back to where you picked us up."

"I can find another way to accommodate these gentlemen if you're unable," Nick said to Zach. He wanted to give him an out.

Zach shook his head. "It's not a problem. I'd be happy to take the doctors back to Houston."

Nick met the man's gaze, but Zach gave him a reassuring nod.

"What a fucking waste," the doctor mumbled as he turned and headed toward the Cessna C560 Citation jet.

The companion, who had remained quiet through the exchange, pocketed his smartphone. "This is very unfortunate." His tone was mild, but something cruel and snarling flashed in his eyes.

Nick narrowed his gaze. "Our priority is safety. We don't play favorites or bend the rules. That's how people get hurt."

A whisper of a smirk tugged at the man's cheek. "We don't want anyone getting hurt, do we?"

The doctor was an asshole. Nick had dealt with plenty of his kind throughout his aviation career. But this guy—he had hardly said a word, and Nick wanted to punch him square in the jaw.

Nick narrowed his gaze. "I'll call the tower personally and make sure your plane's cleared immediately for takeoff. We wouldn't want to inconvenience you any further."

The man held his gaze. "That's very kind of you, director..."

"Nicholas Kincade."

The man's face cracked into a smile sharp enough to cut glass. He looked Nick up and down. "Director Kincade, it's been a pleasure," he said then followed his companion onto the plane.

Nick put a hand on Zach's shoulder. "I know you're single-pilot certified, but I can sit in as your first officer on this run if you don't want to be alone with those two. And you know I'm certified, too. I could take this flight for you. It's your call."

"I'm good, Nick, but thanks for offering. I've flown these guys a few times. Sometimes there's a lady with them. They're a bunch of doctors that get shuttled around by some fancy pharmaceutical company. Their temper tantrums aren't much worse than my toddler's."

Nick glanced at the plane. The man with the dark eyes was watching them.

"Safe flight," Nick said, clapping Zach on the shoulder. "Nobody would fault you if you happened to hit a pocket of turbulence that had those guys with their heads between their knees."

Zach smiled. The color had returned to his cheeks. "Thanks, Nick. I appreciate you backing me up."

Nick crossed his arms and watched the Cessna taxi onto the

runway as the hairs on the back of his neck rose to attention. He would need to keep an eye out for these two.

18

"It's good to see you," Jenna said. She stood on the sidewalk outside a large red brick Victorian home in Kansas City not far from Langley Park. "Welcome to the Rose Brooks Women's Shelter."

Lindsey gazed at the home. A tasteful wrought iron gate dotted with trees and bushes surrounded the building. It was just a couple of weeks into April, and young leaves and tight buds decorated the dark branches.

"It's quite lovely, isn't it?" Jenna said, gazing at the house alongside her.

Two weeks ago, Lindsey had shared her secret with Jenna, Zoe, Em, and Kathy. And in that short amount of time, she had gained their friendship and their loyalty. When she wasn't working, she would spend time over at Em's place, listening to music and eating whatever strange combination of food her new friend had felt like that day. She had joined Jenna and Zoe for yoga at Kathy's studio and met Rosemary for long walks around the Langley Park Botanic Gardens.

The one person missing from her new life was Nick. He would be up with the sun and wouldn't return until late at night. He was keeping his distance.

Lindsey met Jenna's gaze. "It's a beautiful house."

"Here." Jenna handed her a key fob hanging from a chain. "This will open almost every door inside the facility. You'll be teaching in one of the counseling rooms. I thought that would be the most comfortable place to gather."

"Sounds perfect," Lindsey said, holding the key fob. The women's shelter near Houston utilized the same security protocols.

Jenna buzzed the front door and spoke to a security guard through the intercom. They entered the shelter and were met with a wall of teddy bears.

Jenna touched one of the bear's legs. "They're for the children. Most women and kids come here with barely the clothes on their backs. There's often no time to grab toys or even shoes. Rose Brooks does its best to have everything mothers and children need from baby formula to toys. Was your shelter in Texas like this?"

"Yeah," Lindsey said, noting a children's room that looked like a preschool classroom, a large area filled with blankets and clothing, and a large, spacious kitchen with double stoves and two long tables. "Rose Brooks feels more like a home, though."

"It does," Jenna agreed, nodding to staff members passing by in the hall. "Everyone here is meant to feel like family. There's childcare, counseling, play therapy, and a legal advocate on site. We're hoping to raise money to start doing more prevention work. We'd like to help educate the community by raising awareness to help prevent domestic violence."

Jenna led her into a cozy room where people were milling around, filling up coffee cups and chatting. Em, Rosemary, Zoe, and Kathy smiled and waved.

"I didn't know you all would be taking part in the photography project!" Lindsey said, delighted to see her friends.

Kathy pulled her in for a hug. "Rose Brooks is a wonderful organization. We wouldn't miss helping out for the world."

"And Jenna said there'd be snacks," Em added, popping an almond and a pretzel stick into her mouth.

Zoe set a notebook on the arm of a couch. "I'm here to cover the event for Kansas Public Radio. Is that okay with you? It's just a quick piece to highlight the upcoming fundraiser."

"You won't need any pictures of me, will you?" Lindsey asked.

Zoe gave her a sly wink. "Nope, that's the beauty of radio."

"And my name?"

Zoe's expression softened. "I understand the sensitivity of the situation—not just for you, but for all the women taking part. No one will have their name used in the piece unless they give consent. A few of the counselors here said they would be willing to provide their names. That's as much as I need for this story."

"Okay, thanks, Zoe."

Rosemary squeezed her hand. "Are you doing all right? This must bring up some strong emotions for you, dear."

Lindsey let out a breath. "I'm okay. It feels good to be here in a capacity to help. I know it's not much in the grand scheme of things, but it feels like something."

"What you're doing is huge, for you and for all the women and children who rely on this place. I know your mother would be very proud. I certainly am."

Tears welled in Lindsey's eyes. "Thank you," she whispered. But before she could say another word, Jenna addressed the group.

"Welcome, everyone. I'm grateful to all of you for taking part in our Rose Brooks photography project. I'd like to introduce Lindsey Davies. She's a photographer who's traveled the world. She's hung out of helicopters and photographed major cities, and she's also photographed indigenous people in places like South America and New Zealand."

All eyes shifted from Jenna. Lindsey looked around the room and made quick eye contact with each participant. There were ten other individuals in addition to her friends. Three men and three women wore shelter employee badges while four women wore the same visitor's key fob necklace as she was wearing. Lindsey paid particular attention to these women. Their connection went deeper than just working here or wanting to support a good cause. Lindsey sensed a visceral connection as strong as steel between women who have endured abuse.

She let out a breath. The tension in her shoulders and neck melted away. "I'm honored to be here, thank you, Jenna. I do have one thing I can promise you about our time together." She paused. "Nobody is going to be required to hang out of a helicopter. We'll save that for our second lesson."

The participants chuckled, and the atmosphere softened as nervous smiles changed to genuine expressions of interest.

"We could start with all the basics of Photography 101, but this project isn't about shutter speed, aperture, and ISO. The cameras donated for the project are DSLR and mirrorless. They're excellent at capturing shots automatically. We're not going to get into all the technical aspects of photography."

The group gave a collective sigh of relief.

"When you boil it down to its most essential element, photography is about telling a story. A picture doesn't have to be worth just a thousand words. It can be worth ten thousand words, a hundred thousand words. Or, it could be just one single powerful word."

She held up a print of an indigenous woman's face as she gazed down at her newborn baby. "I took this shot almost ten years ago in New Zealand. To me, this is a story about love. To me, this is a story about devotion."

She pulled another photograph from her bag of an aerial shot of the Las Vegas strip. It was taken with the doors of the chopper framing the shot. "When you're telling a story, think of framing. Think of what you could include in your shot to make it unique. If you want to capture the feel of the shelter's children's room, instead of taking a wide shot, focus on a few toys or a child's hands dressing a doll. Think of the picture you want to take and then ask yourself, what little tweak can I give it to add my voice and my touch to this image."

The group nodded. Lindsey smiled as their gazes shifted to different spots in the room. They were already thinking like photographers. Their heads tilted as they imagined new ways to capture the simple, everyday things that surround us.

"Let's talk a little bit about lighting," she continued. "Your cameras are going to do a beautiful job of automatically adjusting to a range of light and dark situations. But there are two times of day I'd like you to pay special attention to. They're called the golden hour and the blue hour."

"I think I've heard of the golden hour," one of the women offered. "It's shortly after sunrise or before sunset."

"That's right," Lindsey said, sharing a smile with the women. "The light is warmer, and it has more of a red tone to it. The other time of day is called the blue hour. This is the time right before sunrise or just after sunset." She held up two photos of sailboats lined up in a marina. "These were taken twenty minutes apart in Greece on the island of Crete. You can see the cool blue diffused hue of the photo taken before sunrise. In this one," she pointed to the golden version of the same boats, "you can see the warmer tones come alive."

The room stilled as the group stared at her photographs.

"Think of the light like a dance partner. Observe it carefully. Move with it. Follow it. Let it guide the shot."

She looked around the room and caught Rosemary out of the corner of her eye. Her godmother was smiling as she brushed away a tear and gave her a knowing nod.

Lindsey blinked back her own tears. "Before I let you loose with the cameras, I wanted to share something personal. Not long ago, I was in an abusive relationship."

The four women she had felt a kinship with gazed at her with wide eyes.

"I was frightened for my life, and I lived in a place much like this shelter in another state. Everyone here has a connection to Rose Brooks. All your voices are important. No matter how you got here, you have a story to tell."

She brought her focus back to the four women who were now holding hands. "Don't move," she said, reaching for her camera bag. "This—your hands." Her mind was moving fast. She saw the shot in her head—four pairs of hands holding tight to each other. "May I photograph your hands? No faces. I promise."

The women nodded, and Lindsey went to work. The light from the late day sun danced and twinkled through the window's lace curtains as specks of dust moved in slow motion like tiny celestial bodies through the stream of sunshine. The glow cast the women's hands in a haunting hue of warmth. Lindsey saw the scars etched into their skin, but she also saw resiliency and strength and courage. The click of the shutter and the sound of her breath disappeared. She framed the shot from above, from below, and at hip level. Then, the light softened like Mother Nature herself had summoned the alteration.

"This, right here," she said and focused on the women's hands. "The clouds must have come in. You can tell by the way the light is diffused. Can you all see the shadows? Can you see the rich layers that just a slight change made?"

Lindsey took one last shot and looked up. "Thank you for indulging me. As you can see, when an image speaks to you, a back-and-forth exchange begins. You'll feel it. The story is there, it's whispering to you. Take your time. Listen. Feel. I can't wait to see how Rose Brooks' story unfolds through your eyes."

She stood up, but doubled back over, releasing a tight gasp.

Rosemary was at her side. "Lindsey, are you in pain?"

Kathy joined them as Jenna, Zoe, and Em came around to her other side.

"Where's the pain?" Kathy asked, rubbing Lindsey's shoulder blades,

"It's low," Lindsey said in a tight breath. "This can't be labor. I'm barely twenty weeks."

She looked up as Rosemary and Kathy exchanged an anxious glance.

Em bent down and took her hand. "Just breathe, Lindsey. Just breathe. Zoe's calling for an ambulance."

She met Em's gaze and squeezed her friend's hand. Tight spasms of pain worked their way through her abdomen.

"I can't lose this baby."

"Hey, boss! I'm glad I caught you."

Nick looked up to see Silas Wright, one of his most trusted members of the airport's ground crew. It wasn't much of a stretch that Silas had caught him. He had been spending almost every waking hour at the airport. Part of it was because he was new on the job. But that wasn't all of it. Lindsey crept into every part of his day. The blue of her eyes, her chestnut hair. Every fucking color of the rainbow made him think of her. He'd managed to avoid her for two long weeks, but her touch, her kiss, the feel of his hands gripping her ass — he hadn't found a way to stop the barrage of memories. He couldn't even escape her in his sleep. With sunflowers tucked in her hair, she haunted his dreams.

"What can I do for you, Silas?"

"Artie just called."

"Oh, yeah! How's retirement going? Is he enjoying the vegetable stand?"

"I think he misses us, boss. He's thinking of buying a Cessna 177 off a buddy of his. The guy keeps the plane in one of our hangars. Artie wanted to know if you had time to take it up, put her through the paces, and see what you thought of her."

"What year?" Nick asked.

"Seventy-eight. Last year they made the one seventy-seven."

"Of course, I can take her up. Is she ready to go?"

Silas gave him a sheepish grin. "She is. She's gassed up and ready for takeoff. I figured you'd say yes. Artie's on his way, but he's stuck in traffic. He said you should go up without him."

Nick nodded and followed Silas out to the tarmac just as a helicopter landed. The helo pilot waved, and Nick waited as the copter's blades came to rest. The pilot exited the chopper and headed his way.

"I don't know how you guys have any fun in those fixed-wing contraptions," the helicopter pilot said, gesturing to the Cessna 177 with a teasing grin.

Nick clapped the pilot on his shoulder. "Joaquin, planes can fly further, faster, and higher than that mechanical sack of metal can any day."

"I guess we have to agree to disagree," Joaquin said with a chuckle.

"Are you going to be around for a little bit?" Nick asked. "I wanted to go over some new helicopter flight protocols that just came in."

"Absolutely, I'll be in Hangar 12's pilots' lounge. Come find me when you get back."

Nick climbed into the Cessna, went through all the checks, and taxied onto the runway. The tower gave the okay for takeoff, and Nick piloted the 177 smoothly into the sky. It was late afternoon and, as the clouds rolled in, the light shifted, softening the glint of light coming off the Kansas City skyline.

He followed the curve of the Kansas River then veered off and headed south toward Langley Park. Everything looks peaceful from three thousand feet. Tiny houses dotted with shrubbery and cars that looked like toys gave the world a surreal quality. So many people, living so many lives. This usually cleared his head, but as he stared into the blue-green horizon, all he saw was Lindsey.

Nick rounded past Lake Boley and headed back toward the airport. He flew north over Kansas City's Country Club Plaza and was about to radio the airport's tower and request permission to land when the plane lurched. He checked his instruments. He'd lost all power.

"Shit," he hissed, but there wasn't time to panic.

He had to maintain the airplane's best glide speed to maximize his range. He was in the heart of Kansas City. There were no empty stretches for miles. He had to make it back to the airport. The alternative was...

He shook his head. There was no fucking way he was dying today.

He attempted to restart the plane.

Nothing.

Nick steadied himself. "Mayday, mayday, mayday. Kansas City Approach, Cessna one-one-seven-four Bravo is declaring an emergency and requests an emergency landing. I repeat one-one-seven-four Bravo requests emergency landing."

His heart was pounding, but his training took over. He could see the airport. The runways were clear. They were ready for him.

"Visualize the path," he said under his breath.

Christ, it was going to be close. He dropped the flaps and secured the engine by cutting the fuel valve. He didn't need the damn plane catching on fire. He held his breath as the Cessna touched down and skidded across the runway.

The plane came to a stop, and Nick released a ragged breath. He looked at his hands, felt his chest and his head. He'd made it. All those hours practicing emergency landings in the flight simulator and all those tedious checkrides where the FAA pilot examiners grilled him had paid off.

Flashing lights and sirens broke his train of thought. He pulled off the headset, opened the door, and started jogging toward the oncoming emergency vehicles.

The door on one of the airport's security vehicles flung open, and Artie and Joaquin came running towards him.

"Nick, are you okay?" Joaquin asked.

"Yeah, I'm good."

Artie put a hand on his shoulder. "What happened up there?"

"I lost power. The engine cut out."

Artie shook his head. "I'm sorry, Nick. I asked if the plane had been properly maintained. My friend gave me his word it had, but that couldn't have been the case. Is this your first emergency landing?"

He nodded.

"Puts everything into perspective, doesn't it?" Artie said, squeezing his shoulder.

Nick nodded again. All he could think about was Lindsey. He had to get to her. His father. Her pregnancy. Her past. None of it mattered. Life was too short. He had missed out on the last sixteen years. He wasn't about to miss out on another sixteen seconds.

"Nick!" Silas ran up to them. "A Michael MacCarron's been trying to get ahold of you."

"Michael? How could he already know about this?"

Silas shook his head. "No, it's about someone named Lindsey. An ambulance took her to Midwest Medical. He said you would want to know."

Everything stopped. The flashing lights. The sound of raised voices. It all disappeared. All he could see was Lindsey.

"Did Michael say what happened? Is Lindsey all right?"

"I don't know. I don't know. He left a bunch of messages. He couldn't reach you on your cell."

Nick patted his pockets for his phone. Shit. He must have left it in his office. He didn't have time to fuck around with finding his phone and fighting traffic. He looked at Joaquin. "Does Midwest Medical Center have a helipad?"

Joaquin narrowed his gaze. "They do, why?"

"Is your helicopter ready to go?" Nick asked. Another hit of adrenaline surged through him. He had to get to Lindsey.

"Nick, are you asking what I think you're asking?"

Nick held the man's gaze.

"What about all this?" Joaquin motioned toward the plane banked in the grass near the runway and the emergency crews securing the site.

"I'll take care of this," Artie said. "You have somewhere you need to be, don't you?"

19

"I hope you have a guardian angel or somebody who owes you a big favor at the FAA," Joaquin said over the roar of the helicopter's blades, "because you're going to have a lot of explaining to do, my friend."

The chopper's lights illuminated the large white cross with a red H in the center, while green lights bordered the periphery of the Midwest Medical Center's Helipad.

"I have to get to her, Joaquin. The other shit, I'll figure out. But this, with Lindsey, I need to be with her. I have to make sure she's okay. I..."

"You're a man in love," Joaquin said with a smile as he lowered the chopper onto the helipad. "Nobody can fault you that."

The door to the roof entrance opened, and a man in scrubs stepped out, shielding his eyes from the wind kicked up by the helicopter.

"I'm not sure if it's a good sign or a terrible sign, but it looks like one of the hospital's head honchos is meeting us on the pad," Joaquin said, flipping a switch.

Nick unbuckled his seatbelt. "Thanks, Joaquin. I owe you."

"I hope your girl's all right."

"Me, too," Nick said. He removed the headset and got out of the chopper, ducking down and jogging toward the safety zone and the man waiting for him near the doors.

"This is a very unorthodox way to arrive at the hospital, Nick, even for the airport's new director of aviation."

"Dr. Stein," Nick said, immediately recognizing Midwest Medical Center's Chief of Surgery and Ben and Zoe's father. "I had to get here. I had to get to Lindsey. Is she okay?"

Neal led him into the hospital. "She's stable, but they've decided to admit her for observation."

"Did something happen? Did someone try to hurt her? You know she's—"

Neal stopped him. "Nick, she's in good hands. My wife, Rosemary, Jenna, Zoe, and Em are all in with her."

Nick knew what Neal was trying to tell him. He didn't need to be here. Christ, he'd been a fool, pushing Lindsey away. And not only that, everyone had noticed.

"I need to see her, Neal. I promise I won't upset her." He swallowed hard and looked the man straight in the eye. "I love her."

Neal's gaze softened. "The women have become quite protective of her."

Nick nodded. "I'm glad she has them, but from this day forward, I'm going to be the one protecting her—if she lets me."

A pang of fear spread through his chest. What if she didn't want him? What if he had pushed her away one too many times? Dammit, he had to try. She could turn him down, but it would have to be after he pleaded his case.

"Good luck," Neal said, gesturing to a door. "This is her room."

Nick took a breath. He was trapped in the space between land and sky. He was either going to take off or crash and burn. Either way, there was no turning back. He opened the door, and six pairs of eyes locked onto him like an F-16 trained on an unfriendly target.

"Lindsey, are you okay? Is the baby okay?"

"Nick, we love you. We really do," Zoe cut in, holding Lindsey's hand. "But Lindsey's had a rough couple of hours."

He looked around the room. The women circled around Lindsey. Mrs. G and Kathy stood on either side of her while Jenna, Zoe, and Em sat next to her on the hospital bed.

The door opened, and Michael walked in balancing a tray of coffees. "Dude, was that you who just got dropped off by a helicopter?"

"You came here by helicopter?" Lindsey asked. She looked tired, but her eyes were sharp and alert.

"Yeah, I had to get to you, Linds."

"Why? Why are you here, Nick?"

He looked around the room. Nobody moved. In fact, the women seemed to circle in closer.

He was going to have an audience.

"Linds, this afternoon, I took a plane up to test it out for a friend. The engine failed, and I had to make an emergency landing."

Her face fell, and her eyes filled with tears. "Are you okay?"

"I'm fine. I'm more than fine because that emergency landing put everything into perspective for me. After I was back on the ground, do you know what I wanted?"

She shook her head.

"You, I wanted you."

A tear trailed down her cheek. She rested her hand on the slight curve of her abdomen. "But what about this?"

Nick took a step closer. The women were still watching him, but the fierce protectiveness that radiated off of them in waves when he had first arrived had cooled to a watchful gaze.

"I want to tell you what the letter that I left you sixteen years ago was supposed to say. What I was too scared and too stupid to tell you, until now." He took a breath. "I didn't want to fall in love."

Lindsey closed her eyes and grimaced. Those words had tortured them both for years.

"But I did," he said.

She opened her eyes.

"Lindsey, what we have only comes around once in a lifetime. I want to wake up next to you every morning, and I want to fall asleep with you in my arms every night. I want to be by your side for as long as I'm breathing, and after that, I'll still find you. My heart will always show me the way back to you."

She wiped away another tear, but she was smiling.

He took a step closer. "Do you remember what we said to each other at Camp Clem?"

"I remember."

He smiled. "This is just the beginning."

She held his gaze. Those blue-green eyes, shiny with tears, cut right into his soul.

"This is our new beginning, Linds. This is how our story continues. I don't need to know about your past. All I need to know is that I love you. I always have, and I always will. And I'm going to love that baby. That baby is part of you, and I will protect and care for you both for as long as I live."

She held his gaze a beat. "This is just the beginning."

"This is our beginning for the three of us."

His voice cracked. He was crying. He couldn't even remember the last time he'd shed a tear. His father had drilled into him that crying was only for the weak. Real men didn't cry. But instead of feeling that deep, biting anger that gripped him like a vice when his father came to mind, he could only feel sorry for the man. His father had never allowed himself to love. He had never taken someone's heart and protected it with his life. He had known a shallow, superficial existence. He had been cruel and abusive—there was no excuse for that. But he'd never known love, and for that, Nick pitied him.

"I think we should give Nick and Lindsey a moment alone," Rosemary said, putting a hand on Lindsey's shoulder.

Nick blinked. He'd forgotten seven other people were watching him spill the contents of his heart all over the floor. He met Zoe's gaze first, and she gave him a wink.

Kathy pressed a kiss to the top of Lindsey's head. "Let us know if you need anything, dear."

"We'll be right outside," Em added, following Michael and the women out the door.

Jenna hung back and patted Lindsey's leg and met Nick's gaze. She smiled at him through teary eyes. "You and Lindsey found each other. Don't let anything get in the way of that love."

He nodded through his own tears.

Jenna shut the door quietly, and Nick sat next to Lindsey on the bed. He took her hands into his. "I'm sorry, Lindsey, so sorry. I've been a fool, a total ass. I let my father and my anger and all my fears cloud what I've always felt for you."

She squeezed his hands. "There are things I need to tell you, Nick. I want you to know everything."

He leaned in and pressed his forehead against hers. He inhaled the sweet cream and summer rain scent that had stayed with him, locked in his heart for sixteen long years. "I love you, Lindsey. There's nothing you could ever say that can stop that." He pressed his palm to her abdomen. "I'm going to love you, too."

"Little banana," she said with a teary chuckle.

He smiled. "You've named the baby, banana?"

"It's just a nickname. The first time I had an ultrasound, my doctor said the baby was the size of a small banana."

"This ultrasound?" Nick asked, shifting to take his wallet out of his pocket.

He handed her the creased ultrasound photograph.

She ran her finger across the baby's little head. "You kept it?"

"Yeah, my heart must have known I could never let you go. It was my head that got in the way." He rubbed her belly. "Is the baby going to be okay?"

She laid her hand on top of his. "They think it's just Braxton Hicks contractions."

Nick furrowed his brow. "The only things I know about pregnancy are what I've seen with Michael and Em. That mostly includes him going out on late-night grocery runs for whatever she's craving that day."

Lindsey smiled. "Braxton Hicks contractions are like practice contractions. My abdomen tensed up. It took my breath away. I could barely stand, but the doctor says they don't cause labor."

Nick brushed back a lock of her chestnut hair. "Linds, that must have been terrifying."

"Luckily, I was with Jenna, Em, Zoe, Kathy, and Rosemary. I'd just finished leading a photography class at the Rose Brooks Women's Shelter. I'm helping them with a photo project. They called an ambulance as soon as I started feeling the contractions."

"Do you know why they started?"

"The doctors think it was dehydration. That's why I have this." She pointed to the IV in her arm.

He looked at the tube. "I'm going to take care of you, Linds."

She touched his cheek. "Every man who said they loved me, always ended up hurting me."

"Not anymore. Not ever again. I'm here, and I love you, and I'm not going anywhere. Tell me you'll have me."

"You're just a prickly pear," she said, through a teary grin. "Of course, I'll have you. You're all I've ever wanted. I've loved you since the moment you kissed me on Rachel and Rory's rock."

Two sharp taps came from the door. A man peeked his head inside and then carted in an ultrasound machine.

"Looks like dad made it," the man said, then shook Nick's hand. "I'm Preston. I'm the sonographer." He nodded to Lindsey. "I met you a few hours ago when you were admitted."

"Yes, I remember. Is something wrong?"

"No, nothing like that. The nurses have been monitoring you and the baby from the nurses' station. Everything is looking good. The obstetrician on call asked that I take a few more pictures and get a little more information. If everything looks good, you'll probably be going home within the hour."

Nick squeezed her hand as relief flooded his system.

Preston flipped through Lindsey's chart. "Looks like you are a little over twenty weeks along. Would you like to know what you're having?"

Nick narrowed his gaze. "She's having a baby."

Lindsey chuckled. "No, silly, he wants to know if *we* want to know if it's a boy or a girl."

"Don't worry," Preston added with a kind smile. "You're not the first dad who's said that to me."

"I'd like to know who this little banana is," Lindsey said through a teary smile.

"Me, too," Nick answered, pressing a kiss to her temple.

Lindsey lifted the hospital gown, revealing a gentle bump, and the sonographer went to work. Nick's eyes danced between the screen and Lindsey's belly.

Preston moved the ultrasound wand across her abdomen. "Let's see what we have here. I can't predict to perfect accuracy, but I'm ninety-nine percent sure you're having a girl."

"A girl," Nick whispered.

He stared at the baby's image. Her little arm was tucked under her chin. He turned to Lindsey. She stared at the screen. All of a sudden, the hospital melted away, and he saw her standing in Camp Clem's dining hall, hair pulled up in a messy bun, dish towel slung over her shoulder, washing dishes and singing that stupid fruit song that he had come to love so fucking much.

"This is our new beginning," he whispered, staring at his daughter.

20

Nick thrust his hips. Lindsey braced herself, one hand on the Cessna's back window, the other, pressed to the center of his chest. He'd had the backseat of the Skyhawk taken out to do some routine maintenance and was just about to reinstall it when Lindsey stopped him, handed him her panties, and climbed into the small space. Never, in all his years of flying, had he done anything like this in an airplane.

Thank God they were just parked in the empty hangar. Had they been cruising at three thousand feet, the air traffic controllers would have gotten to listen to one hell of a show. He wasn't sure how they had worked their way into the tight space, but with Lindsey straddling him and riding his cock, he didn't care if someone had to extract him from the back of his Skyhawk with a fucking shoehorn.

Her body had changed over the last three weeks. The swell of her belly had become more pronounced, and her breasts, which he'd always thought were perfect, had grown fuller and more sensitive. He ran his thumbs over the peaks, and she bucked forward, arching into his touch.

"I'm so close, Nick," she breathed.

She pressed her hands to his chest as he gripped her ass, angling her body the way he knew she liked it.

"Oh, yes!"

Her eyes fluttered closed. She bit her bottom lip.

Christ, she was gorgeous.

He pumped harder. She released a tight moan, and her expression of pure ecstasy edged him closer toward his release.

Weeks ago, he had thought Michael was crazy when his friend had shared the joys of pregnancy sex. Now, like Michael, he too walked around with a stupid grin stretched across his face.

He cupped her face into his hand. "You are so fucking beautiful."

Her core tightened around his cock, and he followed her into oblivion, giving in to complete carnal desire.

Her body slowed, drawing out the last threads of pleasure, and she met his gaze with a sated expression. But her face contorted into a look of disbelief.

She bit her lip to hold back a smile. "That can't be comfortable."

"I'm crammed in like the bus seat to Camp Clem."

A sweet smile graced her lips. She traced his jawline with her finger. "You looked like some kind of giant trying to fit into that bus seat. Your legs were all twisted and smashed against the front of the seat. But we fit in there together pretty well."

"Yeah, we fit so well that you fell asleep." He took her hand and pressed a kiss to her palm. "That's when I knew."

"Knew what?"

"That I was a goner. That my heart wasn't mine anymore. You smelled so good, and it felt so right having your head rest against my shoulder. I could have stayed like that forever."

"Just a prickly pear," she said. "Hard on the outside. Soft and mushy on the inside."

"Mushy, huh?"

Her eyes turned mischievous. "Like lumpy oatmeal."

He shifted his body and rested his back against the side of the plane. "This bowl of lumpy oatmeal has somewhere he would like to take you."

"Oh, yeah?" she asked, curiosity lacing her words.

"Oh, yeah! Do you think you and the banana can handle a little trip?"

"Sure, Dr. Al-Amin says I'm safe to fly."

He smiled. He knew that, too. He had gone with her to all her prenatal appointments, but he had still called and double checked with the doctor that morning.

"I'm going to run inside and clean up. Are we on a tight schedule?" she asked.

"No, we've got some time." He lifted her up and set her gently next to him.

His shirt had ridden up, and she ran her fingers down the hard plane of his stomach. Her eyes grew hooded and hungry. "Maybe lumpy oatmeal is the wrong way to describe you."

He pressed another kiss to her palm. "I never thought I'd say this, Linds, but we better get moving. I've planned out the whole day, and as nice as it would be to make love in the back of my airplane for the next eight hours, I really want to show you something."

"Oh, all right," she said with mock disappointment.

They extricated themselves from the back of the small plane. Lindsey headed for the ladies' room, and he jogged up the stairs to his office. There was one important item locked away safely in his desk drawer that he didn't want to forget.

"It never gets old, does it?" Lindsey remarked, looking out at the horizon. She shifted her gaze to Nick. The sun was playing with the golden highlights in his hair as rays of light glinted off his aviators. He was a gorgeous man, and he was hers.

Nick cracked a smile but kept his gaze forward. "What are you looking at?"

"Just you," she said.

There was nothing sexier than watching this man pilot a plane. If it wasn't so dangerous and her belly wasn't so big, she would climb onto his lap and start round two right there in the cockpit, mid-flight.

"Hey, Linds," he said, gesturing with his chin. "Does anything look familiar?"

They had only been in the air for about forty-five minutes. She figured he was just taking her out and back. Thankfully, he still had his pilot's license. He hadn't gotten into too much trouble for fleeing the scene of an emergency plane landing and then making an unauthorized helicopter drop on Midwest Medical Center's helipad. The investigator sent from the National Transportation Safety Board to assess Nick's emergency landing had a wife who was pregnant. He had told Nick he would have done the same thing had it been him.

She looked out across the horizon. It was early May, and the world had transformed from a barren landscape of spindly trees to a bright green canopy of young leaves and flowering bushes. A large body of water stretched out before them. Beyond that, a steep bluff stood silent and rocky in the distance. Two structures sat near the water.

Lindsey narrowed her eyes. "Is that the dining hall?"

"Yep," Nick answered. Even through the headset, she could hear the smile in his voice.

"And that's the boathouse," she added, leaning forward like a kid pulling up to Disneyland. "Nick, It's Camp Clem."

"You guessed it."

She gazed at the buildings. "There's the lodge, and what used to be the big garden, I think. It looks pretty overgrown."

"Yeah, whoever owns it now hasn't kept it up. I came out last week to check things out."

"You did?" she asked.

He hadn't mentioned this. After she was discharged from the hospital, Nick moved into the Foursquare with her. They hadn't even discussed it. It just happened. She had been with him every day since then, and he hadn't said a word about any trips to their old camp.

"Michael and I flew out this way when I took him up back in April."

"And you've been here since then?"

He was smiling. "Yeah, I wanted to check the runway myself

before I brought you here. Sometimes these private landing strips can be pretty beat up, but this one's okay. I didn't have any trouble."

He circled Lake Langhorne and came in to land, crossing over the bluff and touching down onto the dirt runway. The plane came to a stop, and he jumped out and jogged over to open her door and help her out of the plane.

She took his hand. "It's so weird. It was so long ago, but at the same time—"

"It feels like we were just here," he said, finishing her thought.

"Yeah, it does."

The landing strip was tucked into the highest point of Camp Clem close to the bluff. They walked down a dirt path, and two cabins came into view.

She squeezed Nick's hand. "Those are our cabins. Becky and Sawyer."

Plywood had been nailed to the windows, but a piece had broken off, and they were able to peek inside.

"My cot was over there," she said pointing at the back corner near the window. She turned and wrapped her arms around his neck. "I loved the little sunflowers you would tuck in the screen. It was the first thing I'd look for when I woke up."

He dipped his head, but she stopped his kiss with a finger pressed to his lips. "Gleeful glimpses only, mister!"

"I'll show you gleeful." He nipped at her finger.

"Ouch," she said, feigning outrage.

He pressed a kiss to the corner of her mouth. "Come on! There's more."

They followed the path that led to the lodge. It was boarded up just like the cabins. The sky blue paint had withered to maudlin gray, but the Camp Clem sign was there, sun-bleached and suspended from two rusted chains.

Nick reached up and tapped it. "I wanted to take this and give it to you. I tried to figure out who bought the place. I wanted to offer to pay for it. I even asked Michael to look into it. But even he wasn't able to figure it out. One shell company after another."

"That's weird," she answered, running her hand along the porch railing.

"Michael said it's pretty common. Sometimes people don't want to be identified as the buyer or want to try and skip out on paying the taxes. Some are even fronts for illegal businesses."

"What kind of illegal business do you think they're running out of Camp Clem?" Lindsey asked with a mischievous grin.

Nick wrapped his arm around her shoulders. "Mass production of bug juice?"

"Oh," she said, pressing a hand to her abdomen. "Looks like little banana agrees with you."

He rested his hand near hers. "Is she kicking?"

Lindsey nodded.

Nick sank to his knees and started singing to her belly, "I like to eat, eat, eat apples and bananas."

"I thought you hated that song."

He looked up. "Not when you sing it."

She ran her hand through his tousled blond hair and fingered an errant curl. "You look just like you did sixteen years ago."

"So do you," he said, standing up. He patted her belly. "Minus this. I would have noticed it."

"Aren't you in a good mood, today," she said, eyeing him suspiciously. "What do you have up your sleeve? I can tell, something's up. You're as giddy as a school girl."

"This way," he said and led her toward the lake.

They followed the dirt path down the hill. The old field was overgrown with years of undergrowth packed under the new spring grasses, but a steady trail of what looked like tire tracks wound their way through the foliage.

"Looks like a car or maybe an ATV's driven through here. Probably somebody out exploring," Nick remarked as they veered off the path that led down toward the dining hall.

"Do you want to check it out?" she asked.

"No, we shouldn't really be here either, but I figured I'd take a chance."

He led her to the boathouse and pulled back a ratty tarp. It was just as she had remembered. The sun sparkled blue-green off the water's glassy surface, and she drank in the space. Nick had recreated their night here. The sailboat and the hanging kayaks were gone, but a few faded orange life vests still hung on rusted nails.

She fingered the coils of long-forgotten frayed rope. "Nick, this is perfect."

He'd even constructed a little bed out of sleeping bags with lanterns hanging just as they had that night.

She cupped his strong jaw and gazed into his eyes. "I never imagined a life this full could be possible. I never expected to feel desire or crave intimacy again. You're the only man who could have brought me back to life."

"Your spirit and your strength were always there, Linds."

After she had told him about her time in Houston, he had wrapped her in his arms and held her. She cried all the tears she'd held back for so long. Tears of anger and disappointment and helplessness. It wasn't easy on him. He was furious. The vein in his neck pulsed with fury. He had wanted to get into his plane, fly to Houston, and beat the ever-living shit out of Brett. But he didn't because she had asked him not to.

That life was over.

She was safe.

Nick was the last person who needed to hear that story. The tale of her time in Texas ended with the last retelling of it to him.

He led her to the sleeping bags. "Let's sit down. I have something we need to do."

"Do you?" she asked, tucking her legs beneath her.

His expression turned serious, and he sank to his knees. "I had lunch with your godmother and Kathy Stein last week."

"You did? Did you run into them somewhere?"

"No, I reached out to them." He shifted and retrieved a small bag. "Kathy gave me this palo santo wood to burn. It's a tree in South America."

"We came here to burn a piece of wood?"

"Sort of." A sheepish grin pulled at the corners of his mouth. "Kathy says that people burn palo santo wood because it's believed to have healing powers."

Lindsey cocked her head to the side.

"Stick with me, Linds," he said, shaking his head. "I promised Kathy and Rosemary I would do this."

"Okay, go on."

"Kathy says burning palo santo is a way to welcome love and good fortune into your life."

Lindsey pressed a kiss to his cheek. "I think that's beautiful."

"She also said something about it connecting us to the planet and fostering the inner self, but I kind of lost her at that point."

Lindsey chuckled. "She didn't make you take a Buddha, did she?"

"No," he said, but his tone had turned serious. "I met with Rosemary and Kathy because I love you, and I know they both love and care deeply about you. I told them I wanted to spend the rest of my life with you, and I wanted their blessing."

"Oh, Nick," she gasped.

He struck a match and held it to the wood. Hints of pine, mint, and lemon mingled with the musty scent of the boathouse. He let the wood burn a black ribbon of smoke then blew out the flame. The smoke turned as white as fresh snow. It moved with the breeze, a white stream of air twisting in a slow, hypnotic spiral.

He met her gaze. "Kathy says the white smoke is purifying, and that it signifies new life and new beginnings." He set the small piece of wood into a dish and took her hands into his. "I used to think that the best feeling was the moment right before the plane left the ground, but I don't feel that way anymore because it pales in comparison to what it's like being with you. I've loved you since I was sixteen years old, and I promise that I will love you and protect you and cherish you." He rested his hand on her abdomen. "And I will love and protect our daughter. She'll only know happiness, Lindsey. Love and security and happiness."

It was twilight now, and the lake had come alive with a night's prelude of sounds and scents. The hum of insects threaded into the chorus of bullfrog calls. The water kissed the weathered wood of the boathouse in a lazy, back and forth lapping rhythm.

Lindsey closed her eyes and let it all come back. "This is where our new story begins," she whispered. The intention of her words carried into the smoke and trailed out of the boathouse, becoming one with the wind and the sky and the clouds.

Nick took her left hand and kissed her palm.

She opened her eyes and met his blue gaze.

"Lindsey Anne Hanlon, will you marry me?"

She saw the boy and the man sitting in front of her, and those blue eyes, so sharp, so intense, and so full of love. He had battled the voices inside his head. The whispers that told him he would end up like his father, and he had chosen love over fear.

Her throat grew tight with emotion. "Yes, I'll marry you."

The words encircled them. They filled the room and coalesced with the healing ribbon of smoke, tapering off into one last breath of white like gentle wisps of clouds.

He reached into his breast pocket and pulled out a square of worn fabric adorned with a delicately embroidered sunflower. He peeled back the thin cotton.

"Is that part of the Langley Park flag?" Lindsey asked.

"It is. I went to the Community Center to ask if I could borrow it and ran into Mrs. Quigley."

"The Kids' Camp director?"

"Yeah, she still lives in Langley Park. After I told her what I wanted to do with it, she insisted on cutting off a small square and giving it to me."

Lindsey gasped when she saw the ring. A large blue sapphire nestled between pear and oval shaped diamonds winked at her in the lantern light.

"It reminds me of the sky and..." Her hand flew to her chest.

"Clouds," Nick said, finishing her thought as he slid the ring onto her finger. "When I saw this ring, I just knew, Linds. I just knew it was meant for me to give to you."

She met his gaze and rose to her feet. One button at a time, she undid her dress and let it fall into a pool of linen at her feet. Just like their night here sixteen years ago, he followed, and they stripped in front of each other. She stood in this very spot the first time she had seen him, or any other man, completely naked. Her eyes saw him differently now. He was still a gorgeous specimen of a man. Broad shoulders. Perfectly defined abdominal muscles. And that V that narrowed down and led her eye to his beautiful cock, standing at attention.

Back when they had been camp counselors, she saw the boy with hopes and dreams shining in his blue eyes. Today, she saw the man she was going to raise a child with. The man who had made good on a long-ago whispered promise to love her forever.

"I like you in nothing but that ring," he said in a low growl.

His cock twitched. Nicholas Kincade was done being sentimental. The man had burned sacred wood in a cleansing ritual. He had opened himself up. He'd handed her his heart on a plate. But now his gaze darkened, and Lindsey shivered with anticipation. This man wanted to fuck her and, Christ, she wanted to be fucked.

She pressed her back against the boathouse wall and raised her hands above her head. Nick's gaze traveled up her body. His lips twisted into a sexy smirk as she wrapped her wrists into the coil of rope hanging off an old peg.

She clenched her fingers around the tangled coil. "Did you plan this, too?"

He licked his lips, and Lindsey's core tightened. "No, that's just my good luck."

He pressed a kiss to her lips, and his fingertips traced a line from her bound wrists down to her breasts. He left a hot trail of kisses as he worked his way down, past her collarbone, and kissed the space between her breasts. He took her nipple into his mouth and ran the pad of his tongue over the tip.

Lindsey whimpered. All her senses peaked and her body begged for more. He ran his hands down the sides of her body and cupped her ass as he came to his knees.

They'd had to get creative with her changing body. Nick hooked her leg over his shoulder and nipped at the sensitive skin of her inner thigh. She circled her hips and bucked forward. Her body wanted his mouth and craved his tongue. But he took his time working his way toward her center.

"So sweet," he breathed, rubbing his tongue against her sensitive bud.

Lindsey gripped the rope and rolled her head to the side as Nick went to work, setting her on fire. She thrust her hips, meeting his tongue, while he palmed her ass and steadied her. Her breath came in tight gasps as he sucked and licked a rhythm that had her calling out his name in breathy exhales.

Her eyes fluttered shut. Her limbs tensed. It was like running full speed off a cliff and jumping off into the sky, euphoric and free, knowing that at the bottom, Nick would be there. He tightened his grip on her ass, heightening her pleasure and sending her over the edge again.

When she'd finally caught her breath, she met his gaze, and Nick smiled up at her. He ran his hands up her body and stood.

He wiped his mouth with the back of his hand. "I could do this all day."

He reached up with one hand and held onto the tangled rope, lacing his fingers with hers. With the other hand, he positioned himself and surged inside of her. The sound of twisting rope and his heated breath releasing in sharp exhales combined with the slap of their skin as he worked her body. He lifted her with one steady hand, and she wrapped her legs around him.

His mouth crashed into hers in a frenzy of nips and kisses. He kissed the sensitive skin beneath her earlobe. His breaths were coming faster. He grunted with each thrust.

Nick squeezed their tangled hands together. "You are going to be my wife," he said in a low, primal whisper.

Lindsey flexed her core muscles, and it was just what he needed to push him over the edge. Nick called out her name as she joined him, flying through the air, endorphins surging, riding out each wave of pleasure.

She opened her eyes and met his gaze. "You're going to be my husband."

A warm sated smile pulled at the corner of his lips. He untangled their hands and cupped her face. "This is just the beginning, Linds. It only gets better from here."

"Just the beginning," she whispered.

21

Nick eyed the shutters in the Foursquare's kitchen window. "What do you think?"

When Lindsey had settled on window coverings, he was confident he would have no trouble installing them. But three broken tilt rods, five broken louvers—which he didn't even know were called louvers until he tried to install the damn things—and three misplaced tension screws later, he had relented and let Lindsey call in Terry for some handyman backup.

Terry ran a dry handkerchief along the top and bottom rails then stepped back. "They look good," he said, stuffing the cloth into his coveralls.

Nick had spent the last couple of evenings with Terry installing the shutters, and he could tell why Lindsey had hired him. He didn't fill their time together with idle chat. He was methodical and focused. They worked in companionable silence, drilling holes and assembling the frames.

"Do you want to try to get the last one installed tonight?" Terry asked.

Nick glanced at his watch. It was late. "No, let's call it a day."

"I can come back tomorrow," Terry offered.

Nick shook his head. "I've got a full day of meetings, and then we've got the Rose Brooks fundraiser in the evening. I think we'll have to put off the last window for a few days."

Lindsey padded into the kitchen wearing his old red flannel shirt and a pair of yoga pants. She had the sleeves rolled up, and the rounded curve of her growing belly fit perfectly under his worn shirt.

"It looks beautiful," she said, coming to stand by his side and smiling warmly at Terry.

The handyman blushed. "Nick did most of the work. I was just here to—"

"To make sure he didn't break any more slats," Lindsey said with a chuckle.

"They're called louvers, and don't forget the tilt rods and those damn screws," he said, wrapping his arm around her waist.

Not quite a week had passed since he had asked her to marry him, but life seemed to be moving at top speed. Lindsey's body was changing. A week ago, a loose blouse or high-waisted dress could camouflage the pregnancy. But not anymore. She was almost twenty-five weeks along, and little banana was growing.

"I was craving a cheese quesadilla with sauerkraut. Would you like anything to drink or a little snack, Terry?"

Terry's eyes went wide.

Nick bit back a laugh. Lindsey's crazy food cravings had aligned with Em's.

"That's nice of you, but I better get going," Terry said.

"How many windows do you guys have left to do?" Lindsey asked, frowning as she peered into the refrigerator.

"Just one," Nick answered.

"So close," Lindsey said, grabbing items and setting them on the counter.

Terry closed his toolbox. "I could stop by tomorrow and install the last window. It wouldn't be any trouble."

"It might be nice," Lindsey said. "Especially if we're going to be having everyone over after the fundraiser."

"Are you sure it wouldn't inconvenience you?" Nick asked.

"No, not at all. It won't take me long."

"I'm working from home tomorrow," Lindsey said. "You could stop by anytime."

Terry nodded.

"I'll walk you out," Nick said, gesturing toward the door.

"Nick," Lindsey called from the kitchen just as they were stepping out onto the porch. "I think we're all out of sauerkraut."

"I'll walk up to Pete's Organics and pick some up," he called back and closed the door.

"Maybe grab some rocky road ice cream, too?"

He chuckled. "Sure thing, Linds."

He jogged down the porch steps and found Michael chatting with Terry.

"Grocery run?" Nick asked, clapping Michael on the back.

"Canned peaches and saltine crackers," Michael answered. "You?"

"Sauerkraut and rocky road ice cream."

"That's a good one! I'll have to tell Em. Don't be surprised if you find her raiding your fridge tonight."

"Are you heading up to the bus stop by the grocery store?" Nick asked Terry.

"Yeah, the last bus leaves in about twenty minutes."

"We'll walk with you," Michael said as the men fell into step. "And thanks for coming over last week and helping rehang the bedroom doors, Terry. I love our Foursquare, but these older houses need their fair share of TLC."

"It's no trouble," Terry answered. "Thanks for passing my name on to your architect friend. I've picked up two more jobs in Langley Park this week."

Nick's phone pinged. He held out the text for the men to read.

Lindsey: Can you also pick up some marshmallows and cornichons?

"What are cornichons?"

Michael chuckled. "Ask poor Terry. Em has been eating them by the jarful. She told me she got you to try them."

"They're not half bad. A little sweet for my taste," Terry answered.

"Em had them in France. She lived there and studied music for a while when she was a teenager. They're like little pickles."

Nick pocketed his phone. "You can show me where to find them in the grocery store."

"Do you have any kids, Terry?" Michael asked as they crossed over Langley Park Boulevard and made their way into the town center.

"Yeah, a daughter. She lives in Nebraska with her mother."

"How often do you get to see her?" Nick asked. Little banana wasn't even born yet, and he couldn't imagine a day without her.

Terry stopped. He didn't make eye contact all that much, but he lifted his chin. "I need to tell you something. I want to be straight with you both. I appreciate all the work you've thrown my way, but I have something I need to say."

"Of course," Nick said, sharing a glance with Michael.

"I don't think anyone's run a background check on me. But with all this work coming in, it's only a matter of time."

Nick crossed his arms. He had spent the last several nights working side by side with Terry. He'd never gotten the vibe that something was off.

"When I met Lindsey in the hardware store, I told her about my daughter and how I don't get to see her much because I didn't make the best choices when I was younger." He switched his toolbox to the other hand. "I've got a rap sheet. Nothing big. Some petty theft. But where I really fell into trouble was after I hurt my shoulder. The hospital sent me home with all kinds of painkillers. Bottles of them. The shoulder healed, but I couldn't stop taking the pills."

"Are you using?" Michael asked.

"No, not anymore. When the pills became too expensive, I switched to heroin. Heroin landed me in jail and jail is where I cleaned up." He raised his chin a fraction. "I've been clean and sober for five years. I've got a sponsor. I go to meetings. I support my daughter. I wanted to be the one to tell you that. I probably should have told you sooner. It's just really hard to drum up work after you tell somebody you used to pop pills and shoot up."

Michael put a hand on Terry's shoulder. "It's more common than you think. I was just helping a family adjust their trust to pay for their grandson's opioid addiction treatment."

"I've even seen the effects of addiction at the airport. People who can afford it often charter planes to shuttle family members to rehab facilities. Addiction doesn't seem to care if you're rich or poor, young or old."

Terry shifted his toolbox again.

"We'll vouch for you, Terry," Nick added.

"Absolutely," Michael said. "You can always use us as references."

"I appreciate that. Thank you, Mr. Kincade and Mr. MacCarron."

"It's Nick and Michael," Nick said. "You've taught me how to install shutters, and you've eaten tiny pickles at Michael's house. I think we're all on a first name basis."

The hint of a smile pulled at the corners of Terry's lips as the bus rounded the corner and stopped. He nodded to the men and jogged up the steps. The doors whooshed shut, and the bus rumbled down the darkened street. A couple walked out of Pete's, and the cold rush of air-conditioning followed them out onto the street.

"We've got two hungry, pregnant women at home. We better hop to it," Michael said, gesturing to the door.

They roamed the aisles, silently procuring the strange assortment of items. At eight o'clock on a Thursday night, Pete's was virtually empty. Nick opened the freezer door and tossed a pint of rocky road ice cream in the basket.

"I hadn't thought about the downtown airport being affected by drugs, but it makes sense," Michael said, throwing a box of saltines into the basket.

"It's becoming a real issue for smaller regional airports. We don't have the police presence like the larger airports do. And then, you get people who think if they charter a flight, they can do whatever the hell they want to do with it."

Pete's had four registers, but only one was open.

"Working the till tonight, Pete?" Michael asked, shaking the young man's hand.

The original Pete of Pete's Organic Grocer opened the store in 1935. The family still owned and operated the independent grocery store, and a string of Petes, all named after the founder, had successfully run the business for over eighty years.

"That I am," the man answered.

Michael gestured with his chin. "Pete, have you met Nick?"

"I've seen you in here. You're new in town, right?" Pete asked with an easy smile.

"Yeah, I've been here a little less than six months," Nick answered, but his attention was pulled to a small television Pete had rigged up next to the checkout.

"Oh, sorry about that," Pete said. He reached to flick it off, but Nick stopped him.

Nick pointed to the screen. "I recognize that guy."

Pete had the TV tuned to a cable news station. The caption, *Authorities Make Arrests in Opioid Distribution Ring*, scrolled across the bottom of the screen. The television was muted, but it was easy to tell that the man with an angry red face and wild brown eyes was swearing at the federal agents, spit flying from his mouth, as they escorted him out of a building and into a shiny black SUV.

"That guy was trying to get one of the chartered flight pilots to take him to an unregistered airfield."

Michael let out a low whistle. "You weren't kidding about small airports being impacted by drug trafficking, were you?"

Nick stared at the screen. The story ended, and the network went to a commercial.

"I caught the beginning of that," Pete said, loading their items into a reusable bag. "A whole ring of doctors have been arrested for selling opioid prescriptions for cash and even forging signatures of other doctors to get their hands on more pills. It might even go as high as pharmaceutical sales reps getting in on the action. I think they said the raid spanned several states."

"That's a damn shame," Michael said. "It's no wonder I have to alter wills and trusts to account for rehab. This stuff is everywhere."

Nick shook his head. Jesus, had he been that close to drug trafficking? He made a mental note to meet with the airport's security team. This story hit too close to home to ignore. They had policies and procedures, but he wanted to let his whole staff know how close they had come to a suspected drug trafficker.

"Yeah, it's crazy," Nick said, paying for his items.

He followed Michael out of the store.

They crossed back over Langley Park Boulevard and turned onto Foxglove Lane. The heady scent of lilacs carried on the late spring breeze. Nick was going over the exchange he'd had with the doctor when Michael interrupted his thoughts.

"Looks like you got your Langley Park Foursquare," he said.

Nick could make out Michael's cheeky grin.

"I got a lot more than that."

"I'd say," Michael chuckled. "Have you guys set a date?"

"We haven't gotten that far yet. With the baby coming, everything is kind of up in the air." Nick shifted the bag of groceries to his other shoulder. "How about you and Em? Ever thought of tying the knot?"

"I think we'll get there eventually. She says it's just a piece of paper. I try to explain to her that my whole profession is built on pieces of paper. Lots of fucking pieces of paper. In fact, if the entire law profession disappeared in a poof of depositions and motions, it would probably end deforestation everywhere." Michael's expression softened. "But, Lindsey's doing all right?"

Nick looked up at the Foursquare he now shared with her. "Yeah, she's doing great. I think you and Em being so kind has helped. And then there's Rosemary. If it wasn't for her, I can't even imagine where Lindsey would be now."

"Have you asked Lindsey about going to the police? About filing formal charges?"

"I've tried, but she wants to move on. She feels safe here. We're together. And it's her choice. As much as I want to go and kill the bastard, it would only cause her more pain in the end. So we're focusing on the future."

Michael nodded. "Well, I for one am glad you guys are next door. Did Em tell you, our moms were pregnant at the same time in these very houses? We were born on the same day. She's like three minutes older than me and will never let me forget it."

"It's five minutes, and I'm starving," came a voice calling out from Michael's front porch.

"Duty calls," Michael said with an amused grin.

Nick padded up the steps and unlocked the door to the Foursquare. The deadbolts Terry had installed were good, and Langley Park was a safe place to live, but he was still going to have a security system put in. He closed the door behind him and pulled out his phone to make a note to do it. When he looked up, Lindsey was standing in front of him, white as a ghost.

She bit her trembling lip.

"Linds, what's wrong? Do you feel sick?"

She shook her head. "No, I'm fine. The baby's fine. It's just...Rosemary called. She'd been gone the last couple of days visiting her sister."

"Is she all right?"

"She's fine. The shelter in Houston left a message on her home phone. She didn't get the message until she got back."

"What did the shelter want?" He set the bag on the ground and took her into his arms.

"Claire, you know, Brett's sister-in-law, she called the shelter multiple times saying she needed to get into contact with me. The shelter relayed the messages to my contact person—that's Rosemary."

"Okay," Nick said, rubbing tiny circles across her shoulder blades. "Did Rosemary say anything else? Did Claire say there was a threat or that you were in danger?"

Lindsey shook her head against his chest. "No, I don't think so. Rosemary just said that Claire needed to speak with me."

"Do you think she might just want to make sure you and the baby are okay? She helped you, right?"

"Yeah, she did help me."

"Do you want me to call Claire for you? Do you want me to let her know that you're safe? I don't have to tell her who I am. I can say I know you, and I know that you're all right."

She looked up and met his gaze. "I want you to drive me to Wichita."

"Wichita? Why there?"

Lindsey pulled open a drawer, leafed through some papers then pulled out another drawer.

"What are you looking for?"

A half-empty roll of quarters sat idle next to a handful of paper-clips. "The last time I called Claire was from a diner in Wichita. That's where I want you to take me. There's a pay phone there."

"There are pay phones all over Kansas City, Linds. Why do you want to go to that pay phone in Wichita?"

She was shaking again. "Because it's safe. Because even if Brett checks her phone records, Wichita is far enough away." She closed her eyes, and tears ran down her cheeks. "I'm sorry, Nick. I didn't want to fall to pieces."

He took her into his arms and kissed her forehead. "I love you. I love all your pieces. And I never want you to hide any of them from me."

"Then you'll take me?"

"I'm your copilot for life, Linds. I'll take you anywhere you want, anytime you want. The sky's not even the limit when it comes to us."

22

It was close to midnight when they pulled into the Wichita diner's parking lot across from the bus terminal. The low thrum of the radio mingled with the reassuring purr of the engine running idle. Lindsey tucked her feet beneath her and stared at the building. It was like looking at a piece of someone else's past, like dipping into their darkest parts and pulling out something light.

Nick went to cut the engine, but Lindsey stopped him. "I just want to look at it for a minute."

He laced his fingers with hers. "Okay, take your time."

A beat passed.

"I never knew the name," she said, staring up at red neon letters spelling out Lucero's.

There was nothing remarkable about this diner. A squatty rectangle with blond brick and a bank of windows running along the front. But when she'd stepped off that bus nearly two months ago, walking into this little diner was like hitting the last mile of a marathon.

"It must have felt unreal finally getting here," Nick said

"It was the first place I went after I got off the bus. I remember sitting in a booth. I think it was that one," she said, pointing inside the restaurant. "I kept checking the license plates of all the cars in the parking lot. None of them were from Texas. Something about that kept me together."

Lindsey dropped her gaze to where her left hand was resting on the console, fingers laced with the boy she had loved since she was a girl. In the darkened car, the sapphire of her engagement ring flashed midnight blue, and the cluster of cloud-like diamonds winked each time the high beams of a passing car illuminated the cab of Nick's SUV.

"That life seems a million miles away," she whispered.

"That life is a million miles away, Linds. That chapter is over. No one will ever hurt you again."

There was an edge to Nick's voice—a conviction, stronger than a promise, weaving through each of his words.

The first bars of an acoustic version of "Fast Car" played over the radio, and Nick smiled. "Do you remember this song?"

"No, should I?"

In the light of the car's dashboard, Nick's grin grew sentimental. "This song was playing in the bus when you fell asleep on my shoulder on the way to Camp Clem."

"Was it?"

"Yeah, you told me you liked it. You mumbled it under your breath just before you fell asleep."

"You still remember that?"

He cupped her face. "I remember everything. That strong girl still lives inside of you. I see her every time I look into your eyes. Nobody, not Brett, not your father, could ever take that away from you."

The shriek of brakes sounded off behind them. Bleary-eyed passengers filed off a bus, adjusting backpacks and duffle bags. Lindsey shifted in her seat to get a better view of a young woman clutching a large tote bag to her chest. She was wearing an oversized sweatshirt with the hood pulled up. It cast her face in a shadow.

"That's what I must have looked like," Lindsey said.

The woman crossed the parking lot and entered the diner. She slumped into the same booth Lindsey had taken refuge in all those weeks ago. A waitress held up a coffee pot, and the woman nodded, still clutching her tote to her chest. She turned away as the server delivered the steaming cup. For a fraction of a second, Lindsey thought she had caught the young woman's eye, but the woman's gaze flitted over the parking lot, seemingly unaware of Lindsey and Nick parked less than twenty feet away.

The young woman reached into her bag and pulled out a compact. Shoulders hunched forward, head hung low, a gust of wind could have carried her away. She checked her face in the mirror, wincing when the makeup pad made contact with her cheek. The hairs on the back of Lindsey's neck pricked to attention. How many times had she gazed into a tiny, circular compact, trying to mask the evidence of her abuse?

"You're stronger than you think."

"Do you think she needs help?" Nick asked.

Lindsey met his gaze. "Did I say that aloud?"

He brushed a chestnut lock of hair behind her ear. "Yeah, you did."

A car pulled into the stall next to them, and before the driver had shifted into park, an older woman emerged from the passenger seat and ran into the diner. The driver, an older gentleman, followed close behind. The car was still running, the headlights shining a spotlight on the young woman. Through the glass, Lindsey could see the older couple sprinting toward her. The young woman turned and flung herself from the booth into the woman's arms. The older gentleman wrapped his arms around both women.

"We don't know her situation, Linds," Nick said, brushing a tear from her cheek.

"I know," she whispered.

"It looks like she's got people who love her."

The gentleman threw a few bills on the table as the older woman guided the younger woman out of the diner and settled her in the backseat of the car. Lindsey could have rolled down the window and touched her. She was that close. Tears streaked the young woman's freshly powdered cheeks, and an angry purple bruise stretched from the corner of her eye back to her temple.

I was you once. I lived your life. I felt your pain. I know your fear.

Before Lindsey could even blink, the door closed, and the car pulled away. Its taillights blurred in the distance then disappeared into the darkness.

Lindsey brushed away another tear. "I wish I could do more, Nick."

"You are doing more. You're helping raise money and awareness for the Rose Brooks Women's Shelter. What you're doing will help many, many women and children. You are doing more. Linds," Nick reiterated, giving her hand a little squeeze. "Are you ready to go make that call?"

She stared at the coffee cup left steaming and untouched on the booth's table. That was the only record, the only tangible sign, of what had just happened. All traces of that gut-wrenching reunion absorbed into the tattered, brown booths and the countertops stained with coffee rings. The waitress and a busboy chatted next to a pile of half empty ketchup bottles oblivious that a life had just changed course ten feet away from them.

Lindsey opened the car door, and Nick followed behind her. The SUV's lights reflected against the diner's windows as Nick set the car alarm, the sudden double chirp calling out into the night air. She startled, and Nick pressed his hand to her back.

"Let me get that," he said, holding open the door to the diner.

The waitress perked up. "Need a menu, folks?"

"No, we're just here to make a call," Lindsey answered.

"Pay phone's down the hall by the restrooms," she answered, not even giving them a second glance.

The diner was empty of patrons, and the click of their footfalls echoed off the linoleum tiles. Lindsey led Nick toward the pay phone where the only working fluorescent light buzzed and cracked, bathing the narrow hallway in an unearthly shade of white.

Lindsey patted her pockets. "I forgot—"

He handed her the half roll of quarters.

"Thank you, Nick. Thank you for letting me do this my way."

He nodded and rested his hand on her shoulder, fingering the collar of the old flannel, his old flannel. She was wrapped in his protection. The old shirt might as well have been a bulletproof vest. She lifted the receiver. Last time she had held it, she was a frightened woman on the run.

Not anymore.

With Nick by her side, she was safe. She deposited the coins and dialed Claire's cell phone number. It didn't even ring. A loud prerecorded message spilled out of the earpiece.

The number you dialed is not a working number...

"Could you have misremembered the number?" Nick asked. The recording was loud enough for him to have heard it.

She reached into her pocket and retrieved a scrap of paper with Claire's number. She dialed again and received the same ominously cheery recording.

"It's not working. Do you think I should call her office? I know she has an answering service." Lindsey tapped the receiver against the wall. "I just can't figure out why she would go to all the trouble to try and contact me and then change her number?"

"Maybe she moved to a different medical practice and had to return the phone when she left. Maybe she was getting a bunch of telemarketers calling," Nick said, rubbing his hand down the dark blond scruff on his chin.

"Maybe," she echoed.

"And she just might want to make sure you're okay. I know if I were in her situation, I'd want to know my friend was all right."

Lindsey hooked the receiver back into the cradle.

"It's late, Linds. Tomorrow." He looked at his watch. "More like today, we've got the Rose Brooks fundraiser and then a houseful of people to prepare for."

She leaned into him, and he wrapped his arms around her. "Do you think we should be worried? Do you think Claire was trying to tell me something or warn me? Do you think she's all right?"

"I don't know why she tried to contact you." Nick dropped his chin to rest on the top of her head. "But you're safe, Lindsey."

Brett didn't know anything about Langley Park. Nothing in her past could lead him here. That she knew for sure. She tilted her head and met his gaze. He smoothed back her hair and pressed a kiss to her forehead. This man would move mountains to protect her and the baby.

Lindsey glanced at the pay phone. "Let's go home."

"YOU SAID it would be faster if we showered together," Lindsey gasped as warm streams of water cascaded down her naked body.

Nick kissed her neck and thrust his cock inside of her. "Did I say that?" He braced one hand against the shower while using the other to massage the sensitive bundle of nerves between her legs. "I'm man enough to fess up to being wrong."

Lindsey closed her eyes and pressed her cheek against the cool tiles of the shower wall. "If this is wrong, I want you to be wrong every single morning."

Nick worked her body, rubbing slow, delicious circles over her clit as his cock filled her completely. The warm water and Nick's body pumping into her drove her over the edge. Her body tightened, a coil ready to spring open. One last thrust and she was soaring, her body singing, riding out her orgasm. Nick growled in her ear, called out her name, and filled her to the hilt.

He rested his head against the wall. "I think this is how we should start every morning," he said, running his hand up the side of her body. "The planes can figure out how to take-off and land without me. I'm just a figurehead, really."

She released a sated sigh. "We should probably get out, shouldn't we?"

He pressed a wet kiss to her temple. "We probably should. It won't take me long to get ready. I can start breakfast."

She turned to face him. Water beaded on his chest. She licked her lips and traced a droplet from his abdomen to his cock. "I think I'm hungry for more of something else."

He threw his head back and laughed. His eyes were warm and hooded.

She smiled up at him. "Pregnancy hormones are pretty great, huh?"

"The best," he said, stepping out of the shower and toweling off.

Lindsey turned off the spray of water, and Nick handed her a towel.

"Busy day?" she asked.

"Yeah, but I've got it in my calendar to leave early to pick you up before the fundraiser."

Warmth bloomed in her chest. "I can't wait to unveil the photographs. The work is truly stunning."

The photography participants had risen to the challenge and had captured moving, emotive shots she was sure were going to impress everyone tonight. They had created a breathtaking wall of images pieced together in the shape of the Rose Brooks house. And in the center was her shot of the women's hands serving as a visual symbol of strength and resiliency.

"They had an amazing teacher," Nick said, buttoning his dress shirt.

She stared at him. He was fully dressed and looked good enough to eat. "How do you do it?"

He shook his head. "Eggs and toast sound good?"

"Can you mix some olives and raisins into the eggs?"

He grimaced. "I think you've just outdone Em on the craziest pregnancy craving."

Lindsey dressed and dried her hair, smiling as she listened to the clang of pots and pans and the tap of cupboard doors opening and closing as Nick prepared breakfast. She was coming down the stairs when someone knocked on the front door.

She looked through the peephole and found her godmother standing on her porch.

"Good morning, Rosemary," she said and welcomed the woman inside.

"Oh, look at you," her godmother replied, pressing a hand to her belly. "How are you feeling?"

"I'm good."

Nick craned his head and looked out from the kitchen. "Morning, Mrs. G. Would you like some breakfast?"

"No, no, I'm due in at the office. I just wanted to drop something off before the fundraiser. I thought you might want to wear this tonight."

She opened a small box containing a delicate sunflower hairpin. She touched the warm tangerine colored petals. "I believe these are topaz, and this little spray of leaves looks to me like peridot sprinkled in with tiny diamonds."

The gemstones twinkled in the morning light.

"It's exquisite," Lindsey said. "I'd be honored to wear it."

"I was hoping you'd say that. Your mother gave it to me many years ago. And now, I'd like to give it to you, dear."

Nick joined them in the foyer. "That's a beautiful sunflower pin."

"My mother gave it to Rosemary, and now she's giving it to me," Lindsey said with tears in her eyes.

Rosemary brushed at her cheeks. "It's far too early for crying. I know it's going to be a busy day and then an exciting night at the fundraiser. I wanted to give this to you and let you know how proud I am of you, sweetheart."

Lindsey hugged her godmother. Rosemary was a slight woman, barely five feet tall, but what she lacked in height, she made up for in heart. Lindsey softened into the embrace, allowing her godmother to wrap her slight arm around her.

Rosemary patted her back. "Your mother would be so proud of you. I wanted you to have a little piece of her with you tonight."

Lindsey straightened and ran her fingertips along the beautiful golden petals. "Thank you for everything."

She pulled her hair into a high ponytail and twisted the strands into a loose bun. She dipped her head, and Rosemary slid the pin into place.

Her godmother stepped back and nodded. "I'll see you both tonight," she added through a teary gaze.

They waved goodbye, and Nick wrapped his arm around her waist as Rosemary's car set off down Foxglove Lane. It was almost mid-May, and the gardenias growing nearby added a floral note to the morning breeze while robins and sparrows chirped and busied themselves in the oaks and maples lining the street.

Nick stepped back and eyed the pin. "It reminds me of when you used to wear the flowers I'd leave tucked into the cabin's window."

She touched the pin. "I loved that you did that."

He tilted her chin up and pressed a whisper-soft kiss to the corner of her mouth. "I love you." Then he knelt down and pressed a kiss to her belly. "I love you, too, little banana."

"Nick," Lindsey said on an intake of breath. "There she is." She took his hand and pressed it to the side of her protruding belly.

He hadn't felt the baby kick yet. His gaze shot up to hers and then back to her belly. "Hello there, little banana," he cooed. "It's..."

He looked up, and Lindsey nodded.

"I'm going to be your dad," he said in a tight whisper. "I love you so much."

Lindsey rested her hand on top of Nick's. He met her gaze with tears in his eyes. She ran her hand through his blond curls as the baby's kicks melted into smooth, motionless skin. "I think that's all she's got for us right now."

He nodded and came to his feet. "I love you." His eyes were glassy with emotion, but his gaze was laser sharp and filled with conviction.

She smiled through more happy tears. "You better get a move on. You're going to be so late."

He glanced at his watch. "There's a plate of eggs with raisins and olives on the table."

She pushed up onto her toes and kissed him. "I love you."

He grabbed his satchel from the foyer closet and gave her a wink. "Just the beginning," he said with a grin and headed out the door.

. . .

LINDSEY ROLLED up the long sleeves of Nick's old flannel and plucked a photograph from the pile of images spread out over the kitchen table. The Rose Brooks photography participants had taken thousands of pictures. They had worked as a team to decide on the photographs for the main display, but there were so many awe-inspiring images, Lindsey knew she had to find a way to incorporate them into the fundraiser.

After Nick left for the airport, she went to the arts and crafts store. Glass vases now lined the countertop with sprays of long, decorative twigs, each with several photographs hanging by a colorful string. She secured the last picture when someone knocked on the door. She stepped back and assessed her work. The knock came again.

"It's open, Terry," she called out. He had called an hour ago to let her know he was running a little late. She glanced up at the clock. It was almost half past three.

The door opened and closed.

"I'm back in the kitchen working," she said, lining up the vases. "Thanks for coming over to install that last shutter."

She crossed her arms and checked each centerpiece then arranged a few twigs, so each picture hung smoothly from its wiry branch.

"Terry, is that you?"

The air stilled. Lindsey bristled, and a slow chill worked its way down her spine.

Terry wasn't in her house.

23

Booted footfalls echoed through the Foursquare, and the breath caught in Lindsey's throat. The scent of dried blood—her blood—invaded her nostrils. She wasn't in Langley Park anymore. She was in Brett's house, sprawled on the Italian marble floor, lip split, cheek throbbing, rib cage aching with every intake of breath.

"No," she gasped. "I'm in my home in Langley Park."

She gripped the counter and forced air into her lungs. Her gaze danced between the glass vases and the knife block—anything she could use to defend herself.

The footsteps stopped. He was in the kitchen.

She didn't look up. "How did you find me?"

"Find you," he said, taking a step closer. "I didn't have to find you. You told me all about this place."

She raised her head and met his gaze.

His face was blank and void of emotion, but those whiskey eyes watched her with a surgeon's steady focus. He smiled at her, an icy crack of the lips. "That's the beautiful thing about narcotic pain medications. They make many patients quite talkative."

"I don't understand. I've never taken narcotics," Lindsey answered.

The kitchen island stood between them, providing a physical barrier and hiding her protruding abdomen. She edged toward the block of knives.

"But you have," Brett answered. He took another step into the kitchen. "The week after your mother died, or should I say, the week after I flew to Maine and mowed her down on her morning run."

"You're lying," she said, voice quivering.

"I don't need to lie, Lindsey. I get everything I want. I don't let anything stand in my way. I thought you understood that." Brett put his hands on his hips, revealing the outline of a concealed carry holster and in it, a gun. "Do you remember what I said I'd do if you ever tried to leave me?"

She bit her lip. She didn't want him to see it tremble.

"I'll remind you. I told you, I'd hunt you down and that I'd kill anyone who got in my way." He plucked a banana out of the fruit bowl and peeled it slowly. "I read the emails between you and your mother. I knew she didn't want you to stay in Texas. I knew she was urging you to leave me and move on to your next job. She posed a genuine threat to us, and I needed to respond accordingly."

"No, no! The police never solved the case. You're just trying to frighten me."

He chuckled. "Of course, they didn't solve it. It was a tiny, one-stoplight town. They had no resources to launch a full investigation."

Lindsey shook her head.

"Don't you remember, I had just returned from a medical conference when you got the call." Brett took a bite of the banana and chewed it methodically. "Such a shame. If she hadn't tried to separate us, she might be alive right now."

The room spun. He wasn't lying. It had happened just like that.

"That week, I kept you in an opioid haze, and you talked all about Langley Park, Kansas, and your beloved, Rosemary Giacopazzi."

Her eyes went wide. "Did you hurt her?"

"No," he said and swallowed another bite. "I needed her to lead me to you. And that's exactly what she did this morning." Brett set the banana peel on the counter. "But you've been a busy little whore haven't you. You've already shacked up with your pilot, Nick."

"I don't know what you're talking about," Lindsey said, gaze locked on the floor.

Brett barked out a laugh. "You know, I met him. We flew into his airport. You talked all about him, too. If we had more time, my love, I would put a bullet between his eyes and make you watch. He tried to take what's mine, and there's a price to pay for that. But, unfortunately, some business dealings have run astray, and I've had to make alternate plans. We're going to take a drive. I think you'll be happily surprised where we end up. Remember Camp Clemens? I own it. We're going to pick up a few things and then we're leaving the country."

"No," she whispered.

"No?" he echoed with a harsh, mocking edge. This was the shift. The moment when he'd change from a coolheaded physician to a brutal batterer. "I don't think you understand. You don't have a say. You belong to me."

Lindsey lunged toward the block of knives. Her fingertips grazed the end of the paring knife, but before she was able to pull it from the block, Brett knocked her hand away. She fell back onto the kitchen table and caught herself between two chairs. Brett grabbed her arm, swung her around, and slammed her back into the refrigerator. She raised her hands to protect her face, but the blow didn't come.

He stared at something past her shoulder.

The ultrasound image was hanging from a magnet.

His gaze flicked to her abdomen. The countertop and oversized flannel had hidden her belly until now. He plucked the picture off the refrigerator door and studied it. Then he wrapped his hand around her neck and forced her to meet his gaze. "You're carrying my child."

The fury in his eyes dialed up a notch as she struggled for breath. "So, this is why Claire begged me not to come for you. She knew you were pregnant. You confided in her, didn't you?"

Lindsey couldn't answer. The little air Brett allowed into her trachea was barely enough to keep her conscious. She closed her eyes. When he was this far gone, when the measured doctor had vanished entirely from his persona, there was no reasoning with him. His breath was hot against her ear. "You are going to pay for this betrayal."

A knock came from the door. "Lindsey, it's Terry."

Brett loosened his grip. He wasn't all cool and collected now. He ran a hand through his hair and looked at his watch. "Dammit! Get rid of whoever's at the door. If you do anything to let them know I'm here, I will kill that person. I will kill him right in front of you, and it will be your fault just like your mother's death. Do you want that?"

She shook her head. "It's just the handyman. I can get rid of him."

Brett pulled his gun from the holster. "Be quick."

He followed her to the door but stood hidden from view.

Lindsey took a breath. This was her only chance. She opened the door a fraction. "Hi, Terry!" She glanced over at Brett. "Right now, isn't a good time, but Em next door was telling me she needed your help with something. Could you let her know that I had to go to Rachel and Rory's rock for a photoshoot?"

"Are you sure you're okay?" His gaze flicked above her head and into the house.

She held tight to the door, narrowing the opening as Brett pressed the barrel of the gun into her abdomen.

"Yes, I'm fine." It was taking everything she had to keep it together. "Just pop over to Em's and let her know about Rachel and Rory. I'm running horribly late. I'm so sorry, Terry."

"Will do," he said, giving her a nod.

He turned and left the porch.

As soon as the front door closed, Brett was right behind her. "That's a good girl."

An umbrella sat in the corner, not five feet away. But before Lindsey could lunge for it, a sharp stinging sensation pricked her arm. She tried to stay upright, clawing at anything to remain vertical.

"Easy there," Brett said.

She inhaled the spicy scent of his cologne and threw a punch. But her limbs weren't responding to her commands.

Brett's face came into view, and those whiskey eyes glowed triumphantly. "Sweet dreams, my love."

"NICK, you've got to see this."

Nick raised his head from where he was skimming over some new aviation regulations and met the charter pilot's gaze. "What is it, Zach?"

"Remember those doctors from about a month or so ago? You know, the ones who wanted me to take them to that unregistered airfield?"

Nick's jaw twitched. "I saw on the news last night that one of them got arrested for drugs."

"There's more. The news is reporting that he hung himself in jail last night, and the other two doctors, the lady, and the creepy quiet guy are said to be on the run."

Nick followed Zach out of his office and down to the pilots' lounge.

"It's still on," Zach said, stopping in front of the television screen.

The image on the television changed, and three pictures were plastered across the screen. Zach tried to say something, but Nick put his hand up, quieting the man as the news reporter spoke.

Dr. Mason Mathews, the former prominent Houston surgeon, was found dead in his jail cell this morning. He was awaiting a bail hearing on nearly one hundred and twenty counts of forgery and trafficking of a controlled substance. His brother, Dr. Brett Mathews, has also been charged with forgery and trafficking. However, his whereabouts are currently unknown. He's considered to be armed and dangerous. If you see this man, please contact the FBI task force number at the bottom of the screen. Claire Mathews, the wife of Dr. Mason Mathews, is also being sought for questioning. Her whereabouts are also unknown.

"Mathews," Nick said in a tight gasp. He had been face-to-face with Lindsey's abuser and hadn't even known it. His chest tightened as adrenaline shot through his body.

He pulled out his cell phone and dialed Lindsey. The call went to voicemail.

She could be working. When she was editing photos, she would disappear into her work for hours. How many times had he found her working at the kitchen table at two in the morning, bleary-eyed and having completely lost track of time? Too many to count.

He called again.

Fucking voicemail.

He glanced at his watch. It was almost five thirty. He would need to leave to get home so they could make it to the Rose Brooks fundraiser by six thirty. She was probably just getting the last touches done on the photography project. That had to be it. It was the most logical conclusion.

He glanced back at the screen. Brett Mathew's icy brown eyes flashed vacant and menacing.

Christ, he should have flown down to Texas and beat the ever-loving fuck out of this degenerate when he had the chance. And he'd known those two were up to no good that day he confronted them even without knowing their identity.

Claire Mathews' picture flashed onto the screen.

Hot bile rose in Nick's throat. She had tried to contact Lindsey. Was Claire working with Brett or was she trying to warn Lindsey? There was no way he could know.

An incoming call buzzed on his phone, but it wasn't from Lindsey.

"Em," he said, answering the call, "can you go over to the house and check on Lindsey? I can't get ahold of her."

He didn't want to jump to conclusions. Lindsey had assured him Brett knew nothing of Langley Park or her time here. But the same awful twist in his chest he'd felt when he'd last encountered Brett and Mason Mathews tightened like a vice.

"She's not there, Nick," Em answered. "But Terry's here. He was on my porch when I got home a few minutes ago."

"Did Terry see her? He was supposed to install the shutters on the front window."

The sound of Em's voice grew muffled. She was speaking to someone.

"He said he saw her about an hour and a half ago. He says he knocked on the door. Lindsey answered, but she wouldn't let him inside."

Nick swallowed. That wasn't like Lindsey. There was no reason she shouldn't have let Terry in unless someone was preventing her from doing so.

"Em, Brett Mathews, Lindsey's Brett Mathews, has warrants out for his arrest. He's part of some multi-state, illegal opioid drug trafficking ring and the news just said he was on the run. He's flown into my airport. I don't know if he knows Lindsey's in Langley Park, but we have to assume that somehow, he found out."

Em gasped.

"Ask Terry if he remembers anything else about his interaction with Lindsey."

"Hold on, Nick," Em said.

Nick turned up the volume on his phone, trying to make out their muffled conversation.

"Terry says Lindsey told him she needed to leave to go do a photoshoot at Rachel and Rory's rock. I guess she said it a couple of times. Terry didn't know what she was talking about, but she kept asking him to make sure he told me that."

If he weren't still standing, Nick would have sworn his heart had stopped beating. "Rachel and Rory's rock? This is important, Em, ask Terry if that's exactly what she said."

His heart thundered in his chest. That rock was their place. He was the only other person who would have understood the location.

She was trying to send a message to him.

"Yes, Nick, Terry says she was really adamant about it. Rachel and Rory's rock."

"Rachel and Rory's rock is a place only Lindsey and I know about at Camp Clemens in the Ozarks." He took a breath. "When did Terry last see Lindsey?"

He needed a timeline. It was a four-hour bus ride from Langley

Park to Camp Clem. In a speeding car, it could be anywhere from three to three and a half hours.

"Jesus!" Em breathed. "Do you think he found her?"

"Em, what time?" he asked again, urgency lacing each word.

"Terry says around four." Em paused. "Nick, what should we do?"

"If it is Brett, he's most likely traveling by car. Plane travel would be too risky."

Nick's mind was working fast. Camp Clem was a forty-minute plane ride. It would be close, but he could beat them there.

"Em, I need you to call the FBI. I need you to tell them we think Brett may have taken Lindsey to Camp Clem. I don't know why they'd go there. But that's what she was trying to tell us. She at least believed she'd be going there."

"What if they don't believe me, Nick? This sounds crazy."

"Em, you've got to try. If the FBI blows you off, call the Langley Park police. Ask for Clay. I'm sure he's got contacts."

"But Brett's not supposed to know anything about Langley Park or Camp Clemens." She was crying.

Nick inhaled a shaky breath as the memory of the first time his grandfather allowed him to take the yoke and fly the old Cessna Skyhawk flashed through his mind. He could hear his grandfather guiding him through the headset.

"Steady, Nicholas. Don't let fear get the better of you. You're the one in control."

"Em," he said, calmly, "I need you to focus. There's a good chance he found her. What I need you to do right now is to let the FBI know I'm taking my plane, and I'm flying to Camp Clem. If Brett has Lindsey, and that's where he's taking her, I'll beat him there, and I'll get her back."

24

Lindsey released a sigh as the breeze blew strands of hair across her face, tickling her nose. She was in her parents' Volvo, and the steady thrum of the engine threatened to lull her back to sleep. Where were they going this time? Last summer, she and her parents had visited Sebago Lake. Could they be heading down to Vermont to tour the Ben and Jerry's ice cream factory? Her father had promised he would take her since she had gotten all A's on her third-grade report card.

Lindsey blinked. Thoughts flitted and floated through her mind like the snowy-white, airborne fluff from a cottonwood tree. Real events twisted and morphed into dreamlike scenarios that didn't make any sense. She tried to brush the hair off her face, but her hands were stuck together, bound by something at her wrists.

She opened her eyes a fraction, and a sliver of late afternoon sunlight assaulted her vision, blinding her momentarily.

Where was she?

She focused on her breath and tried to order her thoughts.

A car. She was lying down in the back seat of a car.

She tried again to raise her eyelids. This time, she managed to keep them open. A plane came into view, flying overhead like a white speck darting across a sea of blue. She watched it until it disappeared from her vantage point. The scent of leather hit her next. It was like she had been offline, and all her senses were rebooting. She looked to the side. Black leather seats.

This wasn't the faded, tan fabric of her parents' Volvo, and she wasn't in the third grade.

The haze clouding her brain cleared.

Brett was in her house. Her shoulder throbbed. He'd given her a shot and drugged her with something. The last thing she could recall was a sharp stinging sensation in her arm before a thick, black curtain fell and darkness descended.

"Good, you're up. We're almost there."

Brett's deceptively smooth tone sent a shiver down her spine. He was back to being the controlled surgeon.

"Where?" she whispered. She licked her lips. Her mouth was dry, and the word came out in a cracked syllable.

"Your little summer camp. I own it. I should rephrase. My associates and I own it."

"Did you buy it to punish me?"

Brett laughed. "No, my love. I checked into it after you had spoken so fondly of it. But I wasn't interested in any sentimental value it held. It's remoteness and availability were what piqued my interest. It serves as the perfect midpoint and storage facility between myself and my partners." He met her gaze in the mirror. "And nobody asks any questions in the Ozarks."

A spark of hope grew in her chest. If Terry had gotten to Em right away, and Em had called Nick to try and figure out the Rachel and Rory reference, there could be police waiting for them. Brett was on the run from something. There was no way he would leave a life of accolades and prestige if there weren't a damn good reason.

Lindsey watched him in the rearview mirror. "Where are Mason and Claire? Are they meeting us at the camp?"

His jaw clenched.

She'd hit a nerve.

"Mason proved to be weak." Brett tightened his grip on the

steering wheel. "And Claire proved to be disloyal. You're fortunate I care for you so much, Lindsey. You're also very lucky I've decided to take you back."

"What do you mean, disloyal?"

An icy smirk returned to his lips. "You'll see."

Brett made a hard right, and the smooth pavement beneath them changed to the crack and crunch of gravel. They wound their way up the rough road as the light dimmed under the heavy Ozark canopy of foliage. It was getting late. Close to sundown. Another airplane passed overhead, and tears welled in Lindsey's eyes. They were on the road to Camp Clem. If the police had been called, wouldn't they have stopped them by now? Wouldn't it have been easier to apprehend Brett on the open road?

She had been close to having everything. A career. A community. Real friends. Nick and the baby. She swallowed back a sob.

Do not fall apart.

The light warmed as they pulled into some sort of clearing. She twisted her body to get a better view. It wasn't a clearing. They were near the camp lodge. She recognized the peeling gray-blue paint from when she and Nick had visited.

Brett drove down the sloping hill toward the lake. Through the half-open window, the familiar sounds of the water and the crisp smell of shortleaf pines and bushy dogwoods took her back to another time, a happier time.

She closed her eyes.

Hold on to that. Hold on to the love. Find a way to escape.

The car stopped, and Brett cut the engine. He got out and opened the back door. She tried to look past his looming form. He ran his hand down the length of her calf, and her eyes snapped back and met his gaze. If it were anyone else, it would have been a tender gesture. But from Brett, a gentle touch was a prelude to pain.

He twisted her foot, and the taste of blood flooded her mouth. An excruciating jolt of pain shot through her ankle. He held her there, balancing on the edge of agony. "We're going into the boathouse. If I were you, I'd think very carefully about trying to run. I have very dangerous business associates, Lindsey. One call and I can have your Nick and your godmother killed before breakfast tomorrow. There's also the question of the child. Don't forget, I'm a surgeon. I can make that baby go away, too."

Lindsey gritted her teeth. What hurt worse, the physical torment or the mental? She released a pained whimper.

"Are you going to be a good girl and cooperate?"

She nodded. The pain was everywhere. In her mind. In her body. Her breath came in rapid gasps. Her ankle felt ready to snap—the muscles of her leg burning, the tendons close to tearing.

He twisted her ankle another millimeter. "Answer me."

"Yes, yes," she cried.

Brett released his grip and yanked her out of the car by her bound wrists.

He pulled back the tarp covering the entrance to the boathouse and pushed her inside. She stumbled into the dim space, blinking as bits of dust and earth disturbed by the tarp swirled in a haze of golden light. A person sat hunched near the opening, close to the water's edge. Lindsey steadied herself and locked her gaze on the unmoving form.

"Don't you want to say hello to Claire?" Brett asked, his words flat and void of emotion.

"Claire?" she whispered.

The woman didn't respond.

Lindsey glanced at Brett. His eyes were trained on the water. She took a few tentative steps. When Brett didn't stop her, she rushed to Claire's side.

"Claire! Claire!" Lindsey cried, squatting down next to the slumped form.

She grasped the woman awkwardly with her bound wrists. Claire's head hung loose, and her body slid down the side of the boathouse wall, legs dangling over the edge as one delicate ballet flat slipped off her foot and floated effortlessly on the glassy, golden water. At this angle, the late spring sun bathed Claire's torso in a hazy light. Her features were relaxed. Her mouth hung slightly open.

Lindsey brushed her fingertips across Claire's cheek and rested them on her neck where smooth skin lay still and silent.

No pulse.

"Is she…" Lindsey asked, unable to finish the question.

"Dead?" Brett offered, nonchalantly. "It's remarkably easy to overdose on Fentanyl. At least, that's what her cause of death will look like if she washes up somewhere. Just another junkie nobody will care about."

He walked toward them and nudged Claire's torso with the tip of his boot. Her body slid forward and splashed into the water.

Lindsey sprang up and lunged to follow Claire into the lake, but Brett grabbed her by her hair, knocking out the sunflower pin and pulling her back onto the wooden planks.

Claire floated, face up, beneath an inch of water. Lindsey met her dead gaze as the woman's arms hung limp. She bit back a sob. Claire looked so peaceful. Her hair swayed side to side as her body disappeared under a blanket of water.

Lindsey stared into Claire's watery grave. "Why did you do this? Why did you kill her?"

Brett tightened his grip on her hair and turned her head to meet his gaze. "Would you like to know what years as a practicing surgeon have taught me?" That icy smile was back. "People will do just about anything to escape pain, but they'll do even more in the pursuit of pleasure." He twisted his fingers into her hair and pulled.

"Please, stop," she cried out.

He relaxed his grip but left his hand entwined in her chestnut locks. "I've put in my time, Lindsey. First, I got out of that dead-end Texas shithole. Then, I devoted my life to medicine. But it's not enough. I deserve more, and I found a way to get it. And that's where pleasure and pain come in. As a surgeon, my primary objective was to reduce pain. Now, I'm part of the more lucrative *pleasure* business."

"I don't understand. Why would you kill Claire? She'd never hurt anyone. She helped—"

"Oh, I know Claire helped you. I knew it when your old camera bag disappeared from the house."

"I'm so sorry, Claire," Lindsey breathed.

"Sorry, Claire?" Brett barked. "Claire told me a lot of things before she died. She didn't think I would get to you. She never mentioned the baby. Claire's death is your fault, my love. I told you what I would do to anyone who tried to get between us."

Lindsey closed her eyes. "Oh, Claire."

"Claire had the opportunity to be part of something big. Real money. People want to feel good, and they'll go to great lengths to get that high."

"High?" she echoed.

He shook his head. "Do I need to spell it out for you, my love? The black market. Opioids. That's where the real money is. One kilogram of fentanyl from our Chinese supplier costs a few thousand dollars and can produce hundreds of thousands of pills each selling for twenty dollars apiece, and I don't lift a finger."

"Drugs? You're selling drugs?"

Brett frowned. "I'm taking advantage of an opportunity."

"Where's Mason? Is he okay with this?"

"My brother had no vision. He was weak, and he was threatening to ruin everything. He got sloppy. Started using. He wanted to stay in Houston and keep writing prescriptions and selling off the pills. Small time. Some money, but nothing like what I'm a part of, what I'm building." Brett's gaze narrowed. "Nobody, not even my brother, gets in the way of what I want. You should know that by now, my love."

His eyes had been one of the first things she had noticed about him. The photographer in her had observed the way they changed with the light. The night they'd met at the fundraiser, those golden flecks around his pupils had danced under the ballroom's chandelier, attentive and warm. She had been a fool to fall for him. He'd never loved her. He'd never loved anything. The warmth in his eyes reflected only an affinity for the win, an addiction to the chase. His eyes registered pleasure only in the sense that he was getting what he wanted, no matter the cost.

"Why me, Brett? You could have anyone."

He chuckled. "That's a good story. Mason spotted you at the fundraiser. Every man was watching you that night. He bet me a hundred bucks I couldn't pick you up. He lost. I won. I always win."

A bet! One lousy hundred-dollar bet had turned her life upside-down. A pained expression crossed her face.

"Why that face? You turned out to be worth it. I won one of the most sought-after photographers on the planet. You could have gone anywhere, done anything. But I won you, and I intend to keep you."

"The police will track you down," Lindsey said, but even she could hear the uncertainty in her voice.

"I made sure the trail ended with Mason and Claire. The shell company that owns the camp leads to them. All we need to do is get the product I have hidden here and deliver it to my associates in Chicago. Then we leave the country, and we'll be untraceable."

"Over my dead body," came a voice from behind the boathouse tarp.

25

Nick swung back the tarp and charged inside. His interruption stunned Brett, and Lindsey broke free and pressed her back against the wall, giving Nick room to tackle the bastard. They hit the wooden planks with a hard thud, and something heavy skidded across the floor.

Brett's gun.

He went for it, but before he could reach it, it slid over the edge and into the lake. Panic lined the man's face.

"You're not so fucking tough without your gun, are you?" Nick said, landing a jab to the man's rib cage. "Now you get to see what it's like to fight someone your own size."

Brett wasn't as big as he was, but the man was no lightweight either. Their bodies tumbled across the floor and banged against a post. Nick threw a punch and landed it square on Brett's cheek. But Brett was quick to connect a jab to his abdomen.

Nick sucked in a tight breath.

If this sick fuck wanted to fight, he was ready. He flipped Brett over and pressed his shoulder into the man's chest and searched the boathouse for Lindsey. She stood frozen, still pressed against the wall.

"Run, Linds! Run!" Nick called out.

Brett slipped out of the hold, but Nick pulled him back.

"Linds, go to Rachel and Rory's rock. Go now!"

"I don't want to leave you," she cried out.

"I'll find you, Linds. Run!"

Her footsteps echoed through the air, and the swish of tarp signaled she had gotten out.

Brett struggled, throwing elbows and ramming his shoulder into Nick's chest. He pulled an arm free from Nick's grasp, flipped around, and threw a hard punch, fist cracking against Nick's jaw.

"How do you like that, flyboy?" Brett spit out, scrambling to put space between them.

Nick sprang to his feet, but before he could rush Brett again, the man eyed a broken oar and grabbed it. He swung the jagged, weathered blade in sharp slices, barely missing Nick's face. But the man miscalculated and threw a sweeping blow, giving Nick the opportunity to grab the oar's shaft.

Eye to eye, each man held onto the oar, struggling for control. Brett's lips quirked into a sardonic grin. Nick knew that look. He had watched that same expression beat his mother black and blue. Nick's father and Brett shared no physical qualities, but they were identical in the ways that cut to the core. Neither had the capacity for compassion, and cruelty was their sport of choice.

Nick gritted his teeth and threw his body weight onto the man. Brett crashed against the boathouse wall, and Nick forced the oar shaft under the man's chin, restricting his breathing. Brett struggled and changed his grip. But Nick had all the leverage now.

"You're going to pay for what you've done to her," Nick said, increasing the pressure. He blinked. Two men flashed before his eyes. One real, flesh and blood. The other, long gone, but always scratching beneath the surface of his thoughts.

"Lindsey is mine," Brett let out in a hoarse whisper. "I'll never let her go."

Every protective instinct Nick had ever known coursed through his body. "You'll never get the chance. You'll be spending the rest of your pathetic life in prison."

Brett met Nick's words with a smug, taunting grin. "That baby isn't yours. You'll never be its father."

Nick jammed the oar harder against Brett's neck. "I'll be more of a father to that child than you could ever be."

Brett released a tight laugh. "We'll see about that."

The struggling man shifted his body to the side. In the space of a breath, something sharp and jagged tore into the flesh of Nick's thigh. He jumped back, freeing Brett. The bastard had pulled a rusty nail from the boathouse wall and jammed it into his leg. But Nick wasn't about to let him get away. He raised the oar, and before Brett could dodge the blow, Nick slammed the blade into the man's torso. Brett pitched forward and fell into the lake.

Nick stood, holding the oar like a baseball bat and watched the water. Only a sliver of sun remained visible in the sky. Dusk faded into darkness as he scanned the water, searching for any sign of Brett.

Where the hell had he gone?

He crouched down and peered under the boathouse. The ripple of waves caused by Brett's body stilled, and the lake grew placid. Nick shook his head. He hit Brett hard, but not hard enough to kill. Christ! He didn't have time to hang around and wait for Brett to come up for air. He had to find Lindsey. He had to get her out of there.

LINDSEY PUSHED PAST A BRANCH. Low hanging tree limbs and dense thickets scraped her arms and legs. It must have been years since anyone had trimmed back the tangle of vegetation.

The old Camp Clem trails, overgrown with weeds and tall grass, created a disorienting world of dead ends and dark twists and turns. The last rays of sun cast the forest in an eerie glow. The light would be gone soon, and there was nothing more haunting than a night alone under the thick Ozark canopy with only a sliver of moonlight.

She needed to run but couldn't. Her bound arms and pregnant

belly were slowing her down. She stopped and pressed her back against a tree trunk. She lifted her wrists to her mouth and bit the duct tape. The sticky adhesive tasted as awful as it smelled. She turned her head to go at it at from a different angle when it hit her.

Zoe.

The self-defense class.

There was another way to break free.

She raised her bound hands above her head and slammed them down against her thighs. Just like the demonstration, the tape tore apart. She ripped off the remaining pieces and threw them onto the ground.

Arms free, she ran. The trail disappeared into a mess of thorny bushes, but she worked her way through. The lake was to the east of her, and she continued uphill, edging closer to the bluff. The night sounds bloomed around her. Branches rustled. The familiar chirps and croaks of night creatures grew as the final rays of light disappeared into the darkness.

"You know this place," she whispered. "Get to the rock."

A sharp crack stopped her dead in her tracks. She crouched down and inhaled a ragged breath. It could be Nick. She scanned the darkness. A raccoon appeared from behind the underbrush less than a foot away, and Lindsey pitched backward, knocking into something cold and wet. Her hand swept over a booted foot.

"There you are, my love," Brett cooed.

He grabbed her by the arm and yanked her to her feet. He was soaked. Beads of water trailed down his face. His hand was clammy and damp. Lindsey leaned into him then pulled back, throwing her weight away from him. She broke free and started running.

"You think you can outrun me?" he called out.

He was behind her. His fingers brushed through her hair. But she kept moving. She ran right then left just as Nick had taught the campers to do when playing capture the flag, zigzagging wildly and staying just out of Brett's reach.

It was working.

Brett couldn't react quickly enough to the changing forest landscape and her erratic movements. He cursed and slipped. The crack of branches and his heavy footfalls trailed steps behind her. She closed in on Rachel and Rory's rock and headed toward the edge of the bluff, but a tree root intersected her path and sent her careening to her knees.

Brett swooped in like a bird of prey and scooped her up, holding her in a bearhug, her back pressed to his chest and dragged her to the edge of the bluff. "You try to run again and your godmother's dead."

She stilled, chest heaving.

"Lindsey," Nick yelled, rounding a pair of old maples.

Brett tightened his grip. "You come any closer, and I'll push her over."

Near the edge of the bluff, free of the thick canopy, the tiny slice of moon illuminated the small outcropping. Lindsey met Nick's gaze, and he gave her a reassuring nod.

"Listen to me, Brett," Nick said. He raised his hands defensively. "I've got my plane here. I can take you anywhere you want. But Lindsey's not a part of the deal. She stays here."

"No, Nick! No!" she cried.

Nick smiled a slow, sweet smile that tore her heart into pieces. "I love you, Linds. I love you and little banana more than anything, more than my own life."

"Nick," she gasped, but Brett slapped his hand over her mouth.

"Let me tell you something about myself, flyboy. I don't take kindly to ultimatums. If I don't get Lindsey, nobody does."

Nick took a step forward. "Brett, be reasonable. It doesn't have to end like this."

A low sound buzzed in the distance. Lindsey craned her neck to get a better look.

"What is that?" Brett growled, turning as the searchlight of a helicopter panned back and forth across Lake Langhorne.

Nick took another step closer. He was only a few feet away. "Last chance, Brett. We still have time. Just let Lindsey go."

The thrum of the helicopter blades intensified, and a wide beam of light passed over them.

Nick shielded his eyes as the chopper screamed past them in a burst of air and sound. "Now or never, Brett," he yelled over the roar of the helicopter.

Brett hugged her body against his and leaned in. "You think you're going to get your little happily ever after, don't you?"

She struggled. He tightened his grip, and his hand clamped harder over her mouth.

"If I can't have you, nobody can."

A flurry of lights moved toward her, closing in from the forest. She met Nick's gaze.

"Brett Mathews," came a voice over a bullhorn. "This is the FBI. Release the woman and put your hands up."

"You come any closer, and I'm taking her over the edge with me." He was shaking and breathing hard. His chest heaved against her back in tight, punctuated pulses.

Within seconds, light was everywhere, and the deafening sound of a helicopter hovering above echoed through the camp. The sound rippled across the water. It was like being trapped inside a blender. Bits of earth and branches kicked up in a swirl of wild air.

"I always win," Brett yelled, dragging her a step closer to the edge.

The dark foliage exploded with flashlights and armed men shouting back and forth. The helicopter maneuvered above her, droning on with a steady buzz. Her hair blew across her face, and Brett's hand shifted and covered both her mouth and her nose.

It was hard to breathe, and everything blurred together. Lindsey closed her eyes. She saw her mother. Images of days spent on the Maine coastline and cocoa before bed clicked through her mind like projector slides. Rosemary came next. Their walks around Langley Park. The sun setting over Lake Boley. Her new friends gathered around her, holding her hands and listening as she shared her most painful secrets. And Nick at sixteen, wrapping his flannel shirt around her shoulders. Finally, Nick, singing to the baby. Their baby.

The projector in her mind faded to black. It was peaceful here. Quiet. But before she melted into the darkness, her mother's face broke through like a million flashbulbs in an explosion of light.

"Fight for your life. Fight for your child. Never stop fighting!"

Never stop fighting.

She'd heard that before.

A switch flipped, and she was back. Back to the roaring helicopter. Back to the men yelling. She saw Nick. He was almost close enough to touch.

Fight for what you love.

Lindsey opened her mouth and bit down hard on Brett's finger. His hand flew from her mouth, and he pulled her back. She drove her elbow into his side and kicked her heel into his shin.

"I am not your prize," she yelled, flailing her arms.

Brett released her and struggled for balance. The earth shifted beneath them. Rocks and bits of dirt tumbled off the bluff. He fell back and grabbed onto the hem of her shirt. She was going over the edge. He was taking her with him. She reached out, praying to grab hold of a branch, a tree root, anything that would keep her from falling to her death. The light intensified, the air thickened around her. She stretched. Cool, moist air blew through her fingers until her body pitched forward, and two strong hands took hold of her wrists and pulled.

She opened her eyes and saw Nick's face.

His gaze locked with hers. "I've got you. Hold on."

She wrapped her hands around his wrists and held on for dear life.

The instant Brett let go, Nick pulled her onto the firm ground and wrapped his arms around her. Chaos broke out around them as teams of men emerged from the forest. The light from the chopper swept the water near the base of the bluff.

Agents surrounded them, but Nick wouldn't let go. She buried her face into his chest and breathed in his scent.

"I fought him, Nick. I fought back. I fought for what I loved."

He cupped her face and nodded as tears welled in his eyes. "Yes, you did, my brave, beautiful, Lindsey."

She closed her eyes as the agents' radios exploded with chatter.

"We've got a body. Confirming it's the suspect Brett Mathews."

Nick pressed a kiss to her temple. "It's over."

"No," she said, meeting his gaze, "it's just beginning."

EPILOGUE

Water splashed against the sides of the clawfoot bathtub. Lindsey bit her lip and rolled her head to the side, eyes closed as she gripped the edge of the tub. Her breasts glistened. Beads of water ran down her chest carving sinful trails to her rounded abdomen. Nick squeezed her ass and thrust his pelvis. Lindsey's core muscles tensed, and he released a low growl. She was close. More water sloshed out of the tub, but he didn't give one single fuck.

Lindsey had hit the thirty-seven week mark in her pregnancy, and little banana wasn't little anymore. They had done all the things soon-to-be parents needed to do: packed the hospital bag, assembled the crib, taken the birthing classes, and their friends were on alert. Both Lindsey and Em could deliver any day now.

The early August sun ignited the red and golden highlights in her chestnut hair. She opened her eyes, and he surrendered to her hooded, blue-green gaze. His bride-to-be never looked so beautiful. She rocked her body, grinding into to him as she rode his cock. She set the pace, and he guided her body up and down through the cooling water. Even though it was a tight fit working his six foot four inch frame into the tub, with Lindsey's growing belly, this had become their favorite place. And thanks to pregnancy hormones, they were in here a lot.

Their water bill was going to be a fucking beast.

He slid his hands down her smooth thighs and massaged her calves. Her breath came in shallow pants. He kissed her shoulder and inhaled her sweet cream and summer rain scent.

"Nick, oh, Nick," she breathed.

He gripped her ass with one hand, water swishing, droplets making watery pathways down the tiled wall as she increased her pace. Flying couldn't hold a candle to watching this woman come. She released the sides of the tub and leaned forward. Lindsey gripped his shoulders, and he cupped her face, guiding their mouths together for a scorching kiss.

She slid her hands into his hair and pulled hard. The sensation shot straight to his cock, and he thrust harder. Lindsey released a low, sexy moan, sending him over the edge. Her supple body writhing, wet breasts bobbing, she was glorious. She scraped her nails down his chest and consumed every ounce of pleasure her body could take. He gripped her hips and let loose, his body screaming for release. He came hard in a thunderclap of water, and breath, and skin gliding against skin. If this was just the beginning, he couldn't fucking wait for what life had in store for them.

She curled into him. He wrapped his arms around her and made slow, wet circles on the small of her back.

"Happy wedding day, soon-to-be, Mrs. Kincade."

A slow, sexy smile bloomed on her lips. "I love the sound of that. Say it again."

"Mrs. Kincade," he repeated, kissing the space between her breasts.

She hummed her satisfaction and ran her fingers across his shoulder blades. Cool drops of water slid down his back.

"Do you think this double wedding thing is crazy?" she asked.

He smiled. "Em and Michael are like family. I can't imagine a better way to celebrate."

Em and Lindsey had each traveled to much of the world—Em, as a renowned violinist, and Lindsey as a sought-after photographer. Two weeks ago, they both craved the English delicacies of mincemeat pie and Yorkshire pudding. They had invited Jenna and Zoe over and spent the day baking and watched the BBC's version of Jane Austen's *Pride and Prejudice* with Colin Firth.

Nick had just returned from a trip up in his Skyhawk with Ben, Sam, and Michael when the girls informed them they were going to have a double wedding just like Lizzie and Jane Bennett from Pride and Prejudice. A small tiff broke out between the men over whether he or Michael was the most like Mr. Darcy. Nick was adamant. He was no Mr. Bingley. But all discussion ceased when the girls handed each of them generous slices of Victoria sponge cake.

A few calls later, they had booked the pavilion in the Langley Park Botanic Gardens, found an officiant, and secured a cake from Langley Park's beloved local bakery, and that was that. Double wedding. Except instead of two of Miss Austen's British virgins getting married, they had two very pregnant women. *Pride and Prejudice* 2.0.

Nick would have married Lindsey in a drive-through wedding chapel if that had been what she wanted—anything to help her cope with the nightmare she had survived.

The hours after Lindsey's abduction and Brett's death were frightening and taxing. Their priority was the baby. Brett had injected Lindsey with something to knock her out, and they had to make sure that the baby was safe and healthy. Lindsey spent several tense hours hooked to monitors as the medical staff drew blood and watched and waited. After twelve grueling hours, and numerous visits from the on call obstetrician, both baby and mother were deemed to be in good health.

So when Lindsey said she wanted a double wedding with Em and Michael, he didn't hesitate to say yes.

"We probably need to get going," she purred into his ear.

"Weddings do seem to run more smoothly when the bride and groom show up," Nick teased.

Lindsey played with a wet curl on his forehead. "I still can't believe I agreed to an afternoon wedding. The light at sunrise or sunset would have been so much more romantic."

He laughed. "Do you know what it's like to try and wake you these days?"

She splashed him with a handful of water. "I'm not that bad."

He gave her a dubious grin.

"All right, all right. I concede that I may be a little testy in the morning."

"A little?"

She got him with another handful of water.

He took her wrists and held them behind her back. "When was the last time you stayed up past seven? Last night, when we were sitting on Michael and Em's porch, Michael and I went in for beers and came back to you two snoring on the porch swing."

"That swing is pretty hypnotic," she replied, then her eyes went wide. "I was not snoring."

He winked. "Don't worry, your secret's safe with me—and Michael."

She narrowed her gaze and leaned in. "You know, this hands behind the back in the bathtub could be fun."

Fucking amazing pregnancy hormones.

Unfortunately, they did need to get married, and someone who wasn't incubating a child needed to get this show on the road.

"Come on, soon-to-be, Mrs. Kincade." He craned his neck and searched for his watch. It had been hastily removed and thrown on the floor when she had pulled him into the tub. "The Teddy-cab arrives in less than half an hour."

"Tell me about this Ted. I've seen him around town, but I've never really met him," Lindsey said, rising to her feet.

Nick swung his body out of the tub and wrapped a towel around her shoulders. "Ted's the resident astrophysicist or astrologer. I'm not sure which. But the guy's crazy smart. He works at the bike shop in town, and everybody seems to love him."

Lindsey nodded. "He just seems a little..."

"I'm right there with you, Linds," he said and bent down to retrieve his watch. He shot up when she grabbed his bare ass.

He parted his lips, but Lindsey cut him off.

"I know, I know. No more hanky-panky. Time to get ready for here comes the bride, and all that."

"And all that," he echoed, gazing into the eyes of the girl he had loved since he was sixteen years old.

A THUNDEROUS KNOCKING sound emanated through the Foursquare.

"Nick!" Lindsey called out, putting the lipstick back into her makeup bag.

"It's probably just Ted. Are you almost ready?"

"Just about," she answered.

They had thrown out almost every wedding convention. While many brides didn't want their groom to see them until they walked down the aisle. She wanted Nick by her side every step of their wedding day. She stood back and assessed herself in the floor length mirror. For being thirty-seven-weeks pregnant, she didn't look half bad.

She and Em had gone wedding dress shopping with the girls. Their first day on the hunt ended with uncontrollable giggling as a fussy bridal attendant adorned Em with several giant white bows in an attempt to hide her pregnant belly.

Luckily, Rosemary, who truly was Langley Park's most beloved person, had a former student who was a top seamstress in the Kansas City area.

Lindsey's custom-made, satin wedding dress with an Empire waist and delicate off the shoulder cap sleeves flowed seamlessly over her pregnant belly. An intricate sash with pearls, seed crystals, and sapphire blue beading matched her engagement ring. She turned from side to side. The adornment sparkled in the summer light streaming in through the shutters.

Nick's quick footfalls padded up the stairs.

"I'm coming, I'm coming," she said, drinking in her soon-to-be husband, absolutely killing it in a tailored suit and tie.

She grabbed her camera and took a picture. If a guy with a bike taxi weren't waiting on their front porch to take them to *their* wedding, she would be stripping her sexy groom out of that suit and dragging him back into their clawfoot tub.

"Before we leave, I wanted to give something to you."

"Nick, you shouldn't have," she said, running her index finger down the line of his jaw.

"It's not new. It's not even a gift." He wasn't teasing or being silly. His expression was somber.

"What is it?"

He led her downstairs and opened a small box on the foyer table.

There, sparkling in shades of orange-gold, green and white, was the sunflower hairpin Rosemary had given her the day of the fundraiser. The fundraiser she had missed the day she'd nearly died by Brett's hand.

It had been twelve weeks and two days since she had stood at the edge of the bluff near Rachel and Rory's rock. She'd started attending an abuse survivor support group at the Rose Brooks Women's Shelter. The counselors explained it wasn't abnormal to count the days. They described it as a coping mechanism. A way to help her mind put time and space between the events of that day.

It had been a couple of weeks since the FBI last contacted her. Twenty agents had watched as Brett tried to pull her over the edge with him. There was never any implication made that she had done anything other than fight to survive. But the agents had questions—lots of questions.

Brett was a key player in an opioid ring that included international suppliers and spanned several states. They had been using Camp Clem to store drugs, money, and a treasure trove of forged prescriptions. Hundreds of arrests were made.

Lindsey had surrendered the canisters of film from her old Nikon documenting Brett's abuse to the FBI. They offered to allow her to view the pictures, but she declined. She didn't need to see the gashes and bruises. She had lived it, and she had survived it.

"The pin!" she said, meeting Nick's blue gaze. "How did you get this?"

His eyes shined with emotion. "I knew you were upset that it was lost at Camp Clem. I'd mentioned it to the FBI's victim liaison, but I never thought anything would come of it. I figured it fell into the lake. But yesterday, a messenger delivered it. I thought it was some kind of sign, having it returned the day before our wedding."

She traced the tiny sunflower petals. "My mom," she whispered.

"Yeah, your mom," he replied gently, wiping a tear from her cheek.

"Will you?" She handed him the hairpin and turned her head. Nick secured it in her swept-up waves of chestnut locks she'd fashioned into a twist.

"It's perfect." He tilted her chin to meet his gaze. "I love you. I will always love you, Lindsey."

"It's just the beginning," she said, lost in his blue eyes.

A loud knock at the door startled them.

"Hey, yeah," came a voice from outside. "This sounds like a profoundly touching moment. I just want you to know, I'm stoked to be sharing it with you guys."

"Why is there a surfer dude on our doorstep?" Lindsey asked.

Nick shook his head. "That's the Teddy-cab."

Lindsey chuckled. "We should go."

He took her hands. "Are you okay?"

She nodded. She was okay.

Another knock. "Hey, you two? Are we still on for getting hitched?"

Nick opened the door. Ted sported an easy smile and a shirt that read, Math: Everybody buys 37 watermelons, and no one asks why.

"I decorated the Teddy-cab." He gestured to a mountain bike attached to a two-seater cab covered in white bows.

"Ted," came Em's voice, calling up from the street. "There's four of us. How are we going to fit in here?"

Ted ran a hand through his scruffy hair. "Co-adding."

Michael joined Em at the Teddy-cab. "Not all of us are versed in astrophysics, Ted."

"Right," the man answered, walking toward his pedicab. "So, like when there are stars that are too far away to see, we pick one for reference, and then we do this awesome thing that takes extra images with shorter exposure times. We stack them up to make crazy long exposure times, and then you see way more stars."

Lindsey and Nick joined Michael and Em on the sidewalk.

"You're essentially telling us you extend exposure time and stack images to see stars that aren't apparent in a single frame shot?" Lindsey asked.

"Yeah, but way more complicated," Ted replied.

"You're suggesting I sit on Nick's lap and Em sit on Michael's?" she continued.

"I mean, you could do it the other way around," Ted answered.

"You want Michael sit on me?" Em asked.

"Yeah, technically we're all just molecules bumping around on this crazy planet. But I see what you're saying. Doing it that way might not be comfortable."

Lindsey met Em's gaze, and the women broke into laughter.

"Everybody, ready?" Ted asked. He flicked his thumb against the bike's silver bell, and the familiar "ting, ting" sound skipped through the air.

"Let's do this," Nick said.

The men climbed in the cab and she and Em, with Ted's help, maneuvered their bodies to sit atop their respective grooms.

"Here we go," Ted called out, pedaling furiously.

Lindsey wrapped her arms around Nick's shoulders and held on tightly.

"Jesus, Ted," Em called out. "Can't you do anything about the bumps?"

She was right. It was like being tossed around in a jumpy castle.

"He can't hear you," Michael said. "He's got his earbuds in, and he's listening to music."

"Whose idea was this?" Em asked, laughing.

Lindsey smiled at her friend. "I'll give you a hint. She knows this city like the back of her hand."

Em snapped her fingers. "It was Zoe!"

"Horse and carriage would have been very Jane Austen," Lindsey continued. "But just about every smell makes us nauseous, so Zoe suggested this."

"If Zoe ever gets married, we're sending her out in this contraption," Em said, wrapping her arms around Michael's neck as they hit a bump and bounced.

Ted pedaled the cab up Aster Road and turned into the Langley Park Botanic Gardens. Cars weren't allowed on the grounds, but the pedicab sailed smoothly through the gates. Ted strummed the bike bell and patrons moved to the side to let them pass.

He stopped at the pavilion. The guests were already seated, but everyone turned when they heard Ted's bell.

Sam met the cab, opened the door, and chuckled. "If this doesn't look like a shotgun wedding, I don't know what does?"

Lindsey took Sam's hand, and he helped her out. "You look beautiful," he said with a wide grin and kissed her cheek.

Lindsey met his gaze, but a sharp pain shot through her stomach, and she bent over to catch her breath.

"Are you okay, Linds?" Nick asked.

"Yeah, I think it was just the bumpy ride."

Em met her gaze. "I feel it, too—a sharp little pulse."

Lindsey nodded.

"You guys are a little late," Sam said, apologetically. "The minister said we needed to get started as soon as you arrived."

"Is everything ready to go?" Nick asked.

They had decided on a simple wedding. No bridesmaids. No best men. A gathering of friends and family and the four of them at the altar. But between Michael and Em's close friends and family, everybody at the Chamber of Commerce and the Downtown Airport, it wasn't very small.

"Roger, that," Sam said with a wink.

Sam nodded to a woman holding a violin, a friend of Em's from the symphony. Michael and Em had chosen the music for the ceremony. The hauntingly romantic first notes of "Chopin's Nocturne 20" sailed through the air.

Nick took her hand. "Here we go."

He led her up the steps of the pavilion. All heads turned to watch the couples walk down the aisle. Terry looked handsome in trousers and a dress shirt. She had only ever seen him in overalls. His daughter stood next to him, smiling and holding her father's hand. Kathy and Neil Stein waved. Em and Michael's fathers sat together with Em's mother and a lovely older woman, Eunice Teller, who was wearing a tiara. Sam squeezed into the chair next to Zoe, who was seated by her brother, Ben, and her niece, Kate. Jenna wiped a tear and waved from her place on the opposite side of her step-daughter. Nick's mother sat with his great aunt and Rosemary. The other guests waved and smiled at them as they passed by on their way to the altar.

Surrounded by ivy, winding its way lazily along the beams of the outdoor pavilion, foxglove and sunflowers looked on as she held Nick's hand and met his gaze.

The officiant grinned at the couples. "Dearly beloved..."

Em bent over and let out an audible breath.

Lindsey joined her, squeezing Nick's hands and leaning into his chest. The cramping from the bumpy bike ride hadn't subsided.

"The baby?" Nick asked.

"I think so," she answered.

Lindsey glanced at Em. Her friend's face mirrored her discomfort.

"We need to speed this up," Michael said, eyeing the officiant.

"The thirty-second version," Nick added.

The man's head bobbed back and forth between the women.

"Have they gone into labor?" he asked.

"Yes," Lindsey and Em yelled in unison.

The guests released an audible gasp.

The officiant produced a handkerchief and patted his forehead. "Okay, Lindsey, do you take Nick to be your husband?"

"Yes, please hurry," Lindsey breathed. The contractions were coming faster.

"And, Nick."

"Yes, yes," Nick echoed.

He turned to Em and Michael and sped through the same micro vows.

"Rings?"

Nick and Michael looked at Sam.

"Got'em," he said, tossing a ring box to each groom.

Nick slid the delicate wedding ring onto her finger, and Lindsey followed suit.

"By the power vested in me," the officiant paused. He looked like he was going to faint.

"Blah, blah, blah! Are they married?" Sam called out.

The man shook his head. "I now pronounce you man and wife."

"Are you ready to go have a baby, Mrs. Kincade?" Nick asked, smiling down at her.

She released a tight breath. "I don't know if I'm ready, but little banana certainly is."

"We need a car," Michael called.

Everyone had parked a good fifteen minutes' walk from the pavilion. It was only a quick drive, from where they were. If they could take the lake trail, it would only be a five minute's journey.

Ted strummed the pedicab's bell three times.

Nick cupped her face and gazed into her eyes. "You ready for another wild ride?"

NICK GAZED AT HIS DAUGHTER, swaddled in a pink blanket, cooing in his arms. With blue-green eyes just like her mother, the infant stared up at him and yawned.

"It's a lot of work being born, isn't it little banana?"

Skylar Claire Kincade was born less than an hour after they had arrived at the hospital. Five minutes later, William Noland MacCarron entered the world.

The door to their hospital room opened.

"You guys mind if we join you?" Michael asked, carrying his son while Sam and Zoe wheeled Em's hospital bed into their room.

Nick chuckled. "Of course! But is this even allowed?"

"Zoe's dad pretty much runs the joint. Anybody that gives us trouble can go mess with him," Sam said, maneuvering Em's bed next to Lindsey's.

Another knock and a woman entered with a tray of pink and blue frosted cupcakes.

"I don't mean to interrupt. I'm from the bakery. My grandmother, the baker, heard both brides went into labor, and, since you didn't get to have any of your wedding cake, she wanted you to have these."

The entire wedding had relocated from the gardens to the hospital, but the cake had been left behind in the melee.

Nick stared at the woman. Tall with jet black hair. He'd seen her before. He glanced at Lindsey who was smiling ear to ear.

"Junior kids' camp counselor, Monica Brandt, is that you?" Lindsey asked.

The woman gasped. "Lindsey Hanlon!"

"It's Lindsey Kincade, now."

"You married Brad Pitt and Justin Timberlake's lovechild! Congratulations!" Monica replied.

"When did you get back to Langley Park?" Em asked Monica. "I didn't know you were coming home." Em turned to Lindsey. "Monica grew up in Langley Park. She and Michael's cousin, Gabe, used to—"

A striking man with dark features and Sam's jawline entered the room. "I'm here. I'm so sorry I'm late. My flight from New York got delayed."

"Gabe!" Em called out. "You made it."

The man looked around the room. His gaze landed on Monica.

Gabe opened his mouth to speak, but before he could say another word, Monica grabbed a cupcake and smashed it into his face.

"Congratulations on your weddings and your new babies." Monica wiped crumbs off her hands then whipped around and left the room.

"Excuse me. I'll be right back," Gabe said, wiping frosting out of his eye.

He followed Monica out, and the room was quiet for a beat.

"What was that all about?" Lindsey asked.

"Imagine a tornado colliding with a tidal wave," Zoe said, sharing a look with Sam.

"That about sums those two up," Sam agreed.

As if they sensed the attention wasn't on them, Skylar Kincade and Billy MacCarron released ear-piercing cries.

Nick rocked his daughter. "We haven't forgotten about you," he said, sitting on the edge of Lindsey's hospital bed.

The door to the room opened. This time, it was a nurse with a camera.

"I just need to snap a shot for Dr. Al-Amin's baby wall," the woman said with a warm smile.

Nick wrapped his arm around Lindsey and gazed down at his wife and his daughter. "Just the beginning," he whispered as the camera clicked.

ALSO BY KRISTA SANDOR

The Langley Park Series

A steamy, suspenseful second-chance at love series set in the quaint town of Langley Park.

Book One: The Road Home

Book Two: The Sound of Home

Book Three: The Beginning of Home

Book Four: The Measure of Home

Book Five: The Story of Home

The Complete Langley Park Series (Books 1-5)

The Bergen Brothers Series

A sassy and sexy series about three brothers who are heirs to a billion-dollar mountain sports empire.

Book One: Man Fast

Book Two: Man Feast

Book Three: Man Find

The Complete Bergen Brothers Series (All 3 Books+Bonus Story)

<u>Own the Eights Series</u>

A delightfully sexy enemies to lovers series.

Book One: Own the Eights

Book Two: Own the Eights Gets Married (June 2020)

Book Three: Coming Soon

Sign up for Krista's newsletter to stay in the loop.

www.KristaSandor.com

ACKNOWLEDGMENTS

This book is for all the brave souls whose lives have been touched by abuse. After living through a difficult situation as a child and doing extensive research, I wanted to honor all aspects of Lindsey and Nick's journey. I also wanted to highlight their growth and shed light on the importance of the support of friends and family.

To you, my dear reader, thank you. When everything is said and done, this book is for you. Thank you for visiting Langley Park.

Marianne at Goddess Fish Editing, thank you for making *The Beginning of the Home* sparkle and shine.

Corinne, Chris, Kendra, and Tera, you took my manuscript and helped shape it into an emotive, cohesive, compelling story. None of this would be possible without your keen eyes and editing expertise. Thank you, my friends.

Brandi, thank you for your supportive feedback and for always making sure my *Star Wars* references are accurate.

Dad, I know we're on the third book, but it still must be crazy reading romance novels written by your little girl. You always provide helpful insight and spot-on critiques. I love you and value your support.

Arty, Zach, and Eric, the pilots who were kind enough to answer my aviation questions.

Jessie and Teresa, thank you for sharing your photography knowledge. Thank you for reading over scenes and helping bring Lindsey's character to life.

Michelle Dare, my friend and mentor, thank you for answering all my questions and always providing gentle guidance. It's a gift having you in my corner.

David, my husband, my best friend, my biggest supporter, my home. I love you to the moon and back.

ABOUT KRISTA SANDOR

If there's one thing Krista Sandor knows for sure, it's that romance saved her. After she was diagnosed with Multiple Sclerosis in 2015, her world turned upside down. During those difficult first days, her dear friend sent her a romance novel. That kind gesture provided the escape she needed and ignited her love of the genre. Inspired by strong heroines and happily ever afters, Krista decided to write her own romance series. Today, she's living life to the fullest. When she's not writing, you can find her running 5Ks with her husband or chasing after their growing boys in Denver, Colorado.

Never miss a release, contest, or author event! Visit www.Krista-Sandor.com to sign up for her romance newsletter.

www.ingramcontent.com/pod-product-compliance
Lightning Source LLC
Chambersburg PA
CBHW030241200626
46816CB00002BA/463